The Punishment Room

Glenda Norwood Petz

ISBN#: 9781653938216

Other titles by Glenda Norwood Petz:

A Requiem for Revenge
Ghost Girl
Hurricane
The Children In the Woods
Dream Weavers
Thy Kingdom Come
The Fall of Autumn's Becoming

For Jayda, Eryn, Ty, Tania, Dani Lynn, Steele, Alex, and Andi Jo...simply the best grandkids a Grandma could ever ask for.

Chapter One

Two words.

That's all it took to unlock the vault inside Joey Sheffield's mind that held old, painful memories that she'd struggled for years to put away and keep hidden, finally succeeding after what had seemed an eternity and an endless number of attempts. And years of therapy. In the few short moments it took to answer the phone and hear her sister's voice, every single scab from every single wound was picked away, reopening old sores, unleashing a flow of painful memories like raging flood waters crashing through a broken dam, recalling dark secrets she'd rarely spoken of and had willed herself not to dwell on.

As a child, she'd been helpless in fighting against the wrongs levied upon her, while her own mother stood idly by and allowed it all to happen without lifting a finger to help or protect her because she'd refused to believe what she'd called lies coming out of her daughter's mouth, dismissing the allegations as made-up fairy tales and imaginative fabrications. Joey supposed the fairy tale part was certainly true because there *was* a beast involved, a monster who'd robbed her of her childhood and innocence, never regretting an ounce of the pain he'd caused her.

As a teenager, she'd been stronger and brave enough to speak out against the personal violations thrust upon her, but not strong enough to ward off the evil that resided inside her home, an evil that'd targeted her, never letting a day go by without reminding her of it. To avoid having to face her tormentor or be in the same room with him, she'd hung out with friends as late as she could without suffering dire consequences for failing to adhere to a set curfew. Her favorite hangout had been Nat's Diner, a replica of what Nat referred to as "the old fifties burger joints." It was the one place she could relax without dwelling on the lecherous activities that took place in her bedroom at night. A temporary safe haven where she could laugh and have fun. But the joy and happiness were always short-lived and diminished the moment she stepped over the threshold into that ice-cold mausoleum called home.

With money she'd saved up from working nights and weekends at the concession stand in the local movie theater, and the part-time job Nat had given her after she'd begged him to let her work at the diner, she left home the day she turned eighteen, never looking back or lamenting her decision, vowing that if she ever had to face her tormentor again, she'd kill him.

She'd spent months on the road taking buses from town to town, staying only a few months in each one then moving on to the next. Rat and roach infested motels served as home in each city. Even those unpleasant conditions weren't enough to make her rue leaving home. For the first time in eight years, she was able to lay her head on the pillow at night without worrying about Mac invading her privacy or making unwanted and unwelcome visits to her room while she slept. Waitressing jobs came easily wherever she was, thanks to the training she'd received at Nat's, but serving patrons wasn't always pleasant. From experience, she'd learned that no matter where she was or what size restaurant she worked in, there would always be a certain type of male who thought it acceptable behavior to slap her on the ass every time she walked past his table, then hear him laugh about it to his friends while she gritted her teeth and fought against the urge to slap their faces or drive a fork through their hand in retaliation. No matter how uncomfortable or vile she found their actions to be, she'd tolerated it. Between her small salary and the tips she'd collected, it'd given her the opportunity to save up enough money to get even further away, finally settling down in a small rural town in southern Indiana, working a full-time job during the day and attending college classes at night, determined to make a better life for herself. After four years of arduous work and late-night studying, she'd earned her degree in nursing and was now employed in the cardiac care unit of the local hospital, where she was highly regarded and respected by all her co-workers for her attentiveness and expert care of the patients under her charge.

She no longer had to live in disgusting, filthy motels, eating ramen noodles and crackers because she didn't have the funds to buy anything else, or having to take buses or taxis to work and school because they were the only transportation available. After years of struggling to land on her feet with a fresh start at life, she was finally comfortable and happy, living in peace in her small, one-bedroom apartment.

All those hardships could've been avoided if she'd chosen to stay at home and remain in daddy's will, obeying and bowing to his every demand like a good daughter should. If remaining an heiress meant continuing to tolerate his abuse and sacrificing her own well-being for his demented pleasure, then she didn't want a penny of his filthy blood money. No amount he could ever bequeath would be enough to make up for the childhood he stole from her and as far as she was concerned, he could take all his money and everything else he owned and shove them all up his ass. Her life, mental and physical health weren't up for sale, regardless of the amount written on a check.

He was the reason she had little trust in men. Over the years she'd been on multiple dates, never forming a lasting relationship with any of them. Once they expressed a desire for a more serious relationship, she ended it. She wasn't interested in committing herself to any man.

She'd been in love once, long ago, and had promised to marry him. Instead of tying herself down to Mason Abernathy and remaining in a town where she'd continue to have to see her father, she'd chosen instead to leave and did so without telling Mason goodbye, breaking his heart, and her own. Hurting him wasn't her intention but choosing to leave was an important step she felt was necessary to take. Leaving Cornish was the only way she could ever completely rid herself of Macarthur Sheffield.

She hadn't been back home since leaving but had kept in phone contact with her two sisters. Physical visits with them were rare; however, when they did get the opportunity to see each other, it was always somewhere several miles away from home and without the knowledge of their parents. As far as she was concerned, never seeing her mother again was fine with her. It'd be better for them both if she didn't. She had nothing to say to her and shuttered at the thought of what she might do if she ever had to face her again.

Unfortunately, that's exactly what her sister was asking her to do.

"Joey, did you hear me?" It was Rosemary, her oldest sister, who'd called her with the news.

"I heard you," Joey answered groggily, glancing at the clock on the bedside table. She'd heard everything her sister said, but everything else after her first two words was meaningless, her initial statement ringing in her ears, hanging over her head like a thick, black cloud.

"Are you coming?"

Joey hesitated momentarily before answering. "Rosie, I can't believe you'd even consider asking me to come back there, especially with all the bad blood between me and Helen. I wouldn't feel comfortable doing that."

"He's your father, Joey," Rosemary stated flatly.

"I happen to know who he is," Joey snapped. "Being my sperm donor doesn't change my stance."

"I really wish you'd reconsider, Joey. Robin and I are staying with mom temporarily to help her get through this. We'll both be there, and we need you. Especially Robin. She isn't coping well with this and I'm afraid the stress might cause her to digress and pick up her addictive habit again. I don't believe either of us wants to see that happen, do we? We could use the moral support from our sister, but if you have more important things to do, then by all means, do them. Let me know if you change your mind." She hung up before Joey could respond.

Rosemary Van Allen, always the uppity one with the condescending tone who could make saying good morning sound like kiss my ass. Even her last name sounded snobby. She was her older sister, and she loved her, but God knows the woman had always thought her shit didn't stink.

Joey sat on the side of the bed, the phone still in her hand as she stared into the darkness of the room. Rosemary, like her mother, knew about the abuse she'd suffered. Also like her mother, Rosemary refused to believe a single word of it, always mentioning that daddy was a good man, an excellent provider for his family and would never do something so atrocious. So much for familial support in a time of crisis.

And no, she didn't want Robin to return to her opioid addiction since it'd damn near killed her before she sought professional treatment for her problem. But if she did resort to bad habits, it sure as hell wouldn't be her fault now any more than it was the first time around. She resented Rosemary insinuating that it would be if she failed to go home as she'd requested.

Joey shook her head as she got out of bed, placing her phone on the bedside table before going into the bathroom. Fresh memories flooded her mind once more as she stared at her pale reflection in the mirror, closing her eyes tightly as she tried to put them all back inside the boxes of her mind where they belonged, swearing to never again allow them to rise to the surface and cause her any more agony than they already had. If only she could be so lucky.

With a single phone call and two spoken words, her routine life was upended and thrown into chaos as she again was forced to face the hateful demons of her past, memories put there by the very man she was being asked to honor. On the bright side, if she did go, she might finally be able to bury the past and finally put it to rest. Or at least that's what she told herself as Rosemary's words played repeatedly in her head.

"Daddy's dead."

Chapter Two

"I don't know what surprises me more," Ellen Jacoby said, glancing over Joey's leave request. "That you're asking for time off or that you have a family."

"Did you think I was laid by a chicken and hatched by a buzzard?" Joey asked, smiling as she watched her various facial expressions.

She and Ellen had been friends since she'd settled down in Jeffersonville, having met as they waited in the lobby of the same hospital for job interviews, but for different positions. Ellen, already a nurse, had encouraged her to go into nursing as well, seeing potential in her she didn't know she had. Besides leaving Cornish, it'd been one of the best decisions she'd ever made. She absolutely loved the career path she'd chosen.

On the job, they acted professionally, never letting their relationship interfere with duties or responsibilities. Offsite, however, Ellen was a riot to be around. She had a comical sense of humor and was excellent at telling corny jokes. Her charming personality and contagious laugh were an excellent duo. Whenever they were together, laughter could always be heard. Oftentimes, Ellen had told her it was medicine for the soul and a wonderful detoxifying cleanser.

"Never really thought about it," Ellen replied, glancing up. "In all the time I've known you, not once have you ever talked about your family. Guess it was presumptuous of me to think you didn't have one."

"There's not much to talk about," Joey said, never having shared much of her past with Ellen, other than trivial things like the popular town diner she and her friends had spent a lot of time at, that she'd left home at eighteen while withholding the reasons why because they were too shameful to talk about, and her relationship with Mason. Ellen also wasn't aware she'd come from an extremely wealthy family or that she had two sisters. To divulge any of that information would lead to question after question about her home and family life. As much as she loved Ellen, there were still some things that didn't need to be discussed; therefore, she'd remained silent.

"For what it's worth, I'm sorry to hear about the loss of your father," Ellen said, signing the form and handing it to Joey.

"Don't be. I'm not."

Ellen looked puzzled by her comment, her brows questioningly raised. "Care to elaborate?"

"No," Joey answered, realizing how short and tart her response had been to Ellen's condolences. "Only that I've never been close to my father, that's all."

"I get the feeling there's something you're not telling me. Am I right?"

Joey hesitated, not wanting to lie but also not wanting to tell her why she'd made such a remark.

"Joey, you know you can tell me anything. I'm a good listener and I never judge."

"I know you are, Ellen."

"If you ever need to talk, I'm here for you. No matter what."

"I appreciate that."

"Where is it you're going?"

"Alabama."

"Alabama?" Ellen asked with surprise. "I thought you were from Georgia with that southern twang of yours. I could've sworn you told me that's where you were from. Guess I was wrong again."

"No, you weren't. That's where I'm originally from. Mac relocated us to Alabama when I was a little girl."

"Mac?"

"My father."

Obviously, discussing her father was uncomfortable for her, so Ellen didn't press any further. "Are you flying down?"

"No. I'm going to drive. It'll give me some time to clear my head and prepare myself before I get there."

"Are you expecting it to be that bad?"

"With my family, who knows? Sometimes the drama gets so bad that it's like living in a soap opera."

"Do I detect a note of apprehension about making the trip?"

"Dread, maybe. You'd know why if you knew my family."

Ellen gave a short laugh. "When do you plan on leaving?"

"Early in the morning. I'm going home now to pack."

"Other than attending a funeral, what other plans do you have while you're there?"

"Right now, none. I don't intend to stay any longer than necessary."

"Planning on looking up any old friends?" Ellen asked, smiling slyly.

"If you mean Mason, the answer is no. If I run into him, it won't be intentional," Joey said, returning the smile.

"Sure it won't," Ellen winked. "Okay, come here and give me a hug. You drive safely and let me know the minute you're back. And don't forget to drop that leave form off at human resources if you don't want your paycheck docked."

"Thanks, Ellen, I will," she said, hugging her friend goodbye. "Sorry about the short notice."

"Don't worry about it. It's not as if we can plan death, right?"

"See you when I get back."

Ellen stood in the doorway of her office watching Joey as she walked away, unable to shake the feeling of unease that suddenly washed over her. It was apparent that Joey wasn't thrilled about attending her father's funeral or being around her family, which could explain the reason she had a nagging feeling that Joey was in danger, but from what or who she couldn't even begin to guess. Surely her family would watch over her and protect her, keeping her out of harm's way. Afterall, they were her family.

"Stop being so paranoid," she muttered, returning to her desk. Joey said she was leaving the following morning, so she'd give her time to arrive at her parents' house and get settled in, then she'd call and check on her.

Until then, she knew the gnawing feeling she had wouldn't go away.

Chapter Three

Joey slumped down on the couch, staring at her packed suitcases sitting by the front door. She was having second thoughts about making the trip, not at all eager to face her mother and listen to her bitch about every little thing that didn't go her way or hear her preach about all the mistakes she'd made over the years and how ungrateful a child she'd been.

Not once had Helen told Joey she loved her. She wasn't the type of person who expressed any kind of emotions. Joey was taken by surprise when she'd started receiving letters from Helen within a year of settling down in Indiana. She'd tossed them all in the trash bin unopened because she had no interest in anything Helen had to say. By then, she'd started her therapy sessions and was on the road to healing, so the last thing she'd needed was interference from Helen that would surely lead to a relapse.

Pissed after receiving the first letter, she'd called the one she knew was guilty of disclosing her location.

"What the hell, Rosemary? Did you give Helen my address?"

"Hello to you, too, Joey."

"It was you, wasn't it? After I specifically instructed you not to."

"Relax, Joey. It's not like I started the apocalypse."

"You went against my wishes, Rosemary. Why?"

Rosemary sighed heavily. "You know how mother is. Extremely insistent and persuasive. I gave it to her to get her off my back. What's the big deal? It's only your address."

"I asked you not to tell her where I was. If I'd wanted her to know, I would've told her myself."

"I don't understand what you're so upset about. It's not like she's planning a trip to come there and see you."

"I suppose you gave her my phone number, too."

"No."

"Good. Keep it that way. And tell her to lose my address."

Rosemary obviously hadn't delivered her message to Helen because the letters continued to come for several months thereafter, then abruptly stopped. Helen had finally gotten the message.

Against her better judgment and after much consideration, she decided to make the trip home, knowing her sisters would be disappointed if she didn't show up. To ignore the death and funeral of her own father would drive an uncomfortable wedge between them. As badly as she didn't want to go, she also didn't want to hurt her sisters or destroy their relationships.

Joey exhaled heavily, leaning her head on the back of the couch. "God, give me strength to do this," she said.

The drive was a little over six hours. CD's and audio books would make the trip bearable and help keep her mind off where she was going and why.

She'd packed lightly, not intending to stay long, knowing beforehand she'd be ready to leave within the first few hours of getting there. Hopefully, her sisters would keep her occupied so her interactions with her mother were limited. The less she had to deal with her, the less chance there'd be of her lashing out at her for all the years she'd let her needlessly suffer. If confronted, Helen would still swear it was all a lie or that she knew nothing about what was going on under her own roof. Six of one, half a dozen of another, the result was still the same. Complete and total denial, something Helen Sheffield was a professional at. God forbid any type of scandal should upset her perfect, idealistic world and lifestyle. Pity that her standing and reputation in the community, her afternoon Bridge clubs, her rich, socialite friends had all been more important to her than facing the truth about the horrors taking place inside her cherished mansion.

No matter how many times Joey had tried to forgive her, she couldn't. Her injured heart wouldn't allow it.

With a deep sigh, she rose from the couch and for the third time checked to make sure all the locks were secure and electrical appliances turned off, picked up her suitcase and headed out the door.

Chapter Four

She'd forgotten what a beautiful drive it was between Indiana and Alabama since she hadn't driven it in the fifteen years since leaving her small hometown of Cornish. On the few occasions she'd gotten together with Rosemary and Robin, she'd flown to their chosen location then rented a car.

The rolling hills of Kentucky and mountains of Tennessee were stunning and picturesque as they proudly displayed row after row of trees. Their leaves were beginning to change into Autumn reds, yellows and oranges, a true mountainside inferno basking in its splendor. Pine cabins and houses were visible from the road, appearing to barely be clinging to the sides of the mountain, pinned there to create the ideal optical illusion for spectators. Thin white wisps of clouds covered the mountaintops, reminding her of how the Smokies had gotten their name. Her ears popped as she climbed up one hill and descended another, continuously feigning yawns to clear them.

Traffic on the interstate was moderate but moving along smoothly. Some cars flew past her like speeding bullets, their drivers over-eager to reach their destinations. Others, like her, chose to follow the posted speed limit, also eager to reach their own destinations, but choosing to reach it alive instead of early. Several state troopers had cars pulled over, citation books in hand ready to issue tickets, while others parked off the road and out of sight conducting speed traps.

As a kid, whenever the family took a rare road trip, going no further than Gadsden to visit Helen's family, she'd always enjoyed reading the roadside billboards, especially the ones with a message that was spread out over multiple boards placed several feet apart. Those kinds no longer existed, replaced by advertisements for attorneys, insurance, or real estate.

Mostly, those had been the good and happy days of her life, when her little girl innocence was still pure and intact. Reminiscing about her youth inadvertently called to memory less happier times and horrible incidents that were repulsive. Until receiving the call from Rosemary, she'd learned how to keep them hidden away so she didn't constantly dwell on them.

With the music off, silence engulfed her as she traveled the road that would inevitably take her back to where it all started.

Listening to the soothing sound of tires against asphalt, all those long-hidden memories began spilling out, leaving her with no alternative but to remember.

And there was never a better place to start than at the beginning.

Chapter Five

"Hey, sweetheart," daddy said, his deep voice startling her awake. "Can I lay down beside you for a while?"

"Why?" she asked, sitting up and rubbing her eyes. "Are you scared?"

A quick laugh, then, "Yeah, maybe a little."

"Is there a monster in your closet?" It was the only thing in her young mind that made any sense. What else could scare a grown man so badly that he'd need to ask permission to sleep with his adolescent daughter?

"No," he answered, crawling under the covers and snuggling up close to her. "You're so warm," he whispered in her ear. "And you feel so good to daddy."

The middle child of three daughters, she'd been ten at the time and as innocent and naïve as any other girl her age who saw her daddy as a hero figure, someone she loved and admired, not understanding at the time that daddy crawling into bed with her was wrong, and only the beginning of what was still yet to come. She hadn't been mature enough, mentally or physically, to comprehend that his actions were inappropriate, only that daddy wanted to lie in bed with her and she saw nothing wrong with that.

Until a week later, when the occasional middle of the night visits evolved into every night intrusions, and the hugging and cuddling became more advanced, improper, and uncomfortable.

"Daddy loves you," he said, kissing her lightly on the head.

"I love you, too, daddy."

"You know you're my little angel, right?"

"Yes."

"Lying here with you makes daddy feel so good," he said, slowly running his hand up and down the side of her thigh. "Don't tell the others, but you're my favorite."

"I am?"

"Um hum," he said, moving in closer as he put his arm around her waist and slid his hand under her gown, touching her cotton underwear.

"Stop that, daddy," she said, pushing his hand away. "That's not nice and you're not supposed to touch me on my private parts."

"It's okay," he whispered, slipping his fingers under the elastic band of her panties, proceeding to fondle her. "I would never hurt you."

"You're poking me in my back," she complained, scooting away from him, but he quickly pulled her back.

"Sorry," he said, "I didn't mean to. I'll try not to do it again," he whispered, gliding his hand slowly inside her panties. "Doesn't that feel good?" he groaned.

"No. I don't like it. Please, daddy, stop."

After several seconds, he grunted, exhaled heavily, and removed his hand from her underwear. "This will be our little secret," he said, getting out of bed. "You can never tell anyone, you understand? If you do, I'll swear you're lying and you know what happens to little girls who tell fibs, don't you? They get sent away to live with mean people they don't know in houses where monsters live under the stairs and eat little girls. Remember that my little angel."

Speechless, she nodded as tears streamed down her face, confused and ashamed of what'd just happened.

"Remember, it's our secret," he whispered, putting a finger to his mouth. "I promise to buy you a special present tomorrow, something that'll make you feel better."

As soon as he exited the room, she jumped out of bed and locked the door but hadn't slept a wink for the remainder of the night. Instead, she'd stayed awake, staring at the ceiling, watching the stars from her nightlight dance across the walls, wishing she could be as far away as they were.

At the breakfast table, she'd been unable to look anyone in the eye, certain that if she did, they'd be able to see what she'd done the night before. Not having much of an appetite, she picked at her food, barely eating, anxious to get out of the house and to school. When daddy kissed her on the top of the head and said, "Good morning," she cringed, disgusted by what he'd done to her. But it hadn't fazed him at all. He was smiling and jovial, whistling tunes and acting as normal as he would have any other day.

If anyone had noticed her behavior toward him that morning, they never mentioned it, which was a relief because she didn't want to talk about it.

All she wanted was to forget and pray that it never happened again.

"What have you girls been told about locking your bedroom doors at night?" daddy asked as he sat down at the table.

"Not to," Rosemary, four years older than her, answered.

"That's right. And why is that? Robin, do you know?"

Eight-year-old, know-it-all Robin answered. "So you don't have to break our doors down in case of a fire."

"Right again," he said, looking at Joey. "Josephine, can you explain to me why your door was locked this morning, young lady?"

How did he know she'd locked her door? Had he come back to her room in the middle of the night intending to violate her again, only to find he couldn't get in and would've awakened everyone if he'd tried to force the door open? She was up and downstairs before he exited his own bedroom. So how could he have known?

What she wanted to say and what she should say were two entirely different things. If she told the

31

truth, she'd be laughed at, called a liar, and sent away to live with strangers who kept monsters as pets. "I didn't know it was," she answered, staring blankly into her cereal bowl. "I must've locked it by accident."

"Make sure it doesn't happen again, you understand?"

She knew why he wanted her to keep the door unlocked, and it wasn't for fear of fire. As badly as she wanted to defy his rule, she knew she couldn't. If she did, daddy would get really mad and start yelling and taking his frustrations out on everyone else and be mean to mom. Not wanting to cause all that unnecessary trouble, she knew she must abide by the house rules and do as daddy said.

"Yes, sir," she answered, realizing what he'd done to her the night before wasn't going to be a onetime occurrence, but the first of many more to come.

He'd promised to never hurt her, so perhaps she shouldn't be afraid of what might happen. What a mistake that'd been.

In the near future, he'd betray his promise.

True to his word, he'd presented her with a gift that afternoon. A beautiful rag doll with long, blonde braids wearing a blue and white checked dress and blue buttons for eyes. Fondly, she named the doll Molly. She couldn't hate her. It wasn't her fault she'd been given as a gift to justify daddy's immoral behavior. It also wasn't her fault that she'd caused a major upset in the Sheffield household.

The purchase of the doll resulted in deep ire from Helen. She was furious with Mac because Joey was the only recipient of an unexpected gift for which there was no occasion to receive one. Mac had only made matters worse by giving it to her while Rosemary and Robin were present. Helen accused him of showing favoritism to one while ignoring the other two, having no qualms about making the accusations while Joey and her sisters listened. From that point forward, Helen focused her rage and hatred on Joey, subjecting her to years of mistreatment, exclusion from mother/daughter outings, and making her spend countless hours in the attic punishment room where she was forced to sit for hours at a time in the dark with no food or water until Helen said she could come out.

She'd been too young then to understand why Helen continuously punished her instead of the one who'd violated her. Or why she blamed her for Mac's actions. She didn't think it was possible for a mother to hate her child, but Helen hated her and made no effort to hide her disdain for her youngest daughter.

Those had been some of the darkest days of her life, and Molly became her best friend. One she could talk to for hours and tell all her secrets to, whose dress had absorbed countless flows of tears.

Molly knew everything, and if dolls could talk, she would've had one hell of a story to tell.

Chapter Six

Not much had changed in downtown Cornish in the years she'd been away. A new bank now stood where the old five and dime store once was. As a child, she'd bought a packet of sea monkeys there for her fishbowl, fulling expecting to see chimpanzees grow in the water. Afterall, that's what was advertised on the package and she'd fantasized about having monkeys for pets, going as far as choosing names for them once they matured. After a week's time, disappointment and anger replaced her joy when the so-called monkeys turned out to be parasitic worms. She'd been so angry, she poured them in the toilet and flushed them into the sewer.

The only other new business she saw was an auto dealership where the skating rink used to be. A few of the mom-and-pop stores she remembered had been replaced with more modernized shops selling the same wares as their predecessors. Familiar businesses, like Abernathy Hardware and the flower boutique remained, both upgraded with fresher paint and newer store fronts. Much to her pleasant surprise, Nat's Diner was still open for business and still serving their famous five-pound burger. It didn't *really* weigh that much, but from what she remembered, it was quite large and would've taken someone with a ten-gallon stomach to eat the whole thing. Nat had offered a free dinner to anyone who could. She'd personally never seen anyone do it while she'd worked there and couldn't say with certainty that anyone ever had. If so, rumors surely would've circulated around town, and she never heard about it. The diner was located on the corner directly across the street from the theater where she'd worked as a teenager. Judging by the outside appearance and current movie posters inside glass frames, it also appeared to remain in operation.

Other than a few minor changes, her hometown was exactly as she remembered it. She found the lack of growth surprising considering Birmingham was less than fifty miles away but had failed to advance in any development toward Cornish. Of course, that type of blame could be attributed to the City Council and Commissioners who'd vetoed any proposition that would've given

Cornish a chance to grow, opting instead to keep it a small municipality in lieu of becoming a larger tourist trap that would undoubtedly bring in heavy traffic to an otherwise slow-moving town, giving no consideration to the amount of revenue such positive changes could bring to the town. If remaining at a standstill had been the goal, then Cornish had succeeded.

Only a few short miles from Sheffield Manor, her heart began racing, her stomach tied in knots, dreading having to face her mother after so many years with no contact. If Helen's intentions were to make her visit miserable because she was unwanted there, all she had to do was get back in her car and drive home to Jeffersonville. Problem solved. She was no longer the young girl she'd been when she left, nor was she quiet and withdrawn as she once was. A lot had changed for Joey Sheffield over the years and one promise she'd made to herself was that she would never again allow anyone to mistreat her, regardless of who they were, and Helen Sheffield was certainly no exception.

The mile-long, two-lane paved road leading up to the house was lined on both sides with overhanging Magnolia trees that formed a canopy over the path. Intermittent sunlight beaming through the open gaps had the effect of a strobe light, the constant flashing making her nauseous.

Beyond the last curve of the winding roadway, Sheffield Manor came into view, the expansive white brick home looming on the horizon like a giant Yeti eagerly awaiting its feast. The mere sight of it made Joey tense. To anyone else, it was nothing more than a house, Helen's glorious mansion that she'd always prided herself over. It wasn't spectacular or grandiose. She'd seen plenty of other mansions much bigger, nicer, and more expensive. To Joey, Sheffield Manor wasn't just a house. It'd been her prison, a place where unimaginable evil had dwelt. She never understood why they'd lived in such a huge home when they were forbidden to enter several of the rooms, many that'd remained locked at all times. As a child, she'd played a guessing game of what Helen may be hiding behind the secured doors. Possibly treasure chests full of diamonds, emeralds and rubies. Or dead bodies of those she'd murdered, locking them away so no one would see them. Perhaps there was nothing in the rooms at all, and she was only exercising her extreme greed by not being willing to share what the prohibited rooms held. It hadn't made much difference to Joey whether she was allowed in the rooms or not. Most of her time was spent alone in her own bedroom, doing whatever pleased her, opting to seclude herself from her snobby, stuck-up mother and siblings.

The water fountain in the center of the front lawn either wasn't working or hadn't been turned on, which Joey found strange. In all the years she'd lived there, she'd never seen it not flowing. The rearing stallion in the center of the fountain appeared as though he was prepared to gallop away and run for the freedom he'd craved since being erected in Helen's front yard. The once pristine white stone of the horse's mane and flowing tail was now discolored and teeming with green moss and black mold. The stone horse hadn't seen water or a decent cleansing in years to have accumulated such a high amount of bacteria.

Like everything else she touched, the previously treasured fountain had turned to shit.

All the rose bushes on both sides of the manor were severely overgrown, unkempt and had climbed up and over the surrounding stone walls, making it nearly impossible to enter the backyard without going through the house to get there. Anyone daring to attempt to go around or through them wouldn't escape without injuries from the thousands of protruding thorns.

As she neared the house, she noticed it, too, was in dire need of a paint job or power washing. The same green and black goop growing on the horse was also visible at the base of the house's foundation and was slowly creeping its way up the siding. The black paint on the shutters was chipping away, as was the green paint on the front door. *Odd*, Joey thought, *that Helen would allow her prized possession to deteriorate so badly.* It wasn't like she didn't have the money to pay for the repairs that were so desperately needed. She supposed that after providing tender loving care to it for so many years, Helen just didn't give a damn anymore, choosing instead to spend her money on other things she found more important.

Two cars were parked in the paved circular driveway, undoubtedly both belonging to her sisters. Helen didn't drive and was chauffeured everywhere she went, so neither of the vehicles could belong to her.

Joey pulled up behind a two-door blue sports car, knowing instantly it must belong to her youngest sister, Robin. Rosemary had a family to haul around, which would explain the oversized SUV parked in the driveway.

Before she could get out of the car, the front door opened and within seconds, Robin was running toward her, arms outstretched. "Oh, my God, I can't believe you're actually here," she screeched, wrapping her arms tightly around Joey. "I'm so glad you changed your mind about coming. I was so afraid you wouldn't."

"I almost didn't," Joey confessed. "But here I am." Robin certainly didn't appear to be as distraught as Rosemary had led her to believe and didn't look as though she'd shed a single tear if the clearness of her eyes was any indication.

Robin hugged her again, then took her by the hand, leading her toward the front door.

"What's with this?" Joey asked, tussling Robin's rainbow-colored hair. "Have you morphed into a unicorn since the last time I saw you?"

"Ha ha," Robin replied. "Something different, that's all. You like it?"

"Actually, I do," Joey said, nodding. "It fits you."

Rosemary stepped onto the porch, wiping her hands on a dish towel. "I see you changed your mind, afterall. Thanks for letting me know," she added sarcastically.

"Obviously," Joey said with a smile. "I'm here, aren't I?"

"I'm glad you did. Come on inside." Either she was being paranoid, or Rosemary wasn't too happy to see her, completely void of any emotion and hadn't even hugged her. Then again, Rosie had always been the stoic, uptight one, so she didn't know why she'd expected anything different from the person she'd known all her life.

"I see she still has that stick up her ass," Joey whispered to Robin as they stepped over the threshold.

"You have no idea. Except now it's a log."

Joey felt a rush of anxious adrenaline as she stepped from the porch into the greeting area, the same unsettled feeling she'd always gotten as a young girl when expecting Mac's next visit to her room. Although he was dead, the ghosts of his presence remained, lingering so heavily in the air that she could practically feel him there, watching her with his perverted, lustful glare.

Directly across from the front entry, the sunken living room still contained the same ghastly Victorian-style furniture that'd been there when she left. She'd always disliked the room because it made her feel as though she was sinking through the floor to the pits of hell below. Instead of walking through it, she'd preferred walking around it. Lowered rooms may have been a popular trend in the early nineteen-hundreds when the house was built, but Joey found it unattractive and unpleasant. Living room walls were lined with expensive oil paintings, some signed by famous artists, others by local up-and-comers, all of them as grotesque as the furnishings. Price didn't matter to Helen in satisfying her hunger for the better things in life. Some of the artwork cost more than the average person made in a year.

Beyond the living room were double winding staircases. The set of stairs on the right led to the east wing of the house where she and her sisters' bedrooms had been, each furnished with their own private bathrooms so there was never any arguing over who got the sink or toilet first. The left side stairs led to the west wing where every room there had always remained locked, and entrance forbidden. Also on that side was the entrance to the attic, its trapdoor removed and replaced with a permanent, narrow set of wooden stairs that allowed easy access.

Joey shuttered as she recalled the number of hours she'd spent up there, locked away inside the cold, dark space, listening to critters scurrying around on the roof and inside the walls as she fantasized about the day she could finally get away from that hellhole. Smaller than a jail cell, it was an area on the far-left side of the attic that'd been converted into what she'd long ago dubbed the punishment room. It was a special place where bad girls who did bad things were sent, banished from everyone and everything, and weren't released until Helen Sheffield gave her approval. She was quite familiar with it since she'd spent more time there than either of her sisters.

Helen was standing on the opposite side of the sunken room as Joey entered the house, her hands interlocked across her stomach, displaying the same matriarchal stance she'd always exhibited. Although she still exuded the same air of smugness she always had, tight-lipped and unsmiling, nose high in the air, standing erect like a scarecrow on a post, there was something notably different about her. Maybe it was because she was older now, or it could be because Joey hadn't seen her in fifteen years. She wore an expression of pure contempt as she stared icily at Joey, as if to say, "Aha, I've got you right where I want you," or "what the hell are you doing inside my house?"

Whatever the difference was, it made Joey extremely uncomfortable to where she questioned whether she'd made a mistake in returning home and should turn around and bolt out the door, jump in her car and drive away like a bat out of hell, distancing herself as far as she could, as fast as she could, away from Sheffield Manor.

After what seemed an eternity of silence, Helen finally spoke, the one word sounding strained and forced. "Josephine."

"Mother," Joey replied as icily, hating that she'd chosen to call her mother instead of Helen. She'd certainly never been a mother to her and didn't deserve to be called one.

Helen abruptly turned and walked away. No "glad you're here," "nice to see you," or "thank you for coming." Her animosity toward Joey hadn't changed one bit.

"Give her time," Robin said. "She'll warm up to you."

"No, she won't. And honestly, I couldn't care less if she doesn't."

Rosemary gave her a stern, disciplinary look. "Please tell me you're not going to start a fight with mom while you're here."

"It's certainly not my intention. As long as she doesn't start in on me, everything will be peachy."

"Good."

"Are the girls here?" Joey asked Rosemary. As she did with her sisters, she often spoke with them on the phone and in video calls but had only seen them once since their births. Through their many conversations, she'd grown to love them and was looking forward to seeing them both.

"Not at the moment," Rosemary answered. "Dan will bring them later. Why don't you bring your things in and put them in your room? Once you're settled in, we can socialize."

"Where am I staying?" Joey asked.

"In your old room, of course."

"Hell no, I won't be," Joey stated. "There's no way I'm sleeping in there."

Rosemary rolled her eyes in disdain. "Why not?"

"You know why."

"Don't," Rosemary said, putting up a hand. "Don't even say it."

"Say what?" Robin asked. "Why don't you want to sleep in your old room, Joey?"

"Rosemary knows why."

"But I don't. What's she talking about, Rosie?"

"Nothing important and certainly not worth discussing."

Joey felt the fire burning in her neck and face as her anger surfaced at Rosemary's continued denial, but she kept her temper, and her tongue, under control. No use getting into a spat with her sister after having arrived only minutes before. "No problem," Joey said. "I'll drive into town and rent a hotel room. That'll solve the problem."

"No, you're not," Robin said, glaring at Rosemary. Unless she or Helen had told her about the abuse, then Robin truly was in the dark about what Mac had done to her because she'd never told her either. "I'll take your room and you can have mine. Deal?"

Joey glanced first at Rosemary, her expression one of disgust, then at Robin. "Deal."

Rosemary looked disappointed that she'd refused to stay in a room that had nothing but horrible memories for her, as if Joey had ruined some kind of sinister plot by refusing, making Joey wonder if she really did have something planned, some form of vengeance to retaliate against her for the nasty accusations she'd made against Mac and for walking off and leaving her family behind. Which was a ridiculous thought because she'd had several years to do that, so why wait until now? Unless Mac's death had provided her with the perfect opportunity she'd needed and intended to use it to her advantage.

Stop being paranoid, she scolded herself. *She's your sister, for God's sake. She'd never do anything like that.*

"Come on, Joey. I'll help you bring your things in," Robin said, walking toward the door.

"It's okay, Robin. I only have two bags."

"Then I'll walk outside with you. Fresh air sounds good."

"When you're done, come to the kitchen," Rosemary said. "That's where I'll be."

"What was that exchange between you and Rosemary about?" Robin asked once they were outside.

"It's nothing, really," Joey answered.

"It was most definitely something. I'm not a kid anymore, Joey. If there's something going on that I need to know about, then you need to tell me."

"Remnants of a long-ago disagreement between us, that's all. You don't need to worry about it," Joey said as she opened the trunk of her car. "I'm waiting for you to tell me why your hair is five different colors. You're too young for a midlife crisis and too old for it to have been a defiant act against Helen."

"Because it's different," she answered, running her fingers through her short crop. "Sometimes I'll get a wild hair up my ass to do something I would've been forbidden to do living here. Like this," she said, pulling up her shirt and turning around, revealing a large butterfly tattoo on her lower back that was encircled with red roses.

Joey laughed. "I have one of those, too. In the same place as yours but not a butterfly."

"No shit?"

"I'm serious."

"You'll have to let me see it," Robin said, her green eyes sparkling in the afternoon sun. "I should probably tell you something else, but I don't want you to faint."

"Whatever it is, it couldn't possibly be bad enough to make me pass out."

Robin looked back toward the house, undoubtedly making sure Helen or Rosemary weren't standing there eavesdropping on their conversation. "I have a girlfriend."

"You mean like a new friend?"

Robin smiled. "Sort of, but she's more than a friend, if you know what I mean."

"Ah," Joey said, nodding. "Now I get it. Weren't you dating a guy the last time we talked? Ronnie or Ralph, something like that?"

"Richard. And yes, I was, but it didn't work out."

"Obviously."

"Joey, you can never let that slip out in front of mom. She doesn't know about her, and I'd like to keep it that way."

"Robin, you're a grown woman," Joey protested. "Why do you care what she thinks? Live your own life and be happy."

"It's just…" Robin started, then paused.

"Just what?"

"I'm sure if mom found out, she'd disinherit me and make sure I didn't get a dime of the money dad left to me."

"Because you're gay?" Joey asked with surprise. "That's ridiculous."

"I know that, and you know that, but we both also know how vindictive mom can be sometimes."

"No arguments there. You have nothing to worry about. Your secret is safe with me."

"Thanks, Joey. I really am glad you're here."

"Me, too, if for no other reason than to see you," Joey answered, giving her little sister a quick hug. "Back to the creepy manor?"

"If you insist."

* * * * *

He loved coming in here. It was only a few feet away from the room where he stayed now, so he didn't have to go far to have fun. His new room was nothing like his old one, but it had what he needed to get by. Clothes, television, a toilet. He couldn't recall why he'd been moved up here, only that one day he'd been enjoying the comforts of his large downstairs room and king-sized bed, and the next day, not only was he sleeping in a different bed, but he was staying on a different floor of the house all alone, away from Helen and anyone else who may have been there.

This room was the only one that mattered to him and the only one he cared anything about. It was filled with box after box of old photographs and children's toys and clothing. Helen said the people in the pictures were all family members, but he didn't believe her because she was a mean, lying bitch, always trying to trick him into believing her lies. Sometimes, he sat in the old rocking chair in the room staring at a picture for what seemed an eternity, struggling to make his mind spark an inkling of recognition. But when his brain wasn't feeling too good, like now, the recognition never came. Tomorrow might be different, though, if the clouds in his head disappeared, and he was thinking clearly. In that case, he might be able to identify every single one of them and put names to the faces without a problem if he tried hard enough.

Helen didn't like it when he came in here without her knowledge, telling him he was too clumsy and would fall and break his neck. To hell with Helen, he'd do whatever he wanted, and right now, he wanted to explore. It was a fond hobby of his that

Helen called plundering. What she didn't know wouldn't kill her. Unfortunately.

From a cardboard box, he plucked an old rag doll from the pile and deeply inhaled her smell. A combination of dust, age and another scent felt familiar. He knew he should recognize it, but at the moment, the memory eluded him. He tucked the doll beneath the inside arm of his robe, hiding it in case Helen caught him and made him put it back. As mean as the bitch was, she'd destroy it just to keep him from finding it again. He moved on to the next box, removing individual small dresses one at a time, admiring their flowers and lace, smelling them, then returning them to their cartons.

He didn't understand why all the boxes only contained toys and items for girls, and not toys like train sets, army men and race cars. Even though Helen had told him more than once that they only had daughters, not sons, he knew she was lying about that, too, and was hiding all the good toys away to keep him from being able to play with them. Helen was a mean asshole. She always had been, and that wasn't apt to change, being the old fart she already was. One of these days, he would teach her a lesson for all the hateful things she'd done to him and for keeping him locked away in the attic. But not today. He was too tired to deal with her. The day would come, though, and it would be a glorious one, a day when his thoughts were clear, and when he would know exactly what to do and how to do it. Until that day came, he'd continue to come to his favorite room and search through old boxes, looking at old pictures, toys, and clothes as he tried to remember who in the hell all these people were and what part each had played in his life.

Prepared to return to his small room where Helen would expect him to be if she came looking for him, he was distracted by the sound of nearby voices and car doors slamming. Curious, he felt he should look outside and see what was going on.

Through the sheers of the attic window overlooking the sprawling front yard of Sheffield Manor, inquisitive eyes watched as Joey unloaded her suitcases while conversing with another woman with funny colored hair.

Both looked familiar, but he couldn't quite place them, much less put a name to their faces. Today was a terrible day for remembering anything. His mind was foggy and cluttered, unlike some other days when he could think and remember places and people that he needed to. He wished every day inside his mind could be as clear as a bright, sunny day instead of the starless black sky that it normally was.

There were certain things he could recall when he could think straight, like his library filled with the finest of books where he used to sit in his leather chair while smoking his pipe and reading. Or the garden mazes he'd enjoyed walking through while enjoying the aromas of roses and gardenias. From the window of his new bedroom, he could see the garden below, but all the once colorful flowers were dead now, the labyrinths gone because the shrubbery had not been taken care of. He wasn't allowed to go outside anymore and spent most of his days alone, confined to his locked room, either sleeping or watching shows on television that he didn't care much for.

He knew he'd once had a nurse who sat with him during the night to ensure he stayed inside his room and didn't get up and roam around the house, going into places he shouldn't be in, or was forbidden to enter. He hadn't seen her in quite some time now, so he figured she'd either quit or Helen had fired her. He knew she'd gotten rid of her on purpose, hoping he *would* fall down the stairs or out the window and die so she wouldn't have to deal with him anymore. "Evil bitch," he muttered.

Occasionally, Helen came to visit, but usually it was only to give him his medications, which always made him excessively sleepy and so tired he could barely hold his head up. If he were good during the day and didn't get into any kind of trouble, she'd sit and talk to him for a while, so he always tried to behave because he hated being alone and lonely. Yet sometimes, during the moments when his mind was fuzzy and not working too well, Helen yelled at him and called him awful names, reminding him how stupid he was for disobeying her orders and not doing as he was told.

When she last visited him, she'd told him she had a surprise coming for him but wouldn't say what it was, only that he'd be pleased. He wondered what the surprise was and if it included cake and ice cream.

"My angel," he whispered as he let the sheers fall back into place, unsure why he'd said the words.

* * * * *

Joey slowly climbed the east stairs to the second floor, suitcase in hand, pausing momentarily outside the second room on the left, staring at the closed door to the bedroom that'd brought her so much pain and shame. A part of her wanted to peek inside out of curiosity to see what, if any, renovations had been made. She couldn't bring herself to do it. Instead, she continued down the hallway to the last door, Robin's old room. The door creaked on its hinges as she opened it, startled to see that the room was exactly the way she remembered it when they were all kids. Same bed and dresser, same spread and pillow shams, same curtains. Helen wasn't much into renovations or remodeling, finding it more pleasurable to spend her millions of dollars on things that she found more significant than the upkeep on her treasured mansion.

The room smelled dank and musty, signs of being vacant for a considerable amount of time, making Joey wonder if Robin had been its last occupant or guest. After placing her suitcase on the bed, Joey raised the windows to allow fresh air into the room and was pleasantly greeted by the aroma of magnolias.

Joey glanced around the room, recalling the countless hours she'd spent in Robin's room playing dolls with her baby sister, or sitting on the floor with her talking and coloring, listening to music while they laughed and enjoyed each other's company. All that had changed after her first encounter with Mac and over time, she came to enjoy all those things less and less, then finally, had no interest in them at all.

In the closet, some of Robin's old dolls sat on the shelves staring down at her with their unblinking, black eyes, once favorite toys of her baby sister, now castaways and forgotten about. The clothes rails were bare. Not a single coat hanger remained.

When she and Robin were younger, they'd loved building a fort inside the large walk-in closet, pretending they were camping and hiding from monsters, until she realized that monsters really did exist and had robbed her of that pleasure as well.

As Joey turned to leave, she stopped suddenly, standing quietly as she listened keenly. She was certain she'd heard muffled voices, a male and female exchanging words. The voices were coming from inside the wall. She remembered that the acoustics in the house weren't state-of-the-art, and conversations from downstairs could sometimes be heard through the upstairs vents, making it sound as if they were coming from the room next door. Shrugging it off, she closed the closet door and returned downstairs.

"Is Dan here?" she asked as she entered the kitchen. Robin was sitting at the large butcher-block table in the middle of the room, her arms folded on top of the table as she watched Rosemary cut up vegetables and toss them into the slow cooker.

"Not yet," Rosemary answered, glancing up.

"Is there someone else in the house besides us and Helen?"

"No. Why?" Rosemary asked, dropping a handful of carrots into the pot, then slicing up a potato. "And must you call her by her name instead of calling her mother?"

"I could've sworn I heard a man's voice," Joey answered, taking a seat on the bar stool next to Robin, ignoring Rosemary's question.

"You know how this old house is," Robin offered. "Voices carry."

Joey nodded. "I guess it could've been coming from outside since I had my window open."

"Must've been," Rosemary agreed. "No one else is here but us."

"Whatever you're cooking smells good, but why *are* you cooking? Doesn't Helen have staff for that?"

"Not today," Rosemary answered. "I think mother must've given them some time off because I haven't seen any staff at all."

"I see," Joey said, wondering if her statement was true or whether she no longer employed any help at all. That would certainly explain why the house wouldn't pass the white glove test if one was administered right then. "The gardener, too? I couldn't help but notice how badly the roses around the house are overgrown."

"She let him go a long time ago," Rosemary explained. "He was stealing from her. Or so she claimed."

"And the fountain?"

"Hasn't worked in years and mother has no interest in repairing it."

"Guess that answers that. What's in the pot?" Joey asked.

"Homemade hearty beef stew. I'm making cornbread later," Rosemary answered. "It's what's for dinner."

After several moments of watching Rosemary cut vegetables and throw them into the pot of beef broth, Joey asked, "Shouldn't we be talking about the obvious? Especially since no one's mentioned it."

"What might you be referring to?"

"The reason I'm here," Joey replied. "Mac's funeral."

That disdainful look again from Rosemary pierced straight through Joey. She could practically feel the icicles as they penetrated her soul. "You mean dad?" she corrected harshly.

"Who else? When is his funeral?"

"It hasn't been planned yet," Rosemary answered without looking up.

"Are you serious?" Joey asked with surprise. "Rosemary, I don't mean to sound cold, but I only took a few days off. I have a job to get back to."

"I apologize for your inconvenience," Rosemary replied tartly. "But I haven't had the chance yet to make the arrangements."

Joey was stunned. Shouldn't that have been the first thing to do after Mac's death? Exactly how long was she planning to wait before doing what needed to be done. "How soon before you called me did Mac... um, dad, die?"

"The day before."

"Good grief, Rosemary," Joey exclaimed. "That was two days ago."

Rosemary slammed the knife down onto the cutting board. "You think I don't know how long it's been?" she hissed.

"You called me here to attend a funeral that hasn't even been arranged yet?"

"I didn't call you here," Rosemary said, using air quotes to emphasize her words. "I phoned you to inform you of the death of your father and gave you the option of whether to come."

"Is there something I can do to help?" Joey asked, attempting to avert a heated argument with Rosemary. "Make some phone calls, go to the funeral home?"

"No," Rosemary quickly replied. "I'll take care of everything myself."

"Which funeral home will be in charge of the arrangements?"

"I haven't decided yet."

Robin remained silent during the exchange between her sisters. Her confused facial expression told Joey that she was as surprised as her to hear that no arrangements had yet been made. Either that, or something entirely different had stunned her.

"I can't believe what I'm hearing," Joey said. "If you haven't even picked out a funeral home, then where's his body?"

"The morgue," Rosemary said flatly. "And stop sounding so morose."

"How am I being morose?"

"All this talk about funerals and morgues, calling daddy a body. It's disgusting. Can't you find a better choice of words?"

Holy shit, Joey thought. *Who lit the firecracker in her ass?*

"I'm not trying to be. I'm simply asking questions. Now back to the subject at hand. You said he's at the morgue?" Joey repeated, puzzled by Rosemary's answer. If Mac died at home like Rosemary claimed, then his body would've been transported directly to the assigned funeral home, not to a morgue. Unless an autopsy had been ordered, which would mean there was some suspicion regarding the manner of his death. Rosemary may not be aware of those facts, but having worked in a hospital for years, she was.

"Is an autopsy being performed?" Joey asked.

"God, no!" Rosemary snapped. "Daddy would've never wanted to be sliced and diced into a million pieces. Besides, we know the manner of death, so there's no reason for one to be conducted."

What a crock of bullshit! Rosemary was lying straight to her face. Nothing she'd said made any sense whatsoever. In her sister's mind, it probably sounded like a proper explanation because she wasn't familiar with protocol and formalities when dealing with corpses, but for someone like her who was, everything she'd said was unrealistic and highly improbable. For the hell of it, Joey was eager to see exactly how tight Rosemary was willing to twist her story.

"How did he die? You haven't said."

"A stroke," Rosemary answered pointedly.

"Did he have a history of heart problems?" Joey asked. "High blood pressure, perhaps?"

"Not that I'm aware of."

"Had he been sick?"

"No."

"Yet he died of a stroke?"

"Yes."

"How can you be so sure about that? Did a doctor verify his cause of death?"

"Why are you giving me the fifth degree?" Rosemary asked harshly, irritated by Joey's line of questioning. "I told you it was a stroke. Why are you having a problem believing me?"

"I'm only looking at it from a medical perspective," Joey explained. "Force of habit. I meant no disrespect."

"Could've fooled me."

Rosemary never had taken kindly to being called a liar. Even insinuating that she was dishonest was enough to ignite her temper and jump-start her sharp tongue. Everyone was guilty of telling a harmless lie now and then. Exaggerating about the cost of a name-brand dress or what their annual salaries were. To lie not only about the death of a parent but also fabricating the manner in which they died was beyond Joey's scope of comprehension.

"I'm going out for a while," Joey said, getting up from the table.

"Where are you going?" Robin asked.

"For a drive. I want to check out the town and see what's changed. I'll only be gone for a couple of hours."

"Didn't you see enough on your way here?" Rosemary asked snidely.

"I came *through* town, Rosie. Now I want to go drive *around* town and see what's changed."

"Not much," Robin added.

"Figures."

"You're not going to surprise us by leaving, are you? I'm looking forward to spending some time with you."

"No, Robin. Not yet, anyway," Joey said with a smile.

"Dinner will be served promptly at eight," Rosemary stated. "Don't be late. Those rules haven't changed in this house."

"You and I will talk later, Rosemary," Robin stated bluntly. "I have something I need to discuss with you. For now, I have to get back to work."

"I thought you took some time off to help us with this," she said, prompting a strange look from Joey.

"I did, but it didn't include today. I'll be back later this afternoon."

"Help with what?" Joey asked.

"Staying here and helping mom with things," Rosemary answered, realizing she'd almost said too much. "She can't be here alone right now."

"I'll do my best to be on time," Joey replied to Rosemary as she walked away. Being in the same room with her was like listening to her mother with all her rules and demands. That alone was enough to make her want to leave. The way she was feeling at the moment, she might keep driving and never come back.

There was something besides Mac's death going on with Rosemary. She'd always been haughty and tart with her words, but her current behavior was bizarre, even by her standards. If Joey didn't know any better, she'd say Rosemary was dealing with a guilty conscious over something she'd said or done that went far beyond her failure to make funeral arrangements for Mac. Joey was willing to bet that whatever it was, Helen was at the root of it.

As much as she'd prefer to pack her things and leave, she couldn't do that yet. Something untoward was going on inside Sheffield Manor and she intended to find out what it was and why her family had involved her.

Three days post-death and no arrangements had been made yet to bury Mac? That was unfathomable. The only explanation for a medical examiner not to release a body would be if the coroner found something suspicious during his examination that required further investigation. Rosemary had already confirmed there wasn't going to be an autopsy even though she'd told her Mac's body was at the medical examiner's office. Even if that were true, and Joey knew it wasn't, what kind of person would allow the dead body of a father they adored to lay rotting on a cold, steel slab without taking the necessary steps towards preparing him for his final resting place?

It seemed apparent to her that Rosemary had failed miserably when constructing her cover story for explaining her actions concerning Mac.

First of all, bodies are *never* sent to the coroner to store them while families decide what needs to be done next. Second, the *only* reason he would be sent there at all would be for an autopsy.

Rosemary should've considered that she was a registered nurse employed in the cardiac care unit at a large hospital who dealt with death regularly before concocting such an unbelievable story.

None of it made any sense. Why the delay? Better yet, why be so untruthful about it all?

With those thoughts in mind, Joey decided to stay, if for no other reason than to learn the truth.

* * * * *

"I knew I'd find you in here," Helen scolded. "What were you doing?"

"I don't know," he answered with a shrug.

"Let's get you back to your room," she said, taking him firmly by the arm.

"No!" he shouted, pulling away. "I want to stay here."

"Shh," she hushed. "You want everyone to know about this place?"

"What place?" he asked, looking confused.

"Where we're standing, you idiot. If anyone else finds out about it, they'll want to come in here and take over your space. We don't want that to happen, do we?"

"Um, no," he replied, scratching his head. "No, I suppose we don't."

"Come along now, you crazy old man. It's time for your medicine."

"I don't want it," he argued. "It makes me sleep and I want to be awake."

"Sleep is good for you. It helps to rest your mind."

"If you say so," he said, relenting and taking her hand, allowing her to lead him down the narrow stairs and back to his second-floor bedroom.

"Here we go," Helen said, passing him a hand full of pills and a glass of water. "Take these and rest. I'll open the drapes a bit for you so you can get some sunshine."

"Thank you," he said groggily, the sleeping pills already taking effect.

"I'll be back later to check on you," she said, engaging the door lock before closing it. Once he drifted off, he'd sleep for hours so she didn't have to worry about him coming back out. She kept the door locked from the outside not to keep him from getting out, but to keep anyone from going in. The only key that unlocked his door was in her possession, enabling her to come and go as she pleased, and she intended to keep it that way.

Come tomorrow, some changes were going to be made. Since he loved the attic so damn much and kept returning to it after telling him not to, she intended to move him from his current room to the one place in the house he couldn't seem to get enough of.

And she knew the perfect room to stash him in.

With any luck, during one of his plundering escapades, he'd fall down the stairs and break his stupid neck.

Chapter Seven

Joey scanned the manor grounds as she drove slowly back down the access road towards the exit, but she didn't see anyone. No yard maintenance staff was wandering about, no gardeners were pruning Helen's precious roses, and judging by the absence of any vehicles other than those of Rosemary and Robin, there were no other visitors on grounds. There wasn't a single person anywhere in sight that could explain the voices she'd heard coming from beyond the walls in the closet of Robin's room. Although they were muffled, they were distinguishable as man and woman. The rise and fall of the tempo in their tones told her they were either arguing or in a heated discussion.

Still confused about why Rosemary hadn't yet made plans for Mac's funeral, Joey searched her mind for answers why. Funeral arrangements should be a top priority following a person's death. It wasn't feasible that they'd be left at a morgue or funeral home for an indeterminable amount of time while family members made up their minds about what they wanted to do with them. Not only would that be cruel, but also inhumane.

Rosemary told her that Mac was on hold at the county morgue, but morgues don't hold dead bodies while families make final decisions. Not unless things were done differently in Cornish when it came to taking care of the deceased. She didn't believe it could be *that* much different. Corpses are taken to the medical examiner for one reason and one reason only. An autopsy. Rosemary vehemently stated one was not scheduled for Mac and wouldn't be. Why so much secrecy? Better yet, why all the mistruths and not-quite-so-believable explanations of why she'd made the decisions she had? Was there something she didn't want Joey to know? Something she feared telling her because she knew of the fractured relationship between her and her father? She needed answers, and Rosemary obviously wasn't going to provide them, so she'd have to get them on her own. Either a call or visit to the morgue would alleviate her first question, and since there were only two funeral homes in

Cornish, finding out if Helen or Rosemary had contacted either should be simple enough.

Rosemary could stuff her homemade hearty beef stew and dinner rules up her ass as far as she was concerned. She wasn't a child anymore who needed to be told what to do and when to do it. And thank God, she no longer lived there, so screw the house rules. Besides, there were other things she was more concerned with than eating in silence and watching everyone around the table dab at their mouths with each spoonful because God forbid any of them should show any type of human traits or qualities, like dribbling food on the chin while eating.

She had the rest of the afternoon to begin her quest for the truth, but there was one stop she wanted to make before embarking on her truth quest. Somewhere she could sit and think in solitude while compiling a list of addresses and phone numbers of the places she wanted to call and visit. And she knew exactly where to go. It was the one place she'd been looking forward to seeing since deciding to take the trip back home.

Joey was pleasantly surprised to see that the layout and interior of the diner hadn't changed, and the soda fountain was still in operation. Red faux leather booths lined the walls on both sides of the diner. They were placed in the exact same pattern as they'd been when she'd hung out and worked there as a teenager. In the back left corner stood a jukebox, its scratchy, mono vinyl 45's now replaced with CD's. Red-cushioned stools with silver, wine glass stem-shaped trunks were bolted to the black-and-white checkered floor around the bar, most of them occupied by patrons. Joey chose the last booth on the right side of the diner next to a large plate-glass window.

After ordering a cup of hot lemon tea, Joey placed her phone and a writing pad on the table, eager to find answers to the questions that were plaguing her.

"Do I need a Wi-Fi password?" she asked as the waitress served her tea.

"No, ma'am. It'll connect automatically. Let me know if I can get you anything else."

"Thank you."

Joey was busily writing the address to the first funeral home when she was startled by a man's voice.

"Well now, slip a pair of boots on my feet and call me a cowboy," he proclaimed. "As I live and breathe, it's Josephine Sheffield."

"Mason?" Joey beamed, slipping out of the booth and hugging him.

"In the flesh," he said, taking her by the shoulders and holding her at arm's length. "Let me get a good look at you," he beamed, shaking his head. "You're wearing your hair differently, but you're still just as beautiful as ever."

"You're too kind, but thanks," she said, running a hand over her light brown bobbed cut. Mason had known her as a blonde. It was one more thing she'd changed about herself in her quest for a new beginning.

"I mean it," he said. "May I sit for a minute?" he asked, motioning to the seat opposite her.

"Of course," Joey replied. "I'd be delighted if you joined me. I have to admit that never in a million years would I have expected to see you in here."

"Is that right?"

"To be truthfully honest with you, I didn't expect to see you at all."

"Any day of the week that you choose to come in here, you'll see me here as well."

"Still come here a lot, do you?"

"I reckon you could say that," Mason said with a smile. "Since I own it."

"You bought the diner?" Joey exclaimed. "How did you ever talk Nat into selling?"

"Didn't have to. Nat died about three years ago."

"Oh," Joey said sadly. "I'm sorry to hear that. I didn't know."

"When he died, there were no family members willing to take over. The city and county both were hell bent on demolishing it to make room for a different type of commercial business, but I couldn't stand the thought of losing a valuable piece of the town's history. After talking it over with my dad and getting his approval, I left the hardware store in his hands and invested all my savings on the purchase and renovations. I considered doing a complete overhaul on the place and making it more modern, but I finally decided against it because I felt it should maintain its original atmosphere. Afterall, that's what made it so much fun to hang out in, right? Enjoying a taste of the fifties while living in the present? I did buy more modern furniture and tables though because the vinyl on the old booths and chairs were cracked beyond repair, and who wants to sit down and eat with a piece of broken plastic constantly poking them in the butt?"

"I love it, Mason. That was a wise investment, and I'm sure the townsfolk appreciate your desire to keep alive a diner that holds a special place in a lot of hearts around here. You did a wonderful job on it."

"Thanks, Joey. I appreciate that."

"I did notice that your jukebox has CD's instead of forty-fives."

Mason gave a short laugh. "There's a reason for that."

"Do tell."

"You're going to love this one, so get ready," Mason told her. "Shortly after I reopened, a group of kids from the high school came in. Probably Freshmen, Sophomores at the most. Young kids. One boy asked me what that machine in the corner was and what did it do, so I told him it was a jukebox and it played records. He gave me the strangest look, like I was speaking a foreign language that he didn't understand. I explained that if he put coins in the slot then punched in the number on the keypad of the song he wanted to hear, the chosen record would be selected by a robotic arm and placed onto the turntable and his song would play through the speakers. This kid is giving me a look like I was insane, shaking his head and making faces at his friends. Not wanting to embarrass him, I asked him if he knew what a record was. And do you know what that kid said to me?" he asked with a wide grin.

"What?"

"That kid looked up at me and in a smartass tone said, 'Duh, it's a big, black CD.'"

"Oh, no," Joey laughed. "Can you imagine what they'd do with a rotary dial phone?"

"Stare at it and scratch their heads, I reckon, since they've never seen one. Or a phone booth. So, yeah, after that, I replaced the vinyl with CD's. It keeps me from having to explain it repeatedly."

"CD's or vinyl, still works the same."

"That it does," Mason agreed. "It was touch and go there for a while in the beginning and I wondered if I'd made a mistake by putting all my money into it, but it's finally paying off and I have no regrets. We stay pretty busy around here."

"I can see that," Joey said, glancing around the small restaurant.

"Enough about me and the diner," Mason said. "Let's talk about you now. I have to start by asking you a question."

"Okay," Joey said. "Go ahead.

"After all this time of being gone, what brings you back to Cornish? Not that I'm not happy to see you, but you could've blown me over with a feather when I saw you sitting here."

"A funeral."

"I'm sorry. Whose?"

"My father's."

"Mac's dead?" Mason asked in a surprised tone.

"Yes."

"When?"

"A couple of days ago."

Mason's brow furrowed as he chewed absently at his bottom lip, staring blankly down at the table.

"Is something wrong?"

"Wrong, no. I'm surprise, that's all," Mason answered. "I consider myself to be well informed of what goes on in my community, but this is news to me. I haven't heard anything about your dad dying, nor have I heard anyone say anything about it. You'd think that the death of a man like your father who's a highly regarded and prominent figure in Cornish, would have everyone talking about it."

"His obituary wasn't in the local paper?"

"If it was, I certainly didn't see it, and I still read the paper every day. I think I'd remember seeing that. Want me to ask around and see what I can find out?"

"No," Joey answered, shaking her head. "That's probably one more thing Rosemary hasn't taken care of yet."

"When's the funeral? I'd like to attend if that's okay with you."

"It would be fine with me, but I don't even know myself. It hasn't been arranged yet."

"He's been dead for two days?" Mason replied, his voice rising a pitch. "And there aren't any services planned?"

"No."

"I'm sure Rosemary has her reasons for delaying. Are more family members expected to come in?"

"I don't think so. Most, if not all, of Mac's family is deceased. So is Helen's. I'd be surprised to learn that anyone else is coming."

"If you do find out the information, can you please let me know?" Mason asked, rising from his seat.

"Sure."

"Here's my number," he said, passing her a napkin with his cell phone number on it. "I've got to get back to work for now, but I'd really like to get together with you while you're in town. We can talk about old times and catch up on what each other's been up to."

"I'd like that," Joey said, taking the napkin and ripping off the bottom piece. "Here," she said, passing him the jagged piece of paper. "My number in case you need to call me."

"We'll talk some more later," Mason said, rising from the booth and disappearing through the swinging door that led into the kitchen.

"I know who you are."

Joey glanced up from her phone to see an attractive brunette occupying the seat that Mason had just vacated. "Then you've got one up on me because I don't know who you are."

"You don't remember me?"

"I'm sorry, but no, I don't."

"We went to school together. Cassidy Foreman. Cheerleader, Homecoming Queen."

"The name sounds familiar, but remembering you is alluding me right now."

"Doesn't matter. Like I said, I know who you are. I know about your past with Mason and that the two of you were in love and were going to get married. I also know that you walked out on him without even saying goodbye."

For the second time that day, Joey struggled to keep her anger intact. Leaning forward, she folded her arms on the tabletop and stared directly at Cassidy. "You seem to know an awful lot about me, yet I don't know a single thing about you."

"The only thing you need to know is that I'm with Mason now, so if you're even thinking about reconciling your romance with him, let me give you some advice. Forget about it."

Joey smirked at the brazenness of the strange woman whom she honestly did not recognize, interpreting her words as a threat. "You said your name is Cassidy, right?"

"Yes."

"Cassidy, let me take this time to advise you I am not, in any way, shape, or form interested in getting back together with Mason. In fact, that's the furthest thing from my mind. But if you think for one second you can sit there and dictate to me which friends I can associate with, then you are sadly mistaken. If I want to get together with Mason, as a *friend* and talk, I really don't see where that's any of your business so I won't be asking your permission to do so. Now, is there anything else you'd like to say while you have a chance?"

"I've said what I came over here to say, and I hope I've made myself clear. Stay away from Mason, or else."

"Cassidy, you should know I don't take kindly to threats, so you may want to back off and watch what you're saying. For what it's worth, I didn't know Mason owned this diner and running into him was a complete surprise and nothing more than a coincidence. As I said, I'm not looking to get back together with him. As soon as my father's funeral is over, I'll be heading back home to Indiana, so don't go worrying your pretty little head over me. You have a lovely day now, you hear?"

Joey dropped a five-dollar bill on the table, grabbed her purse and left the diner with Cassidy's words resonating inside her head.

What she wanted to tell the arrogant bitch was that she'd already had Mason multiple times, but there was no reason to say something so hateful and personal as a means of retaliation. Her envy was well-noted, but undeserving. She meant it when she'd said she wasn't interested in a reconciliation. Her confrontation with Cassidy brought out even more buried secrets. One of the most painful ones being that when she and Mason had their first sexual encounter, she'd faked being a virgin, letting him believe he'd been her first and she'd hated herself for it. But it was a lot better than telling him the truth.

That Mac had beaten him to it.

Chapter Eight

As time went by and she grew older, the nightly visits from Mac decreased in number, yet increased in intensity whenever he did come to her room. Fondling and groping her became his choice of assault, slobbering all over her while blasting his whiskey-filled breath into her face as he lavished his revolting, sloppy wet kisses all over her face. Before Mac began launching his incestuous desires upon her, she'd never known it was possible to hate anyone as much as she did him. Girls were supposed to love and adore their fathers, not despise them. Because of his twisted outlook of being "daddy's little angel," he'd taken away any inkling of love or affection she may have once felt for him the first time he embarked upon his midnight pleasure outings, making her a victim of his twisted and disgusting sexual desires, touching her in places she knew he wasn't supposed to touch her, making her perform sickening and grotesque acts on him to fulfill his pleasures, covering her in his stinking man juices every time he'd reached his climax, always careful not to get any on the sheets but plenty on her skin and clothing. If the servants had ever been suspicious about the hardened stains left on her pajamas and nightgowns, they'd certainly never brought it to anyone's attention.

The profane and vile acts inflicted upon her over the course of the years had always brought joy and pleasure to Mac but had made her purely sick. No number of showers or baths had ever seemed to wash his stench away, nor did he heed to her requests to stop hurting her. In fact, it'd always seemed to her that the more she begged him to stop, the more he enjoyed it.

At the tender age of thirteen, the assaults still hadn't ceased; however, she was willing to suffer the consequences of defying house rules by locking her door at night to keep him out. Whatever punishment would be issued for disobeying couldn't be any worse than the punishment Mac had been inflicting on her since she was ten years old. Locking the door proved futile because Mac always found a way in. If he'd done so by picking the lock, he'd done it expertly every single time because he'd never made a sound, which gave him the advantage over her on that horrible night so long ago that'd changed her forever.

Chapter Nine

After leaving the diner, Joey drove around town long enough to pull herself back together. She'd maintained her composure while in Mason's presence, but between the melancholy stir of emotions she'd felt seeing and talking to him again, and the confrontation with Cassidy, the tears began free-falling before she could even get in her car. It'd been bittersweet seeing Mason after such a long absence, especially since she'd left Cornish so abruptly and without anyone's knowledge, and had she known he owned the diner she would've never gone inside and taken a chance on running into him. The exchange of words with Cassidy was both nerve-wracking and unexpected, angering her more than it should have, possibly because of all the personal accusations she'd slung at her. The sting of her words was painful but couldn't make her feel any more guilty about her actions than she'd already dealt with for fifteen years. What was one more wound added to the list of many? Although she'd said enough to Cassidy to get her point across, she could've just as easily said so much worse. She was glad she'd been able to control her temperament and not cause a public scene. Afterall, she was only going to be in town for a few days and there was no sense in causing unnecessary rifts with people she'd likely never see again.

In the rearview mirror, she checked her eyes to make sure her tears hadn't caused her mascara to run and give her raccoon eyes, and that they weren't too red or swollen. Giving herself a stamp of approval, she exited the car.

The medical examiner's office was only a few blocks from the diner, situated next to the small, and only, one-story hospital in Cornish.

Other than a white van with *Bristol County Coroner* stenciled on the side in black lettering, the parking lot was empty. Joey feared she'd come too late in the day and wouldn't be able to obtain the information she needed.

The front door opened when she pulled on the handle, a bell chiming as she stepped into a small office area void of furniture and reeking with the smell of formaldehyde. No one was at the reception window, but someone had to be there or else the front door would've been locked.

"Hello?" she called out.

A man's voice answered, but she didn't see him. "One minute, please."

Joey crossed her arms and waited anxiously. She hated being there. But her visit was a necessary first step in verifying Rosemary's claim. Dead people and funeral homes had always been a difficult challenge for her, even in nursing school when she'd had to work with cadavers as part of her clinical training. It hadn't been easy, but she'd succeeded, hoping, and praying she'd never have to deal with corpses in that way again, especially after being told that sometimes dead bodies have muscle twitches, burp, fart and have even sat up on morgue tables. While she knew it was impossible for a dead person to hurt her, if she ever saw one make movements like that, they could certainly make her harm herself while running away as fast as her legs could go.

"Can I help you?" A middle-aged man with graying hair and horn-rimmed glasses appeared at the reception window wearing green scrubs and wiping his hands on a small, green towel.

"I'm sorry to bother you so late in the day, but I just drove into town from Indiana."

"What brings you here?" the man asked. "To the medical examiner's office, I mean."

"I'm in town for the funeral of my father and I was told he was here."

"I'm sorry for your loss. I'm Dr. Ford, the attending M.E." he told her as he folded the towel and put it in a pocket of his scrub shirt. "Is your father scheduled for an autopsy?"

"Not that I'm aware of. My sister informed me he was being held here until arrangements are made and a funeral home is chosen."

Dr. Ford cocked his head slightly. "There must be some kind of mistake, Miss...?"

"Sheffield. Joey Sheffield. My father's name is Macarthur, but everybody calls him Mac."

"Of Sheffield Manor?"

"Yes."

"I know your father. Or I guess I should say I know of him. He's an important person in this town, so I'm sure most everyone does know him."

"You said there's been a mistake. What did you mean by that?"

"Only that your father's body wouldn't be here unless he was being autopsied. It's not customary to store corpses here while families make funeral arrangements," he explained. "I hope that doesn't sound cold or rude, but I really don't know another way to explain it."

"I understand," Joey replied. "I'm in the medical profession as well, so I'm not offended. If it's not too much trouble, do you mind double-checking just to make sure he's not here? I'm certain this is where my sister said he was, unless there's another coroner's office in town and I misunderstood her."

"No, this is the only one. I'm the Chief M.E., and I can assure you Macarthur Sheffield was not brought into this office. However, if it'll help, I'll check my records to make sure."

"It would help, thank you."

"Wait right here. It'll only take a few seconds to find out." Less than a minute passed before he reappeared carrying a clipboard. "When did your father pass away?"

"Two days ago."

Dr. Ford shook his head as he scanned a finger down the board. "Nope. No Macarthur Sheffield has been brought here."

With confirmation from Dr. Ford, she no longer assumed Rosemary had lied to her. She now knew factually that she had. Why would she be dishonest about something that was so easy to verify? Had she honestly expected Joey to take her at her word and ask no questions? Unfortunately for Rosemary, she'd terribly underestimated her.

A heart-to-heart chat with her sister would be forthcoming, but not until after she paid visits to the two funeral parlors. She preferred having all the ammunition before confronting her because it would be difficult to deny the accusations with proof on her side. If it turned out that neither one had been contacted about Mac, then Rosemary, Robin and Helen all owed her an explanation, beginning with the reason she'd been summoned back to Cornish to attend a funeral that'd never existed.

"Thank you, Dr. Ford. I appreciate your time."

Joey checked her phone when she got into her car, seeing that she'd missed a call from Ellen. She'd silenced it before entering the coroner's office, not wanting to chance being interrupted while speaking to the doctor. She'd return Ellen's call later that night once she was alone in her room and could talk without anyone listening in.

One last stop needed to be made before returning to Sheffield Manor, an errand she hadn't planned to tend to, nor would she have ever thought she'd need to do what she was about to. Knowing this trip would be the last time she'd ever be in Cornish, and since the issue at hand was a pressing one, there was no better time than the present to do what must be done. If her suspicions proved correct and she'd been enticed to return home under false pretenses that had nothing at all to do with Mac's death, then they could blame themselves for their own comeuppance because they'd given her no other choice than to do what she had to. All three of them would be more than deserving of the final outcome.

As she headed back to the manor, she wondered if anyone had become suspicious about the length of time she'd been gone and what had been so important that it'd kept her out for more than four hours. Not that she cared about what they thought, but for now, it was important that she act normal and maintain control of her emotions and behavior. The slightest change in either could alert them to the fact that she was more than skeptical about what was really going on at Sheffield Manor and why she'd been called home for the funeral of a man that didn't appear to be dead.

Chapter Ten

"Aunt Joey, Aunt Joey!" the girls squealed, running and throwing their arms around her waist as she entered the front door.

"My goodness," Joey exclaimed, hugging Julia and Jackie, Rosemary and Dan's two daughters. "Let me get a good look at you both," she said, holding them at arm's length. "You're both growing like wild weeds." Julia, ten and the oldest of the two, was the spitting image of her mother when she was the same age as Julia was now. Two long, blonde braids hung over her shoulders, her bright blue eyes glistening beneath the dim lighting of the foyer. A sprinkle of freckles spread across her nose and cheeks, and she was missing a front tooth. Jackie had celebrated her eighth birthday only the week before. She resembled her father, inheriting his red hair and green eyes. Her hair was also braided, with pink ribbons tied on the ends to match the pink and yellow dress she wore. Contrary to the belief that freckles were inevitable with redheads, Jackie didn't have any. Her skin had no blemishes and was as smooth as porcelain. "Who knocked your tooth out, Julia?" Joey teased.

"Nobody, silly," Julia said, then laughed. "It came out all by itself. And guess what? I got a whole dollar for it from the tooth fairy."

"Wow, that's a lot of money for one tooth. Bet you can't wait until the others come out. If the tooth fairy keeps leaving you money like that, you'll be rich by the time you're eleven."

"Goody," Julia replied, taking hold of one of her hands as Jackie took the other, leading her toward the dining room where everyone sat around the table.

"You're late," Rosemary said without looking up. "Girls, if you're finished with your dinner, go wash up."

"Mom," Julia groaned. "Can't we stay here and visit with Aunt Joey?"

"You heard me," Rosemary said, casting an icy glare at them. "Now go. You can visit later."

"You're looking well, Joey," Dan said, lifting a glass of white wine in the air. "I suppose life's been treating you well?"

"Can't complain," Joey answered, pulling out a chair and sitting down.

"Nice of you to come for a visit. Guess you three are planning a sisterly reunion?"

Before Joey could answer, Rosemary cut her off. Obviously, Dan didn't know why she was there, which meant he, too, was unaware of the supposed funeral. This ordeal was getting crazier by the second. "You missed dinner," Rosemary reprimanded. "House rules still apply, no matter how old you are and regardless of whether you reside here. You're a guest and should be more respectful."

"Doesn't matter. I'm not hungry, anyway."

"Where have you been all afternoon? I thought you were only going to be gone for a short time."

"Riding around, taking in the town, admiring the changes," Joey replied sarcastically.

"I'm guessing you stopped by your old stomping grounds?"

"If you mean the diner, then the answer is yes."

"Run into anyone you know?" Rosemary sneered.

"As a matter of fact, I did."

"Rosemary, stop it," Robin stated with a scolding tone.

"It's okay, Robin," Joey said. Turning back to Rosemary, she said, "Why don't you go ahead and ask me if I saw Mason. That's what you want to know, isn't it?"

"Did you?"

"I did."

"And?"

"And what? There is no and. We spoke briefly, I drank a cup of tea then left."

Helen hadn't spoken a word or even so much as looked at her since she'd sat down, but suddenly she hissed, "Trash," as she scooted her chair back, threw her napkin down into her empty bowl and angrily left the table. Within seconds, the loud bang of a slamming door caused everyone to jump. Joey wasn't sure if Helen's comment was directed at her or Mason, and she had no intentions of asking her. "Was it something I said?" Joey frowned. "Or is it because she's still the same old bitch she's always been?"

"Joey!" Now Robin was scolding her.

"Some things never change, do they?" Rosemary asked condescendingly.

"Not in this house, they don't," Joey answered, hoping Rosemary would tell her she'd taken care of the arrangements today and fill her in on the information she needed. Instead, Rosemary remained silent, staring down at her bowl. Joey desperately wanted to confront her and tell her about her visit to the M.E., but she knew it wouldn't be wise to do that quite yet, not without all the facts first.

"Mason's done a lot to improve the diner, hasn't he?" Robin asked, trying to lift the heavy fog that'd suddenly settled over them.

"He has," Joey agreed. "Renovations combined with some of the old features gives it a homey feel, almost like it did in high school."

"It's always busy in there. Sometimes there's a line of customers waiting outside to get in. He did a good thing for this town when he took over."

"I think so, too."

Dan glanced at his watch, then finished his glass of wine. "Guess I'd better get going," he said, rising from the table. "You and the girls have everything you need?" he asked Rosemary.

"Yes."

"You're staying here?" Joey asked, surprised that Rosemary would even consider spending the night since she had her own mansion to go home to. Coming from a wealthy family had never been good enough for her. She'd also married into money.

"I told you when I spoke with you on the phone that Robin and I were staying here temporarily."

"Guess I misunderstood. I thought you meant during the day. My mistake."

"Dan's going out of town on business, and I don't want to be home alone with the girls. Besides, mother needs me here. Is that a problem for you?"

"Not at all," Joey replied dryly, striving to keep her cool in the face of her sister's obnoxious and arrogant attitude. Rosemary had always been curt and quick with her words, but Joey felt her intentional hatefulness was directed solely at her, and she had no idea why. She hadn't come back to Sheffield Manor to fight and quarrel with her eldest sister, but she felt as though that's exactly what Rosemary was trying to get her to do. Was she intentionally endeavoring to get her to leave? And if so, why would she do that when she was the one who'd asked her to come? Had she done something she now regretted and the only way she could deal with her guilt was by treating her like shit, hoping she'd pack her things and go back to Indiana? It wouldn't take much for her to do exactly that and tell them all to go fuck themselves as she walked out the door the same way she'd done fifteen years before. She'd been tempted to do it ever since Rosemary informed her that no preparations had yet been made for Mac. Now that her curiosity was piqued, she needed to fight that urge until she found out exactly what the hell Rosemary and Helen were up to and why she'd been called back to a place she'd sworn she'd never return to again. She hadn't come out of love or respect for Mac because she felt neither of those emotions for him. She came because she loved her sisters and was there for them. There was definitely something weird going on with Rosemary, however. Although they hadn't seen each other in quite some time, Joey acknowledged she was acting odder than usual and out of sorts in her behavior. Joey's mind was suddenly filled with the vision of a horror movie she'd watched as a kid where humans were replaced by replicas of themselves that were born from a pea pod, making Joey wonder if Rosemary was really Rosemary, or an excellent replica of her sister in alien form. Joey felt certain that Rosemary was exhibiting either shame or regret, perhaps both, and the only way she knew how to deal with those two things was by lashing out at the one person who made her feel that way. Unfortunately, it was her that Rosemary's wrath was aimed at.

"Guess I'll see you all in the morning," Joey said, getting up from her chair.

"You're going to bed this early?" Robin protested. "It's not even nine."

"Not going to bed, but I am going to my room. I have a couple of phone calls to return, and I think I might read for a while. You're spending the night, too, right, Robin?"

"Yep," Robin answered, nodding. "I'll be in your old room if you need me."

"See you in the morning."

She needed to call Ellen back and let her know she was okay. She had no plans to read since she hadn't brought a book or even a magazine, but it'd been a good excuse to break away from Rosemary's hostility. Who thinks about reading when they're supposed to be planning for, and attending, a funeral? She absolutely couldn't bear being in the same room with Rosemary a second longer for fear that if she did, she'd end up slapping the piss out of her and she really didn't want that to happen.

Hopefully, by distancing herself from her egotistical sister, it'd help alleviate the anger and hard feelings between them.

A good night's sleep for both would bring a fresh start for everyone the following morning.

Chapter Eleven

"I can't even stand to look at that devious bitch," Helen seethed through clenched teeth, balling her hands into fists. "Whenever I do, I get the urge to knock her head off. All the lies she's told over the years, the trouble and shame she brought to this family. It's all unforgivable. She's such a disgrace to the Sheffield name."

After storming from the table, she'd retreated into the small den down the hallway from the kitchen, expecting Rosemary and Robin to join her once Joey retreated to her room and wouldn't notice their absence. She sat erect in a floral print wing-back chair, drumming her talon-like fingers on the arms as she stared blankly ahead.

"Well, mother, getting her to come back here was your idea, not mine. You knew how you felt about her from the get-go, so if you knew ahead of time she'd get under your skin this way, why did you even bother?"

"Not just my idea," Helen corrected, snapping her head around to look at Rosemary. "Or have you forgotten that fact?"

"No, mother, I haven't forgotten. I'm sure you'll never let me forget it."

"You'll mind your tone with me," Helen seethed. "I've already got one ungrateful and disrespectful daughter to contend with, I sure as hell don't need two."

"Rosemary, what the hell?" Robin yelled as she entered the room. "You told Joey daddy was dead? What were you thinking?" She'd been surprised that morning when Joey questioned Rosemary about funeral arrangements but hadn't confronted her about it until now because she'd left for work right after. By the time she got back to the house, Dan and the kids were there, eliminating any chance she may have had to address the issue further. Once Joey announced she was retiring for the night, she knew her mom and sister would be meeting in the den and that would provide the opportunity she needed.

"It was the only thing I could think of to get her to come back," Rosemary snapped, forgoing telling her it wasn't her idea at all, but their mother's.

"Surely to God, you must know she's not going to stop prying until she gets the answers she's looking for, especially after the debacle this morning. I'd be willing to bet that's what she spent her afternoon doing. It's only a matter of time before she learns the truth."

"If you had any better suggestions on how to get her to come home, you certainly didn't share them with us. I did what I had to do. Besides," she said, plopping down on the matching chair opposite her mother. "It worked, didn't it?"

"Yes, but you brought her here under false pretenses," Robin argued. "You never mentioned to me what you'd done to make this work. What, exactly, are you and mother up to? You told me you were planning a surprise for her and daddy. That's the only reason I agreed to participate."

"Enough," Helen demanded. "I'll not sit here and listen to the two of you bicker. What's done is done. She's here, and that's all that really matters to me. I couldn't care less how Rosemary got her to agree."

"Don't include me in this sick plan of yours," Robin protested. "I won't be involved in something as sinister as making Joey think our daddy's dead."

"You're already involved," Helen stated firmly, rising from the chair, turning to face Robin. "Do I need to remind you that you also have a stake in this?"

"A stake?" Robin asked. "What the hell could be worth tricking Joey by lying to her?"

"I think you already know the answer to that question," Helen said, nodding her head toward Rosemary. "As does your sister."

"Wait a second," Robin said, holding up a hand in protest. "Are you trying to tell me that receiving my inheritance is contingent upon whether I take part in this disgusting scheme?"

"Why don't you ask Rosemary," Helen sneered. "Wills can be changed with the stroke of a pen, and might I remind you, I maintain an attorney on my payroll for such purposes. Do you need further clarity?"

"You know what, mother? If I'm forced to make a choice between collecting daddy's money and lying to Joey about what's really going on here, then let me say this as clearly as I know how. Shove it," she stated, opening the door to leave. "I won't do that to Joey."

"Oh, Robin," Helen called pompously, her nose high, lips pursed. "Claiming your inheritance isn't only about participating in what you have referred to as a scheme. There are other conditions. Would you care to know what they are or is your mind already made up?" Helen sat back down, a queen on her throne, satisfied that she'd made her point so eloquently.

Closing the door, Robin leaned against it as she glanced at Rosemary, who sat straight-faced in her chair, arms folded, knowing the twisted consequences she could face if she dared to speak out against Helen, the matriarch to end all matriarchs. Rosemary shook her head and looked away.

"I'm listening," Robin said finally. "Enlighten me, mother."

"You will keep your mouth shut and not breathe a word about any of this to Joey. If you do, I will know about it and there will be repercussions, that much I can guarantee you. If you can't do that, then perhaps the best thing for you to do is to stay away and avoid any type of contact with Joey. I'll also add that my lawyer is on standby if you choose to not comply with my wishes. Do you honestly think you could continue your way of living on that measly salary you make?" Helen said with an evil laugh. "What a joy it would be to watch you try. And may I also remind you that the deed on the home you live in is in my name? Eviction from such a lovely house doesn't suit you, but with the money you make at your dreadful job, you can afford to buy yourself a mobile home. There's a cute little trailer park on the outskirts of town that would be suitable for relocation. But the choice you make is entirely up to you. However, my suggestion is that you choose wisely."

Robin stormed out of the den, slamming the door behind her.

"Way to go, mother," Rosemary said sarcastically. "You've managed to piss off another daughter. Are you seriously planning on expelling and disinheriting her, too?"

"If she fails to heed my warnings, I most certainly will, and I won't bat an eye while doing so. That's the price one pays for being disloyal. What's the old saying? Never bite the hand that feeds you.

Even if Robin does choose to backslide and live like a pauper, I still have you to count on, as usual. You've never let me down before, so I hope you're not planning on starting now."

"No, mother, I wouldn't dream of it," Rosemary replied dryly. "God only knows what you'd do to me if I did."

"Good. Your father will be proud."

"Tell me something, mother," Rosemary said, glancing at Helen. "Is all this reunion planning really for daddy? Or is it you who wants it so badly?"

"Whatever do you mean?"

"Even when he's half-ass coherent, he barely knows where he is or what his name is. Do you really expect me to believe, in his deteriorating frame of mind, that he begged you to get Joey home so he could see her one last time?"

"I expect you not to question the motives here," Helen replied. "Why else would I want this if not to please him?"

"I think the answer to that has yet to be determined."

"Think what you wish, it doesn't change a damn thing."

"Speaking of daddy, where is he?"

"Adhering to the plan," Helen answered. "Staying out of sight for now." Rosemary didn't need to know she was keeping him heavily sedated, even more so than what had been recommended by his physician. He sometimes roamed about, and she needed to make sure Joey didn't see him before she could take care of the business that needed to be dealt with. If she saw the man whose funeral she was there to attend, the likelihood that she'd pack her things and head back to Indiana asking no questions was great, and she refused to let that happen. She'd never allow her to get away again. "When the time is right and everything's in order, he'll make his appearance and do what needs to be done."

"Out of curiosity, exactly what is it he's planning on doing? Considering his state of mind now, do you really think he's going to know who Joey is? He barely knows who I am half the time, and I'm the one who's here the most to help you with him.

When you *allow* me to see him, that is. Can I go up for a quick visit now?"

"No," Helen answered, the frown on Rosemary's face telling her that she'd answered too fast and a tad bit harsh. "What I mean is, he's sleeping, and I don't want you to disturb him." *What I don't want is for you to see that he's totally knocked out, compliments of a vast amount of Alprazolam because I'm not in the mood to deal with the lousy bastard nor do I want him up and about wandering from room to room, making noise and drawing attention.* "You can go up and visit when he wakes up." *If I'm lucky enough, that'll be never.*

Helen hadn't told Rosemary and Robin everything. In fact, she hadn't told them the truth at all. As far as they were concerned, bringing Joey home had been Mac's idea, requesting to see her one more time before his illness took full control of his mind, rendering him nothing more than a vessel once occupied by her headstrong husband. Rosemary and Robin, both of whom dearly loved their father, had agreed to help her persuade Joey to come home, but only Rosemary had been aware of the lie that needed to be told in order to convince her that she needed to come. Anything for daddy. Truth was, Mac didn't even know she was there. All she'd told him was that she was arranging a surprise for him. It didn't matter to her whether he knew and recognized her or not. She didn't bring Joey home for his pleasure. She'd brought her back for her own.

"That's for me to know," Helen said, opening the door to leave. "And for you to find out. Trust me, you will soon enough. That's a promise."

* * * * *

Rosemary hated that she'd allowed herself to get drawn into her mother's diabolical plot. After being threatened with exposure of her one and only indiscretion against her husband and not wanting to face the possibility of an ugly divorce that would leave her homeless and penniless, she hadn't been left with much of an option. Against her better judgment and protesting the whole time, she'd even allowed her mother to convince her that her father needed to be moved to an upstairs room temporarily to ensure Joey didn't see him until it was time to act. That was three weeks ago, so why had her mother insisted that he needed to be moved so far ahead of Joey's arrival? Additionally, that'd been the last time she'd seen her father. Every time she asked to visit him, he was either resting or sleeping. Mother wasn't allowing her or Robin to visit with him, and since she was the only one with a key to his room, there was no way to get in short of breaking the door down. On a couple of occasions, she'd knocked on the door hoping he would answer but he never did, and if she banged too loudly on it, surely mother would come running, ready to hand out a good tongue lashing for daring to disturb him against her orders. She'd unexpectedly fired his nurse, insisting that a jackass could've taken better care of him than she had. Rosemary knew that wasn't true because the nurse had administered excellent care and was shocked when she'd been relieved of her duties without notice. Daddy's care was now solely in mother's hands. If she told her and Robin that he was fine, her word was to be taken as the gospel and neither of them dared to doubt her word or tell her to prove otherwise. They both knew better than to call or insinuate that Helen Sheffield was a liar.

Initially, the plan had been to fabricate a believable story that would entice Joey to come for a visit, but every time a plan was voiced, it was dismissed quickly, knowing Joey was too smart to fall for any of their unbelievable cover stories. According to her mother, the entire idea benefited their father, claiming he desperately wanted to see Joey once more because he knew his illness was progressing and he wished to see her before he forgot who she was, so making sure it all happened took top priority and excuses for failure were unacceptable. While the part about his illness certainly was true, Rosemary was having doubts about it being her father who wanted Joey home, especially considering that it was her mother, not her, who'd concocted the lie of his death as a last-ditch effort to get through to Joey. Even that almost hadn't worked. In the end, Joey finally relented and came home, unaware she'd taken the poisoned bait and walked right into the spider's web.

Even as kids, her mother had treated Joey as if she were the proverbial red-headed stepchild, excluding her from mother-daughter outings, sending her to the attic dark room as punishment although she'd done nothing wrong, debasing her and calling her hateful names, practically ignoring her existence. She and Robin both had shrugged it off because they knew how their mother was and how harsh she could be with words and actions, even toward them. On multiple occasions, she'd informed them that the reason Joey wasn't joining them on their excursions was because she didn't want to, and they had no reason to believe otherwise.

Under the circumstances, Rosemary didn't blame Joey one bit for leaving home when she did and would've done it sooner if she could have. Hell, she was anxious to get out of the house herself, so when Dan proposed to her, it'd been a Godsend.

From the moment Joey had arrived, her guilt over what she'd done had been in overdrive. Not knowing what her mother was planning gnawed at her, even frightened her because her mother could be unpredictable. What she really wanted to do was take Joey to the side and tell her to gather her things and get the hell out of there, but to do that would be to suffer the wrath of Helen, who was more than capable of giving Satan himself a run for his money. As much as she hated doing it, being a bitch to Joey was the only thing she could think to do, hoping Joey would get fed up with the abusive treatment and leave on her own, but that didn't seem to be working either. All she could do now was keep a watchful eye on her mother, agree to go along with whatever she had planned, and monitor the situation. If her mother were planning on harming Joey, she'd stop her, regardless of the consequences. Lying to her was one thing. Allowing Helen to hurt her was a whole different ballgame, and one she had no interest in playing in.

Chapter Twelve

"Ellen, I'm telling you, something strange is going on here. I don't know what it is, but it has me a little on edge," Joey told her friend as she stood next to the window looking out into the darkness. In the distance, she could see the intermittent flashing of red lights from the radio station tower in downtown Cornish. "My entire family has always been a little on the eccentric side, but I believe they've all reached a whole new level of insanity."

"What do you mean by strange?" Ellen asked. After Joey finished explaining, Ellen said, "Maybe I'm just being paranoid, but I've had a bad feeling ever since you left. I can't explain it."

"A bad feeling about what?"

"To be honest, Joey, I'm not sure. All I can tell you is that I can't shake the feeling that you're in danger. I know it probably sounds crazy to you because I don't even know your family. Like I said, it's paranoia."

"Don't worry about me, Ellen. I'm a big girl and I can take care of myself and deal with my family.

To tell you the truth, more than once I've considered leaving this place and coming home. Something just doesn't feel right."

"Always trust your gut," Ellen said. "Isn't that what you've always told me?"

Joey laughed lightly. "It is."

"Other than a make-believe funeral, is anything else going on? Are you enjoying yourself?"

"I ran into Mason."

"No," Ellen exclaimed. "How did that go?"

"Awkward and pleasant, sad and happy, all at once. I held myself together in his presence, but I shed a few tears afterwards."

"I'm sure. That must've been hard, even painful. Did the two of you talk?"

"Briefly, but not about anything of importance. He did say he'd like to get together while I'm here and catch up."

"Are you going to?"

"Thinking about it, even though his current girlfriend basically threatened me and told me to stay away from him."

"Well, if I know you the way I think I know you, that only made you *want* to spend time with him."

"You know me too well," Joey began, then paused, holding the phone away from her ear. She was certain she heard muffled voices again. "Ellen, hold on a sec," she said, going to the closet and stepping inside.

"Is everything okay?"

"I'm not sure," Joey answered, pressing an ear to the wall. She distinctly heard a man's loud voice. He sounded either extremely irritated or outright angry. Then came a woman's voice, followed by another. It sounded like they were arguing. After listening for a few moments, the voices began to recede, then disappeared altogether.

"Joey?"

"It was nothing. I thought I heard someone calling me."

"Please be careful," Ellen pleaded. "If you don't feel safe, do us both a favor and get the hell out of there and come home where you belong."

"I have a couple of errands to run in the morning," she explained. "And if I discover what I think I'm going to find, I'll be doing exactly that as early as tomorrow afternoon."

"You'll keep me informed?"

"Of course. If you don't hear from me right away, don't call out the cavalry, alright?"

Ellen laughed. "Don't make me."

"See you when I get back. Love you."

"Love you, too."

Joey disconnected the call and laid her phone on the bedside table, curious about whose voices she'd heard. Whoever they'd been, they weren't there now. It wouldn't do any good to ask Rosemary about it because she'd continue to deny that anyone else was there, even if someone was. And if they were alone in the house, then the voices could only belong to those who were already there, all of whom were women and none of them had deep voices.

* * * * *

"You told me he was sleeping," Rosemary said gruffly. "You said that's why I couldn't come up to visit. What in God's name have you done to daddy? He looks horrible."

"He was sleeping when I last checked on him," Helen answered. "Sometimes his medication

126

causes him to sleepwalk. And don't blame his appearance on me," she barked. "I'm dealing with him the best way I know how."

"If what I'm seeing is your best, then you might want to consider hiring another nurse. This is unacceptable, mother."

"If you think I'm not properly caring for your father, then by all means, feel free to take over since you seem to think you can do a better job."

"Get your fucking hands off me, both of you," Mac yelled as he tried to pull away.

"Stop that, you stupid old fool." Helen reprimanded. "Will it be necessary for me to tether you to your bed?"

"Mother!" Rosemary gasped. "You wouldn't dare!" Yes, she would, especially if it kept him inside his room so she didn't have to deal with him. If she didn't know any better, she'd swear her mother was trying to kill him. No wonder she hadn't allowed her or Robin to see him in weeks. He looked like shit and had deteriorated drastically in the weeks since he'd been moved to his new room. "I can't believe you left him unattended. What if he fell down the stairs?" She couldn't hide the disdain in her voice over Helen's total disregard for his safety. An accidental fall down the stairs would undoubtedly kill him. Maybe that's what her mother wanted. She'd be overjoyed if she no longer had to look after a man whose mind was failing him a little more with each passing day.

"He didn't though, did he?" Helen answered sarcastically. "Now shut up and help me get him back to his room," she said, heading toward the end of the corridor.

"You have *got* to be kidding me," Rosemary exclaimed as she stared at the narrow wooden staircase at the end of the hall. "This is *not* the area I helped you move him to," Rosemary said angrily, more familiar than she cared to be with Mac's newest living quarters. At the top of those stairs was the room that, as kids, she, Robin, and Joey had been sent to whenever they misbehaved. Which, according to Helen, was quite often. During those times of punishment, they were forced to stay inside the dark room with no lights, nothing to keep them occupied and no food until they were released on good behavior. Upon their releases, they were forced to offer apologies for being such rotten kids. "With all the extra rooms in this house, you're keeping daddy up here? How could you stoop so low? Is he being punished, too? He's not an animal, you know?"

"For crying out loud, Rosemary, stop being so melodramatic. I needed him in a smaller area so he'd be more manageable. He was constantly snooping around, plundering through boxes and leaving behind awful messes. Quite frankly, I got tired of cleaning up after him. He's fine up here. It's only temporary." No it wasn't. She'd moved his things to his current room the day after Rosemary had helped her move him to a second-floor room, knowing she would've never agreed to place him inside what they'd always referred to as the punishment room. Yet that's where he belonged because he was a bad, bad man and deserved whatever punishment she decided to dish out. "I moved him up here to keep him out of view to prevent any chance of Joey seeing him."

"Why don't I believe that?" Rosemary asked, shaking her head. "He was out of the way in the room downstairs."

"Get your damn hands off me!" Mac shouted again. "You dreadful whore!" he spat in Helen's face.

"Keep your voice down, Macarthur!" Helen scolded. "And mind your language."

"I'll do no such thing!" he shouted louder. "I was only taking a damn walk, and you had to come along and spoil things like you always do," he sneered, revealing unbrushed, yellowing teeth. "Whore, whore, whore," he spat, poking his finger in her face.

"Shut your mouth this instant," Helen hissed. Softening her voice, she added, "Or else you'll spoil your surprise."

"A surprise?" Mac asked, his voice softer. "For me?"

"Yes, but not right now, Macarthur. Not tonight, but soon."

"Soon," he repeated. "Who the hell are you?" he asked, glaring questioningly at Rosemary.

"I'm your daughter, daddy. Rosemary."

"Who?"

"Rosie, daddy."

"I don't know no damn Rosie," he huffed. "And stop calling me daddy, you sniveling brat."

"Come along now, Macarthur. Time for you to go to sleep."

"I don't want to sleep! I want to walk! Can I go look at the pictures?"

"You've had enough exercise for today, dear," Helen said, opening the door to his room. "Let's get you tucked into bed."

"This is temporary?" Rosemary asked as she entered the room. For someone who'd proclaimed that she needed assistance with the initial move, she'd certainly had no problems with his relocation to the topmost part of the house, which would've required multiple trips up and down the attic stairs to deliver his personal belongings. Bare necessities were all daddy had in the punishment room, which had become his living space. Rosemary noticed there was one extremely important item missing, shocked by her mother's cruelty. "Son of a bitch," she exclaimed. "You're making him sleep on a cot? Where's his bed?"

"The cot is closer to the floor," Helen argued. "Less chance of him getting injured if he should fall off of it. It's for his comfort and safety." She didn't bother telling Rosemary the truth about her beloved father. That he'd ruined his mattresses by repeatedly shitting the bed. She'd scrubbed and scrubbed trying to get the stains and stench out, but not even bleach had worked. Weary of constantly cleaning up his shit, she'd decided he could either sleep on a cot or in his own dried excrement. If she shared that with Rosemary, she'd only insist on buying him a new bed, and she couldn't be bothered with such trivial things. More important matters took precedence as far as she was concerned. Mac's needs were secondary, and much less important.

"Besides, he has the only thing he really wants in here. His television."

"Is it time for my westerns?" Mac asked. "I like cowboys."

"If you say so, mother," Rosemary answered, not buying a word of her explanation. *Comfort and safety, my ass,* she thought. *More like out of sight, out of mind.*

"Here, Macarthur," Helen said, removing the top from a thermos she kept on the bedside table next to the cot. "I made your favorite tea. Drink up. Then it's nighty-night."

Why wouldn't it be? She'd put enough sleeping pills in the tea to bring down an elephant. Some might find that to be rather cruel, but it'd certainly keep him asleep for several hours, ensuring he wouldn't be able to roam around freely and cause any more trouble for the rest of the night.

"Is it time for my westerns?" Mac asked again, sipping tea from the thermos cup. "I like cowboys."

* * * * *

Regardless of what Rosemary might say, Joey knew she'd heard a man's voice, but she couldn't identify it. It couldn't have been Mac's because he was dead, and supposedly Dan had left town on business. She didn't know who else it might be, unless it was one of the staff. They generally weren't allowed inside the main house unless it was an emergency, or they were reporting to work. She supposed it was possible that Helen or Rosemary had invited a staff member in but it was doubtful. She hadn't seen any manor staff since arriving, so she quickly put that thought to rest.

Joey took a deep breath and shrugged. "Let it go," she muttered.

Stepping into the hallway to look around, she was surprised by the sound of a familiar voice coming from inside her old room. The door was ajar enough that her words were clear and audible.

It wasn't Julia talking to herself that bothered Joey so much. It was what she was saying that sent a cold chill down her spine.

Never one to eavesdrop or impinge upon one's privacy, Joey put those rules to the side as she stood outside the doorway of the room where Julia was playing, listening closely to what she was saying to make sure she hadn't imagined what she'd heard.

Her childlike voice was harshly reprimanding someone inside the room with her. For a moment, Joey thought it might be Jackie. When no response came from her, Joey concluded Julia was either talking to a doll or an imaginary friend.

"You know better than to touch her down there," she scolded. "That's not nice. You're a bad, bad boy and you're gonna get an ass whoopin'."

Joey shut her eyes and swallowed the lump that rose in her throat. Julia's words were all too familiar to her. They were the same ones she'd scolded herself with after Mac violated her the first time. Whether it was Mac, Dan, or another adult at Julia's school or in the family circle of friends, it was evidently clear that she, too, was a victim of sexual molestation and was exhibiting her anger and experience through role playing.

Joey poked her head inside the room. "Can I come in?"

Julia jerked her head toward the door, startled by Joey's presence, quickly hiding whatever she was holding beneath her folded legs. "I guess so," she answered with a shrug.

"Who were you talking to?"

"Nobody."

"Julia, I heard you talking right before I came in," Joey said softly. "It's okay to tell me."

"No, it's not. You wouldn't believe me, anyway."

"Why don't you try me and see?" Joey asked, sitting on the floor in front of Julia and crossing her legs. "You may be surprised."

"Promise you won't tell?"

"It'll be our secret," Joey assured her, crossing her heart to seal her promise.

"I was talking to Molly," Julia said as she stared at the floor.

"Molly?" Joey asked with surprise. "Who's she?" This *had* to be a coincidence. There's no way Julia could be referring to the only Molly that Joey knew. It would be too strange for her to grasp, even in a house where strange was the normal repertoire.

"Her," Julia answered, pulling an old and worn rag doll from beneath her.

"Where did you get that doll, Julia?" Joey asked in a near whisper, eerily realizing it wasn't a coincidence afterall. Julia's Molly was the one and same.

"I found her."

"Where did you find her?"

"Out there," she answered, pointing toward the hallway. "She was lying on the ground by one of

136

Memaw's rooms, so I picked her up and brought her in here to play. Am I in trouble?"

"No, sweetheart, of course not," Joey answered, playfully tugging on one of her braids. "Julia, who told you her name was Molly?"

"She did."

"The *doll* told you her name was Molly?" Joey prodded, her voice taking on a pitch higher than she'd intended, surprising her and disappointing Julia.

"See, I said you wouldn't believe me," Julia said, angrily folding her arms and pouting.

"No, no, honey, it's not that I don't believe you. You just took me by surprise, that's all."

"Then you *do* believe me, Aunt Joey?" Julia asked, hugging the doll tightly to her chest. "Molly said you would."

She'd been witness to a handful of unexplainable events in her lifetime, like the cardiac patient she'd had a couple of years before that'd coded, was pronounced dead and taken to the hospital morgue, only to wake up in the refrigerator with absolutely no memory of what had happened or how he'd gotten there but fully recovered and released to go home two days later. Or, what she referred to as the case of the disappearing man, an elderly gentleman who'd appeared out of nowhere as she sat eating her lunch at one of the patio tables on hospital grounds, begging for food and money. She'd only looked away long enough to remove a couple of dollars from her pocket to give to him. When she turned back, he was gone. It was as if he'd disappeared into thin air without a trace. That incident had haunted her for days afterward because she couldn't stop wondering how in the hell he'd been able to move rapidly enough to vanish without making a sound or accepting the money he'd asked for. Where he could've gone remained a mystery since the only access door led from the patio back inside the hospital corridor and she'd neither heard the door open or close.

But this? This was a whole different kind of strange. There was absolutely no way Julia could've known that the doll she was holding had once been hers, a friend named Molly, the only one she could hug and cry to about the abominations thrust upon her and never be judged or called a liar or other vulgar names. She'd left

Molly behind when she'd absconded, feeling her assistance was no longer needed once she was out of Sheffield Manor. She was shocked to discover the doll was still inside the house and Helen hadn't either given it away or destroyed it. Julia said she'd found it lying in the hallway of the west wing, which meant it hadn't remained in her old room, the one Julia was now playing in. Where had the doll been stored? A different bedroom? The attic? If that were the case, how did it get from there to the second floor of the house and left where Julia could find it?

Maybe Julia had overheard Rosemary or Helen, perhaps both, discussing the childhood atrocities she'd faced and was parroting what she'd heard. Joey doubted it, considering that neither of them had ever believed a word she'd said about it and discussing it would be way beyond taboo for two non-believers, unless they'd been doing it in jest, making fun of her and laughing about it, because a serious conversation relating to the subject was forbidden inside the walls of Helen's beloved mansion.

Joey cleared her throat and glanced at the door to make sure she and Julia were alone. "What else did Molly tell you?"

"That she was your friend one time, too, and that you got hurt when you were a little girl."

"Molly told you I got hurt?"

Julia nodded.

"Did she tell you how?"

"No, only that you cried a lot and got into trouble a bunch of times, and that Memaw was really, really mean to you. She said she could always make you feel better." Julia picked at one of the loose buttons on the doll's blue and white checked pinafore. Without looking at Joey, she said, "She makes me feel better, too."

Recalling the conversation she'd overheard from the hallway; Joey knew what Julia was referring to and exactly how she felt. Those feelings of loneliness and betrayal could both be overwhelming and destructive. "Julia, is someone hurting you or doing something to you that you know they shouldn't be doing? Is that what you were talking to Molly about?"

Julia remained silent. A knot formed in Joey's stomach as she waited for Julia to answer.

"Julia? Look at me, sweetheart. Whatever you say to me is just between us, alright? You can trust me."

Julia finally raised her head and looked at Joey with tear-filled eyes. "You promise not to tell?"

Joey nodded.

"Yes," Julia whispered.

"Yes, someone's hurting you?"

"Yes."

"How, Julia?"

"He touched me down there," she said, pointing to her groin area. "And he made me touch him back. He said if I told anybody about it, monsters would come out from under the bed and get me. The kind that eat little girls who lie."

Joey felt nauseous. Blood pounded in her temples as she imagined what had been done to her being done to Julia. "Is it your dad?"

Julia shook her head.

"A teacher?"

Another shake of the head.

"Who, Julia? Who's hurting you?"

"Grandpa," Julia murmured, cupping her hands around her mouth.

Dear God! Joey thought. *That son of a bitch was one sick, twisted, and perverted man. Molesting his own daughter was bad enough, but his granddaughter?*

"It's okay, honey. Come here," Joey said, pulling Julia over into her lap and hugging her. "Don't cry. Everything's going to be okay."

"Swear?"

Joey nodded, silently vowing to herself to do everything within her power to keep Julia protected from the same evil that had destroyed her own childhood. "Has he done it to you a lot, Julia?"

"No, only one time when I spent the night. I don't like sleeping here anymore, Aunt Joey. Grandpa comes out of the walls at night."

"Out of the walls?" Joey asked, perplexed by such a statement. "How so?"

Julia shrugged. "I don't know how he does it. He must be magic or something."

"Or something," Joey replied. "Have you actually seen Grandpa come out of the walls?"

"No, but I heard him."

"Can you tell me what happened?"

"I was asleep."

"Which room were you staying in?"

"This one."

Imagine that, Joey thought. *My old room, where bad habits never die.* "Did you know this used to be my room?"

"Really?"

"Um, hum. I spent a lot of time in here reading and listening to music."

"I don't like this room, Aunt Joey. Playing in here is okay, but not sleeping."

"Don't blame you one bit, kiddo. I didn't much care for it, either. Go on and finish your story."

"I woke up because I heard something in the closet. I was too scared to get out of bed because I thought there was a monster in there, so I pulled the covers up over my head so I wouldn't have to look. But it wasn't a monster, Aunt Joey. It was Grandpa."

"He came out of the closet?"

"Yes," Julia answered. "See what I mean? He must've gotten into the closet through the wall because he sure didn't use the door to get in. After he came out of the closet, he got in bed with me."

"Is that when he did those unpleasant things to you?"

Julia nodded. "He kept calling me a funny name even though he knows my name is Julia."

Joey swallowed back another lump as she felt the bile rising in her throat. "What name did he call you?"

"Angel," Julia answered. "Over and over. He said I was his special little angel."

That warped bastard knew he was in my room, and he thought Julia was me. Talk about habits that never die.

"Have you told your mom or dad about this?"

"I told mommy, but she said I was only having a bad dream and I shouldn't make up stuff like that about Grandpa because he's sick and doesn't know what he's doing sometimes. She said if I did it again, I'd get a spanking."

Or sent to the attic to sit in the dark for hours at a time? Joey thought. *He was sick alright, but not with an illness that requires a doctor or medicine to fix him.*

"She didn't actually say spanking, did she?" Joey asked with a smile.

"Are you gonna tell on me for saying a bad word?"

"What bad word?" Joey said, lighting tapping the end of her nose. "I don't know what you're talking about."

Joey knew all about those types of threats because Helen had never believed her and had done the same thing to her, threatening severe punishment for telling such elaborate lies. To Joey, it was incomprehensible that Rosemary refused to believe her own daughter when she'd made the same allegations against Mac that she had. Was Rosemary so set on the fact that her father could do no wrong, or was she afraid that if she spoke out against him, she'd be disinherited as well? Surely to God her daughter was more important to her than money.

"You don't have to worry about Grandpa hurting you anymore, Julia. He's dead now and can never harm you again."

Julia glanced up at her, eyes wide. Shaking her head, in her shrill, little girl voice, she sang, "Ohhh nooo, he's nooot!"

Joey opened her mouth to respond but was interrupted when Rosemary burst through the door.

"What are you up to, Joey?" she asked angrily. "You're not up here filling my child's head with garbage, are you?"

"Relax, Rosemary, we were only playing and talking."

"I'll bet that's all you were doing," she snapped. "I'd better not find out you've been speaking ill of daddy to Julia, do I make myself clear?"

"Perfectly," Joey replied, feeling the urge to tell Rosemary right there and then that her precious Mac was doing the same thing to her daughter that he'd done to her, but she couldn't betray Julia by breaking a promise. Still, she needed to know what Julia had meant by her last remark. The chances of ever being left alone with her again were slim if Rosemary had anything to say about it.

As she stared down at her small, helpless niece, she made the decision that if Mac weren't dead afterall and she came face to face with him, she would kill him. Death was the only solution that would prevent him from preying upon another young, innocent victim. No way in hell would she allow Julia to be subjected to the same type of abuse and suffering that she'd endured.

This time, unlike fifteen years before, she wouldn't tuck her tail and run away like the scared, timid, youthful girl she'd been then. If being a victim of sexual abuse had taught her anything, it was to stand strong in the face of adversity and fight for what was right and what was good. Julia was good, and she was an innocent victim. Mac, on the other hand, was not a decent man. His soul was dark and evil, full of hatred and ill-will. Ruining one life was enough. She wouldn't allow him to ruin Julia's as well.

"Bye, Aunt Joey," Julia waved as Rosemary dragged her forcefully from the room.

Within seconds, Rosemary stepped back inside, shutting the door behind her. "I know you claim daddy did some unspeakable things to you, and your therapist has probably planted even more falsehoods in your brain by making you talk about it and believe it even more than you did before you started your therapy. What you believe is your business, but when you put that kind of shit into my daughter's head, it becomes my business. Do us both a favor and keep your mouth shut about it."

Before Joey could rebut, Rosemary slammed the door and walked away, leaving Joey dazed by her rancid accusations, pissed that she'd once again called her a liar. "What a bitch," Joey muttered as she retreated to her room, closing and locking the door behind her. The urge to pack up and go was strong; however, knowing what she knew now about Julia, she couldn't walk out on her and leave her to be devoured by a predatory wolf who was supposed to be dead.

She intended to find out what was going on, who was responsible for it all, and why they'd taken such extravagant steps to lure her back to Sheffield Manor. And when she did find out, someone was going to have an awful lot of explaining to do.

* * * * *

When a knock came at Joey's door, she expected to open it and see Rosemary standing there, ready to chew her ass some more.

"What was that all about?" Robin asked as she entered Joey's room.

"Rosemary being Rosemary."

"She looked pissed when she slammed the door."

"What's new?"

"More so than usual. What's going on between the two of you?"

"Nothing that I know of. She was ticked because Julia was playing in your room."

"I told her she could," Robin said, sitting down on the side of the bed. "Something tells me it's more than that. Perhaps it's a continuation of your earlier conversation?"

"Only Rosemary knows the answer to that," Joey replied, refusing to go into detail about their differences.

"Joey, did something happen to you that I don't know about? An issue you don't want to talk about, but that Rosemary has knowledge of?"

"Nothing that's worth mentioning."

"Whatever it is, it seems the two of you need to iron it out. That's the second argument you've had with her in one day."

"Not arguments, Robin. Differences of opinion."

Robin shrugged. "Same thing. Still needs to be settled before you scratch each other's eyes out."

Robin inhaled deeply and laid back on the bed, hands folded behind her head. "We had some fun times in here, didn't we?"

"Yes, we did."

"I used to love it when we built forts inside the closet and pretended we were being stalked by vampires. How many times did we scare the shit out of ourselves in the dark with our flashlights?"

Joey laughed. "Too many to count."

"We would sit in there for hours playing with our dolls and listening to records."

"I remember."

"Those were good times, weren't they?"

"They were. It was always fun to watch you use a hair brush as a microphone and pretend you were a rock star performing on stage while you sang along with the songs."

"And you never had the heart to tell me I couldn't carry a tune if it was in a bucket."

"Never saw it that way," Joey said. "I was too busy having fun to notice."

"Liar," Robin said, sitting back up. Turning to face Joey, she asked, "What happened?"

"What do you mean?"

"To us. To our play time together. There was a time when we were together practically every night, then your visits began to dwindle away until they no longer happened at all."

"We got older, Robin," Joey replied with a shrug. "Guess I lost interest in those things." *I lost interest in a lot of things, Robin. You can thank Mac for that.*

Robin shook her head. "It was more than that. *You* changed, Joey. The way you looked, the way you acted, everything about you. It was like watching you morph into a different person, one that became a stranger to me. I felt as if I'd lost my best friend."

Her words stung because they were true. Even she knew she'd changed drastically over the years. Continuous sexual assaults do that to a person.

"I never meant to hurt you, Robin," Joey told her. "It wasn't intentional and I'm sorry that I did."

"You went through a lot here, Joey. I know that, and so does Rosemary. We used to talk about it amongst ourselves."

"Discuss what, exactly?" Joey asked, wondering if Rosemary had told Robin about her allegations against Mac, and now Robin was attempting to get her to give specific details about those accusations.

"How mean mom was to you, how much she picked on you and sent you up there," Robin said, pointing upwards. Joey knew she was referring to the attic where the room from hell was encased. "We used to get so mad at her for the way she treated you, but what could we do?"

"Nothing, I suppose. It's still nice to know you cared and were concerned about me."

"Of course, we were. You're our sister and we love you."

"I love you both as well."

"I felt I needed to say that as much as you needed to hear it."

"Let's talk about something else."

"Alright. Can I see your tattoo now?"

"Some other time, okay?" Robin's words were certainly nice to hear, and somewhat comforting. Yet Joey wasn't ready to let her off the hook yet and pretend she didn't have a hand in what was going on. It was hard for her to imagine that she was involved after everything she'd said, but Joey stood firm on the belief that Rosemary had not acted alone.

"No problem," Robin replied. "I'm sure you're probably tired, what with that long drive and all."

"A little," Joey agreed.

Robin glanced nervously at the door, then back at Joey.

"I have to tell you something," she said, frowning.

"Before I do, you have to understand that it wasn't me."

Joey rose from the bed. "What is it, Robin?"

"It's about daddy," she started, glancing at the door again.

"What about him?" Was Robin on the verge of confessing everything? Was she going to confirm that Mac wasn't dead and his death was a hoax, a fabricated story manufactured for the sole purpose of getting her to come home? A lie her and Rosemary had concocted because they knew she had a weak spot for her sisters, knowing she'd give in and come for them?

She may have found out the answers to all her questions had Rosemary not intruded on them, telling Robin that Helen was demanding to see her downstairs right then.

With the multitudes of rooms inside the manor, how had Rosemary known exactly where to find Robin? Had Helen overheard their conversation through the vents and sent Rosemary to get her to keep her from telling Joey what they'd done? Was the room bugged? Helen was certainly evil enough to do that, so it wouldn't surprise her in the least to learn that she had. If so, she had a message for her. *"FUCK YOU, HELEN SHEFFIELD!"* she shouted. If the room was tapped and she'd heard her, then she knew exactly how she felt about her. As if she didn't already know.

Joey relocked the door behind Robin and Rosemary, not wanting any more uninvited or unexpected intrusions.

Her conversation with Robin reminded her of all the changes she'd gone through during that time period, and why. She'd transformed from pupae to larva overnight, thanks to Mac. Not until she'd escaped Macarthur Sheffield and his years of abuse had she been able to complete her transformation from caterpillar to butterfly, freed from the suffocating cocoon at last, never to be imprisoned again.

As she lay back on her pillows staring at the ceiling, tears rolled from the corners of her eyes as she recalled the dreadful and fateful night that'd set in motion her life-altering metamorphosis.

Chapter Thirteen

She awakened to find him hovering over her bed, leering down at her, his eyes and teeth glistening in the dim glow of her mermaid nightlight. She gasped when she saw him and tried to get away, but his lightning-fast move kept her pinned down. Clamping his hand tightly over her mouth, he crawled on top of her, his breath stale with the smell of whichever liquor he'd chosen that night to get drunk on. She didn't know the difference between Whiskey, Bourbon or Scotch, only that they all stank and shared the same result if too much was consumed at once. In Mac's case, that was every single time because he never knew when to put the bottle down.

He looked different that night than any of the other times he'd been in her room. His eyes were those of a wild predator stalking its prey. Instinct warned her she was in serious peril, but there wasn't anything she could do to stop his attack. He leaped onto her before she could react. She was trapped in her room with a man whose intentions weren't of the good kind, and no one was going to come and save her from his brutality. No knight in shining armor, no loving and compassionate mother, no fairy Godmother. She thought she'd already experienced the worst of his assaults; however, nothing could've prepared her for what was about to take place.

"You're not going anywhere," he panted drunkenly in her ear.

She fought against him, bucking and kicking like a wild horse, but her small-framed body was no match for his massive, masculine physique. Her eyes wide with fear, she breathed fast and heavily through the narrow nasal passage that wasn't obscured by his gigantic hand.

Not knowing what else she could do to save herself from his attack and prevent him from hurting her any more than he already had, she bit down hard on the fleshy area of his palm, between the thumb and index finger, her jaws as powerful as a vice grip, until her taste buds were overcome by a bitter, coppery taste. She'd bitten through his skin, wounding him.

In anger, Mac snatched his hand away, seething in pain. "You stupid bitch!" he seethed through clenched teeth, drawing back his fist.

"NO, DADDY, NO!" she screamed. "PLEASE STOP! DON'T DO THIS DADDY, PLEASE!"

The hard, backhanded blow rocked her head sideways, stunning her. Within seconds, Mac's hand was over her mouth again. "Won't do you any good to scream," he blasted in her face, covering it with fine droplets of spittle. Clutching her cheeks, he forcefully turned her to look at him. "No one can hear you."

With his free hand, he clumsily groped at her underdeveloped body, gliding over her chest, then her stomach, and finally, into her panties. The hardness of his manhood pressed against her leg as he began grinding back and forth, dry humping her while groaning.

"That's my girl," he whispered. "My special little angel." He ripped off her underwear as she frantically kicked out, squirming beneath him as she fought to get away. "Daddy loves it when you fight, my little angel," he said, forcefully spreading her legs apart.

Tears streamed down her face and into her ears as she continued to fight what she knew would be a losing battle, but she refused to give up. Her heart pounded faster than it ever had before, feeling as though it were on the verge of bursting. Never had she experienced such intensive fear.

When he thrust himself forcefully inside her, she was certain she would pass out from the almost unbearable pain. How she'd wished she would have instead of being subjected to such excruciating agony. Fortunately, it was over quickly, and when Mac was finished, he exited through the bedroom door as if nothing had happened. She could hear him whistling as he disappeared down the hallway.

All she wanted afterwards was to get out of bed and lock her door, but she couldn't move. The pain. Oh, Dear God, the pain. It felt like her entire insides were on fire. Her groin throbbed in perfect rhythm with her heartbeat.

After several minutes, she was finally able to get out of bed, but she could barely walk. Every step she took felt like there was a piece of gritty sandpaper rubbing between her legs, scraping away pieces of tender flesh with every movement.

Cold liquid trickled down her inner thigh. Initially, she thought she'd peed herself, until she turned on her bathroom light and saw the thin trails of blood covering her flesh. She wanted to scream or run to her mother and tell her what daddy had done to her, but she knew she wouldn't believe her, just like she didn't believe her when she'd told her about daddy coming into her room at night. Instead of addressing the issue like any mother should, she'd told her to stop fabricating stories and cease trash talking about her father.

She had no one to confide in, no one to tell what had just happened to her, except for Molly. And what could a stuffed rag doll possibly do to help her? As usual, she was utterly alone and forced to deal with it on her own.

She'd had to change her panties three times that night because of excessive bleeding. Unable to go back to sleep, she'd sat in her bed with her back against the wall, legs drawn up, trying to figure out how to dispose of her soiled underwear. She couldn't put them in the laundry because the housekeeper would see them and bring it to Helen's attention, who would then accuse her of doing something filthy and issue punishment that wasn't warranted. Same scenario if she threw them in the trash, so she decided to put them all inside a brown paper bag and stuff it in her backpack to toss in the dumpster once she arrived at school.

As she did every other day, she got up and dressed, unable to move at her normal pace because of the intense pain between her legs. She felt a deep void inside, a feeling of emptiness, and although she wasn't to blame for what Mac had done, shamefulness. Her body ached all over. Her cheek was sore to the touch, but not bruised. It was difficult to walk and sit, not knowing if she'd be able to hide her discomfort but knowing that she must. If she failed to show up for breakfast, undoubtedly, Helen would come looking for her, ready to dish out undeserving punishment.

Mac was sitting at the dining table when she entered the kitchen, sipping coffee, laughing, and talking with the others, acting as innocent as a newborn baby with not a care in the world. His hand was wrapped in white gauze and first-aid tape, but no one seemed to be concerned about why his hand was bandaged, unless he'd fed them a lie about how he'd hurt his hand before she came in, and after expressing their oohs, ahhs, and poor daddies, were satisfied with his explanation. Too bad he'd chosen to cover it up. Had they seen the teeth marks in his skin, perhaps they wouldn't have accepted his lie so blindly and gullibly.

Rosemary and Robin may not have seen his guilt, but she did. Because of one atrocious act of betrayal upon her, she no longer viewed him as a father, but as a vile, evil man, unfit to receive love or respect from her, and she'd never give either to him again. From that moment on, he became Mac, because the title of daddy was reserved for men who loved and cared for their children, and he wasn't worthy of such an honor.

A phrase often spoken by Helen played through her mind that morning. "Things will only get worse before they get better." She wondered how many more times she'd have to suffer through Mac's abuse before he finally relented altogether.

When she was too old for him? When she began fighting back? Or would it continue to go on until she could leave home and get away from him?

She'd never considered hurting anyone or taking another human's life. Except that Mac wasn't human. He was a perverted beast who took pleasure in sexually assaulting his own daughter over and over again.

Mac's rape had changed her. Not only physically, but mentally.

For the first time in her life, she began envisioning scenarios in which she killed him, each fantasy becoming more savage than the one before, all with the same finale. She believed she could do it without even batting an eye, and without an ounce of remorse or regret.

Until that time arrived, she knew she wasn't safe. Not as long as Mac was alive, and she continued to reside at Sheffield Manor.

Chapter Fourteen

Joey awoke with a start, springing upright, certain that someone was standing over her bed. It was the exact same eerie feeling she'd had on the night Mac had sneaked into her room and violently raped her. The sound of heavy breathing as loud as a lion's roar in the silence of the darkness had awakened her.

She supposed it could've been a dream, a product of her subconscious working overtime. She had, afterall, plucked yet another memory from her vault of terrors as she'd relived Mac's torturous assault on her so many years before. Recalling it had made it seem as fresh in her memory as it had been immediately after it'd happened.

Throwing back the covers, she scrambled out of bed, turned on the light and checked the door. It was still locked, so there was no way anyone could've come into the room from the upstairs hallway. Opening the closet door, she stepped inside.

Either her imagination had gone haywire, or she hadn't been dreaming or imagining things afterall.

Still hanging in the air was the faint scent of a man's cologne that she instantly recognized as the same spicy smelling aftershave Mac had always worn. A slight aroma of cherry tobacco was also present. The same particular flavor Mac had preferred in his pipe, leaving trails of the putrid smoke hanging in the air as he puffed and sucked on the stem to keep the tobacco lit.

Either someone was going out of their way to make her believe Mac was still alive and residing inside Sheffield Manor, continuing to taunt and tease her, or her suspicions were correct. That he *was* alive and the invitation to his funeral had all been a façade, a scheme to get her back to the manor. What reason could there possibly be for them to go to such extravagant lengths to ensure her return? Were they *all* involved in the elaborate hoax? Surely Robin wasn't. Then again, pretending to be happy to see her could've been a part of the master plan. Rosemary had always been a bitch, so her behavior was certainly no surprise. To have acted in a nice, kind way would've made her suspicious from the onset. Same with Robin had she behaved arrogantly and uptight the way Rosemary usually did. The opposite of their usual behaviors would've been out of character for both of them and would've immediately produced distrust. Helen was Helen. She'd always been a bitchy snob with her nose stuck up in the air as if her shit didn't stink. That was just one of the many self-assertive traits Rosemary had inherited from her. Ms. Goody-Two-Shoes Helen, who never had a nice word to say about anyone, nor had ever performed an act of generosity or a random act of kindness in her life. Her precious money, finely built home and standing reputation in the community was all she'd ever cared about. Many times over the years Joey had surmised that when Helen finally died, she'd bust Hell wide open and give Satan a run for his money vying for his fiery throne so she could rule the roost.

"What the hell is going on in this house?" she whispered, spinning around when she thought she heard a shuffling sound, expecting to see Mac standing in the doorway, wearing that awful sneer of his that she loathed. But he wasn't there. No one was. Only the ghosts of her past were present.

Stepping into the closet, she was greeted with a light draft of musty-smelling air wafting in her face, strong enough to whisk strands of hair that hung loose from her ponytail. The air was coming from the back corner of the wardrobe. Running a finger along the mid-wall border, she felt a small crack between the back and side wall, too small to get her hand or fingers through to open it wider. She'd need something small and sturdy to slip through the crack and give it leverage to allow her to pull it open.

Hoping to find a nail file or scissors as she rummaged through the pair of bathroom drawers, she found nothing that could pry open the panel. Other than a dirty cotton ball and a long-dead spider, both were empty.

In the middle drawer of the small desk inside the room, she found a silver letter opener buried beneath several sheets of notebook paper. "Perfect," she muttered, taking the opener from the drawer and returning to the closet. Slipping the sharp end through the tiny crack, she twisted and turned the opener's blade until a space large enough to slip her fingers through appeared.

Son of a bitch, she thought as she slid the thick wooden panel aside, noticing that it didn't make a sound as it glided smoothly along its oiled track, built about an inch below the closet wall, making it undetectable from the inside. On the outside of the door was a bronze handle that provided easy access from the hallway to the interior of the bedroom.

Reluctant to step beyond the door into the unknown, she chewed her lip in thought as she contemplated what to do. The hallway beyond the door was dark and reeked of the same musty odor she'd smelled earlier. She had no idea if there were light switches inside the hallway and she wasn't about to go wandering around in the dark to find out. What she needed was a flashlight but there wasn't one in the room. If she went in search of one at such an early morning hour, she'd be sure to awaken someone who would interrogate her about what she was up to, why she was rummaging through drawers and cabinets, and what she was looking for.

"There's a flashlight app on my phone," she whispered, remembering she'd downloaded it only a few days before so she'd have it if she ever had to walk to her car alone at night. Hospital parking lots could be scary, especially in areas where there wasn't adequate lighting. Drug addicts and other miscreants frequented the area, begging, and looking for handouts. She'd feared being mugged by a desperate junkie who'd gladly kill his own mother for the benefit of getting high. She'd also bought a can of pepper spray for her keyring, hoping she'd never have to use it but feeling safer because she had it. At the moment when she desperately needed a flashlight, she was glad she'd downloaded it.

Joey stepped out of the closet and into the hallway, immediately hearing the distant sound of a door closing. She wasn't sure if the sound came from somewhere inside the house or in the corridor she was about to explore. Armed with her phone and the letter opener, she slid the panel back in place, leaving a small crack so she could identify which room was hers in case she lost her sense of direction, or was chased back to her room by Mac or anyone else who felt threatened by her discovery of the secret panel and passageway.

* * * * *

Tonight was a good night. He felt more like himself than he had in weeks, even recalling his own name and where he lived. Helen brought him his medication earlier, but he'd only pretended to take it because he'd felt so good and knew he didn't need it. He even allowed her to lock his door when she left. Tonight, he was lucid enough to take a walk around, and that's exactly what he intended to do the minute he'd given Helen enough time not to return. Had he taken all those pills, he'd be in bed sleeping like a baby and that was the last thing he wanted to do.

Once she was gone, he picked the lock with a piece of durable plastic he'd found inside one box he liked looking through and confiscated it without Helen's knowledge. Judging by the dark blue color, he guessed that at one time, it might've been part of a child's toy. He'd put it to much better use now. As his makeshift key.

Unlocking the door was easy as pie. All he had to do was slip the plastic between the jamb and latch bolt to free himself from his prison.

Quietly descending the stairs to the second floor, he used the plastic once more to unlock the door to his old room, where he'd stayed comfortably until Helen took it upon herself to move him to that godawful room in the attic. She knew how much he hated that tiny space, which was probably why she did it. She'd punished him for what she'd deemed as unruly behavior.

Closing the door behind him, he was pleased that he remembered why he needed to go there. Inside a bureau drawer, he kept a wooden box with an elephant carving on top. It held his smoking pipe and favorite cherry flavored tobacco. Also in the drawer was a bottle of his favorite cologne, all items he'd brought with him when Helen first moved him from their bedroom on the first floor. He'd done so without her knowledge. If she'd caught him, she would've called him a stupid old fool for hanging onto sentimental items that were of no use to him anymore. He had to keep them hidden because if she found them, she'd toss them in the garbage or burn them like she had everything else that'd meant anything to him, then scold him harshly for having them in his possession. He spritzed his green satin smoking jacket with the cologne then lit his pipe, puffing hard on the stem until trails of white smoke billowed from the pipe bowl. On a night such as this, when his head wasn't stuffed full of cotton, he remembered these were two of his most treasured belongings and by utilizing them, it helped him to remember other things as well.

Macarthur Sheffield felt like the man he once was, the man he was meant to be. Suave, debonair, and classy, he glided down the stairs puffing on his pipe enroute to the one room he knew would lead him to where he needed to be. Of course, he could've simply gone to the east wing, second door on the left and walked in, but where's the fun and challenge in that? Chances were that she'd have the door locked anyway, so he'd have to double back to the library and take the secret stairs to the closet entrance the way he used to. He didn't have time to waste on useless and time-consuming maneuvers.

Inside the walls, he stopped at the second panel with the brass handle, gently and quietly sliding it open. Rainbow-colored hair splayed out on the pillow told him he'd entered the wrong room, surprising him because he knew he was at the right door, but his angel didn't have multi-colored hair. She must be teasing him by playing a game of hide and seek, forcing him to play if he wanted to find her. Exiting the closet, he moved to the next door, excited by the game of cat and mouse. So excited, in fact, that he felt a throbbing sensation in his groin that he hadn't experienced in several years, pleasantly surprised to discover he had an erection, the hardness of his cock begging him to release it from its confines and relieve it of its tension.

At the last panel, he gently slid it aside and stepped into the closet that he remembered as being Robin's room and was greeted by a familiar scent that could only belong to her, his precious and beautiful angel. The aroma of rose scented lotion or perfume filled the air, awakening his senses and further arousing his erection. In the darkness of the closet, he freed his aching manhood and began stroking it softly, enjoying the satisfaction and ecstasy it brought him, groaning and panting as he pleasured himself. It felt so damn good. He wished the feeling could last forever, but he knew it wouldn't because the urge to climax was already beginning to peak. Unable to hold back, he stroked harder and faster until the volcano erupted, blasting a stream of semen onto the carpeted floor of the closet. "Ahh," he groaned, using the bottom of his shoe to grind his ejaculation fluid into the carpet fibers.

Striding away from the closet, he stealthily made his way toward the bed. She was lying on her side facing the wall, oblivious of his presence. He meant her no harm. He only wanted to look at her and watch her while she slept, the way he used to when she was a little girl. She was older now and even more beautiful, a positive and welcome trait she'd inherited from her mother. He longed to touch her hair, feel her warm skin. He knew he shouldn't. If he did, she'd wake up and he'd have to leave, and he wasn't quite ready to do that yet. He wanted to admire her for as long as he could while his continual, failing mind would allow him to.

"Josephine," he whispered, wondering if she was the surprise Helen had referred to. If so, it was much better than any double chocolate cake or two gallons of ice cream ever could be.

As he reached out to stroke her hair, she took a deep breath and rolled over, startling him, causing him to recoil. He mustn't take any chances on waking her or else Helen would be furious with him, and he didn't want her spoiling his good mood. Back through the closet and out the sliding panel, he closed it quietly and retreated to his lonely room, grateful for a lucid mind, if only temporarily, that'd allowed him to see and recognize his daughter. They were memories he'd cherish as long as he could, until the thick fog rolled in again, wiping away any memory he may have had of her.

* * * * *

Several feet beyond the entrance to her closet was an identical panel with the same type of brass handle. She didn't need to slide it open to know what lay beyond. It was an entry to her old room, the one where Mac had repeatedly violated her, the same room she'd refused to stay in when she'd first arrived, where Julia had played with Molly only hours before. All three of their bedrooms had secret entryways accessible from the hallway, and with the same type of brass handle. Exactly where did the dark corridor lead to, and why had a secret passage been built in the first place? Neither Rosemary nor Robin had ever spoken a word about being mistreated by their father, the secret doors making her question whether they had been and either chose to forget about it or had completely blocked it all from their minds as though it'd never happened. Denial doesn't make sexual assaults any less real, but perhaps it'd been the coping mechanism they'd each opted for. It was certainly easier than verbalizing the truth. What possible, logical reason could Mac have had for installing secret doors if not for nefarious reasons?

The hallway was empty except for cobwebs dangling from the walls and wooden rafters, their shiny silk strings swaying slowly in the breezy hallway. It reminded her of scenes from old vampire movies where the damsel in distress wandered dark corridors alone, carrying nothing but a lit candle or torch in search of an escape from the monster's dungeon. It was a monster's lair, sure enough, but not one that had fangs and could morph into a bat. Macarthur Sheffield was the worst kind of monster that'd ever existed. He was a predator and a pedophile. He didn't need sharp teeth, claws, or wolf fur to make him scary. His very existence was frightening enough. And to think he may still be hidden away somewhere inside Sheffield Manor, waiting to pounce on her and force himself upon her once again, was enough to give any horror movie lover a bad case of the creeps.

There were no doors or windows along the right side of the corridor. Walls were unfinished, exposing bare wooden beams. She believed the secret passageway existed for only one reason. To gain access to the bedrooms that'd once belonged to her and her sisters. Strange she'd never known it existed. Especially having grown up in the house. She didn't recall any type of construction work ever being done there and a project like that would've taken quite some time to complete. It must've already been there when Mac inherited the property, including the sliding doors.

Did that mean Mac's late father, Grampy Sheffield, had also violated his daughters and Mac had inherited that abominable trait from a corrupt gene pool? Like father, like son? Mac's two sisters were dead now, so that was a question that would forever remain unanswered. But why three doors and only two daughters? Had he molested his son as well? Was it possible that Mac himself had been a victim of his father's sexual lusts and desires? What an appalling thought. Was that the reason Grampy had willed the house with secret halls and entryways to Mac, so he could continue his father's profane legacy?

Mac probably considered it all a bonus package, knowing beforehand the use he'd get out of it without having to pay for the work himself. He nor Helen had ever spoken a word about it in her presence, and as far as she knew, Rosemary nor Robin knew about it either. There was no way

Helen wasn't aware of its existence because nothing happened at Sheffield Manor that Helen Sheffield didn't know about or approve of first. For all Joey knew, the bitch may have had it built herself to please her sadistic husband, staying on his good side in order to remain wealthy, which meant that the entire time she denied the allegations against him, she knew damn well what Mac was doing and chose not to step in and make it stop. Was money seriously more important to her than protecting her own daughter?

At the end of the hallway, she stopped and leaned her back against the wall, listening to make sure no one was standing there waiting for her to come around the corner so they could snatch her and do whatever it was they were planning to do. Joey breathed a sigh of relief when she was greeted by the sound of silence. The right side of the walkway ended at an "L" shaped corner junction. Joey turned left down yet another dark and empty corridor, void of any windows or access to any of the other second-floor rooms. Was it possible when she'd heard voices talking, they'd been coming from where she was standing now? Were the voices coming from Helen and Mac while they held secret meetings to discuss what came next? Which was what? Mac springing out from behind a curtain and yelling, "SURPRISE, JOSEPHINE!?" Or would they all stand huddled together, laughing and pointing because they'd been successful in playing a huge trick on her by getting her to come home for the funeral of a man who wasn't dead, mocking the fact that the joke was on her?

Joey shook her head at the thought, hoping Rosemary and Robin hadn't been cruel enough to do such a horrible thing to her. If they had, it'd cause irreparable damage to their sisterly relationships, and she never wanted that to happen. They both knew how much she hated it there and how badly she'd wanted to leave, and when she finally had, she'd sworn she'd never return. Yet, here she was, falling right back into the pit of vipers. Why was she in such a situation? Because she'd thought it was the right thing to do for both of her sisters by showing them respect and support in their hour of sorrow, although the decision to return had gone against every personal rule she'd set for herself over the years and resulted in her breaking the most important promise of all by returning. That decision made out of love might turn out to be the worst mistake she'd ever made.

Her heart pounded, her palms damp with sweat as she recalled her conversation with Ellen earlier in which she'd expressed concern for Joey's safety, feeling she may be in peril. Even though Rosemary knew why she'd left, she'd still called her and informed her of Mac's so-called death, her tone filled with contempt when Joey had initially refused. When that hadn't worked, she'd exploited her with a guilt trip, hoping that would change her mind. By the end of their conversation, Joey still hadn't committed herself to making the trip. It wasn't until several hours later, after giving Rosemary's call careful consideration and thinking about how disappointed she and Robin would be if she didn't show up, had she changed her mind. Yet knowing how Joey felt about the dreadful home she'd grown up in, Rosemary made up a fictitious story in order to lure her there. The one question that kept resonating through Joey's mind was why? Why would Rosemary do something so heinous and participate in an act so mean, hateful, and cruel? Could it be that Helen had manipulated her into doing it by threatening to withhold her inheritance if she failed to comply with the queen's request, or had pressured her in some other way that was conniving enough to sway Rosemary into doing her dirty deeds? She couldn't blame Robin because she was clueless about the reason she'd chosen to leave, so she couldn't imagine her being involved in this convoluted conspiracy, if that's what it turned out to be. Being unkind and demeaning was behavior she expected from Helen, but not from either of her sisters.

"One thing at a time," Joey whispered, continuing down the hallway, shining her flashlight intermittently at the ceiling, then the floor and naked walls. The corridor ended abruptly and had she not had adequate lighting, she would've fallen head-first down the winding, wooden stairs that led to the floor below.

Startled by a sudden scratching, scurrying noise overhead, Joey dropped her phone, the loud clamber echoing through the hollow corridor. Joey stood frozen in place momentarily, hoping the noise hadn't been loud enough to wake anyone in the upstairs rooms. If it did and they investigated and found her nosing around in an area where she shouldn't be, she'd have to explain why, and she wasn't prepared to give answers. Quickly scrambling to retrieve it, fearful of what might be hiding in the dark corners or the stairwell, she snatched the phone up from the floor and stood motionless as she waited for Helen, or Mac, or Rosemary, to appear. Her hand was trembling as she aimed the beam down the hallway behind her, relieved when none of them rounded the corner in search of her.

Whatever the noise was that'd surprised her came from the attic, specifically from the punishment room, which she estimated to be right above her. It was likely that birds or squirrels had found their way inside and nested in there, wondering why a human was invading their privacy and waking them up in the middle of the night.

Satisfied that she was still alone, she proceeded cautiously down the uncarpeted stairs, cringing every time one creaked, until she reached the bottom of the stairway. It ended only a few feet from a door. This one had no brass handle like the ones upstairs. Instead, it had a lever.

She felt sure she knew what was on the other side of the door, but the room was generally entered from the interior of the house, not through skeletal passages which made pinpointing her location confusing. She'd come too far to give up and turn back. She needed to know with certainty what lay beyond. Pulling down on the lever, she took a step back when the panel slid open, exposing a room familiar to her, confirming her suspicions.

A desk lamp was on, illuminating the room clearly enough for her to see inside. It wasn't the presence of light that told her the room had only recently been vacated. The smell of Mac's cherry scented tobacco hung heavily in the air. Tendrils of smoke were still visible around the lampshade. Besides the afterglow of Helen's putrid perfume, the scent of Rosemary's lavender body lotion was also distinguishable. She recognized the smell from the encounters she'd had with her twice that day, in the kitchen and in Robin's room when she'd spoken with Julia. Apparently, the three of them had gathered there in Mac's library. From the fragrances emanating through the air, it hadn't been long since the meeting adjourned. Was that their normal gathering place to plan and prepare for whatever it was they were working on together?

Joey stepped inside the library and looked around but didn't see anything out of the ordinary. Certainly nothing that would alert her to any type of evil goings-on or sinister planning.

The seat of Mac's green leather reading chair had a fresh groove in it and was still warm to the touch. Who'd sat there? Mac, Helen, or Rosemary?

There was nothing extraordinary about the desktop. It contained most of the same items any desk would. A phone, a blotter, a cup filled with pens and pencils, and a legal pad with yellow paper. There were no indentations in the paper that would indicate anything had been written on top of it, and after scanning through the pad, she saw there was nothing written on the inside either.

Joey pulled on the middle drawer only to discover that it was locked, as were the other four drawers. She could force the drawer open with the letter opener she had in the pocket of her robe, but it's destroy the lock. If Helen discovered it, she'd instantly know who the culprit was, so that was out of the question. *This must be where he kept all his legal documents,* Joey thought, surmising that Helen had a key and could access the desk any time she chose. It was a good bet that Mac had made no business deals or changed his will without Helen's input and assistance, so whatever was locked away inside was nothing Helen didn't have full knowledge of.

Row upon row of books lined the built-in shelves, all in order and aligned neatly and properly. There were no empty spaces. If Mac *was* still around, he wasn't busying himself by reading one of his favorite books while sitting in his favorite chair smoking his favorite pipe.

On the wall behind Mac's desk hung a large, framed oil painting of his millionaire father, unsmiling, staring down his nose in judgement at anyone who dared to cross in front of him. Joey remembered the portrait was there to hide a wall safe, but she didn't know the combination so it wouldn't do any good to try. Still, she was curious to know if the safe was still there.

Whoever had been in the library must've heard her coming and quickly vacated, scurrying away like the rats they were before she could walk in and catch them all red-handed. The portrait was partially misaligned, leaving a gap between the wall and the frame. When she pulled on the corner, she was able to move the portrait completely away from the safe. In their haste to get away, whoever had opened it had been careless in securing the safe, failing to close and lock it, giving Joey access to all of its contents.

Manila file folders, each individually labeled, contained legal documents and other miscellaneous papers, none of which appeared to be of extraordinary importance. The safe held no money or anything else of monetary value, so why be so secretive about what was kept inside?

Beneath the last folder was a small, brown accordion file bound by a single piece of jute string. Joey found it odd that everything else had been placed inside folders with identification labels, yet the brown file was blank. Whatever was inside must hold something of importance, either monetarily or legal-wise, or else it wouldn't be locked away with all the other documents that Mac felt needed coded security.

Joey removed the folder from the safe and opened it, revealing a single sheet of beige, folded paper. As she removed it from the envelope, she felt an impression in the bottom left corner of the document that could have only been produced by an embossing stamp used by notary publics and other legal representatives.

Underneath the light of the desk lamp, she unfolded the document, gasping as she read its contents. Through tear-filled eyes, she stared in disbelief at the legal document she held in her hand, suddenly feeling nauseous and light-headed.

"Oh, my God," she breathed, clutching onto the edge of the desk as her knees went weak, feeling as though she were on the verge of passing out. "Oh God, Oh God, Oh God, this can't be real," she cried, shaking her head in disbelief.

It was now clear to her why Helen had always hated her so much, why she'd continually mistreated her, and why she'd done nothing to help or protect her against Mac. It was because she didn't care what happened to her and was no doubt delighted by the inane acts imposed upon her. In the blink of an eye, everything about her past became utterly clear and made perfect sense.

Did Rosemary know about this? Or Robin? Which one of them had been in the safe and was the document she held what they'd been after?

Joey refolded the paper and placed it in her pocket, putting the empty brown folder back inside the safe, leaving it ajar as it had been and returning the portrait to its previous position.

There was no way she was letting the document out of her possession. She intended to use it as ammunition against Helen when she confronted her with the truth, and she intended to do so in the presence of her sisters because they both deserved to know the truth about everything.

Joey closed the door to the library using the lever, returning to her room the way she came, sliding the closet panel back in place behind her. If Mac decided he wanted to pay her another visit before the sun rose, he'd be in for a huge surprise when he opened his secret door to find her standing there, ready to plunge her letter opener into his neck and rip his throat out.

"You were right, Julia," she whispered into the emptiness. "Mac *did* come out of the walls."

Sleep would not come to her for the remainder of the night. Tucked safely back in her bed, she pulled the covers up to her chin and leaned back on her pillow. With the bedside lamp on, she stared in astonishment at the legal document she'd discovered, becoming more dismayed each time she read it.

Distressed and stunned over the painful truth she'd uncovered, she tried not to cry.

But her eyes disobeyed.

Chapter Fifteen

It'd been so hard to hide her pain and discomfort following the rape. Her gait was slower, she could barely sit, she kept her head hung down lest anyone could tell by looking into her eyes what had happened to her, and she'd found it extremely difficult to focus on anything other than her attack. Friends noticed her behavior and questioned her about it, but she'd lied and told them she'd fallen off her bike and injured her back. Satisfied with her answer, they pried no further, accepting her excuse as a bona fide reason for her unusual conduct. Truth told, she didn't even own a bike and never had. What they didn't know couldn't hurt them or make them none the wiser.

She carried her bloody panties to school in a brown paper bag tucked inside her backpack and disposed of them in the girls' bathroom trash bin immediately upon arriving. Even if they were discovered, no one would ever know where they'd come from or to whom they belonged.

Although that was the one and only time Mac had ever forced himself on her in such a horrid manner, his visits to her room continued. On multiple occasions, she'd awakened in the middle of the night to find him standing over her, lusting after his own daughter.

Years of sexual abuse had taken their toll on her, negatively affecting her friendships, grades, and all-around sense of self-worth. Irrational thoughts began invading her mind. She started fantasizing about the multiple ways she could end her own life. Drugs, alcohol, a razor blade. Anything that would get her away from Macarthur Sheffield permanently so he could never hurt her again.

But then the rational part of her brain began shining through, reminding her of the many reasons she had for not wanting to die. She decided that Mac was the one who deserved death, not her. The turn-around awakened a whole new being inside her. She became determined to end Mac's abuse. Exit thoughts of suicide, enter probabilities for ending Mac's life, not caring if she went to prison for his murder. If she did, at least she'd be out of that dreadful house and away

192

from him permanently. She began keeping a journal, logging in excruciating detail all his assaults on her, beginning with the very first one and ending with his traumatic rape. In a separate journal, she began entries on the best way to kill him, realizing how many ways were possible. Poison, a gun, a knife, anti-freeze in his decanter of Scotch. Whichever one she picked would be the dealer's choice and would have the same result, but she preferred whatever would be less messy and bloody.

Countless nights she'd lain in bed pondering all her choices, wondering if she would actually have the courage to do it if the opportunity ever arose. Never having been one to have violent tendencies or thoughts, as far as Mac was concerned, she honestly believed she could and wouldn't hesitate for a second to carry through with it.

Thanks to an extremely attentive English teacher, she was spared having to make that choice, if only temporarily.

When she'd been summoned to the Principal's office a week after her rape, she wasn't sure why, but thought it was because she'd failed a test or was overheard using profanity. It was neither.

When she entered Principal Clemmons' office, two other women were present. She didn't recognize either of them.

"Josephine," Principal Clemmons said, greeting her when she walked in. "Please come in and have a seat," he told her, getting up to close his office door.

Joey glanced back and forth at the two women, who remained silent and let Principal Clemmons do the talking.

"Josephine, I've been made aware that you may be having some issues you haven't discussed with anyone."

"Issues?"

"It's been reported to me by one of your teachers that she believes you may have been..." he hesitated, trying to find the right way to express what he needed to say. "Harmed in some way. I brought you to my office to give you the opportunity to talk to professionals. If you need to, that is."

"Josephine," a woman of around forty wearing a black pantsuit spoke first. "My name is Brynne Peacock. I'm a social worker from Child Protective Services. My colleague here," she said, pointing to the other woman, "is Lynda Raineri. She's a nurse. We're both here because one of your teachers has expressed a great concern for your welfare and believes you may have recently suffered some type of physical abuse. Is there something you'd like to talk to us about?"

Joey gulped down the large pool of saliva that'd formed in her mouth, staring wide-eyed at both women, wondering how they'd come to that conclusion because she hadn't told a soul about what Mac had done to her.

"Principal Clemmons," Brynne said, turning to face him. "Do you mind loaning us your office so we can talk privately to Josephine?"

Once he was out of the office, Brynne returned her attention to Joey. "Josephine, it's just you, me and Lynda in here now. We're not here to judge you. Quite the contrary. We're here to help you. You can be honest with us. We're here for you."

Joey began to cry, not out of fear, but embarrassment. "What did my teacher say to you?" she asked, hanging her head.

"Josephine, you don't need to be embarrassed to speak with Lynda or me. You understand that, right?"

Joey nodded. "Please call me Joey," she'd requested, wiping a tear from her cheek. "I hate the name Josephine."

"Joey it is, then," Brynne replied, removing a file from her briefcase, and opening it on her lap. "To answer your question, the complaint we received didn't supply us with specific details, only suspicions of some form of physical abuse. That's why we need to talk to you and give you the opportunity to either verify or deny the allegations," she said, pausing for a few moments before continuing. "Joey, has someone hurt you?"

Joey sniffed and raised her head, realizing this might be the moment she'd been waiting for, an opportunity to disclose every horrible thing Mac had ever done to her and she wanted to seize it, to spill her guts to someone who could do something about it and hopefully lock him away in prison for the rest of his life. With Brynne and Lynda on her side, she might not have to plot the killing of Mac any longer. Instead, she'd put her faith and trust in the law and let them oversee it for her.

"Yes," she stated.

"Can you describe to us how you were hurt?"

"Describe?" Joey asked with a frown, uncomfortable about going into the sickening details of such a personal attack.

"Was it a physical assault?"

"You could say that," Joey answered.

"Can you be more specific?" Brynne answered.

"It's embarrassing," Joey said, her voice low.

"Joey, were you sexually assaulted?" Brynne asked.

Joey nodded, burying her face in her hands. "He raped me," she moaned.

"Who, Joey?" Brynne pressed. "Who raped you? Was it someone here at school? A teacher or another student?"

"No."

"Do you know your attacker personally?"

"Yes."

"Was it a relative? An uncle, perhaps?"

"It was my father!" Joey wailed, her whole body trembling. "My daddy did it."

"Dear Lord in Heaven," she heard Lynda whisper.

Brynne and Lynda were silent momentarily as they glanced at each other, both shaking their heads.

"Joey?" Brynne said, reaching out and taking Joey by the arm. "How old are you?"

"Thirteen."

"Then you were a virgin prior to this happening to you?"

"Yes."

"Was this the first time your father has ever sexually molested you?"

"No."

"But the first time he's ever penetrated you?"

"Yes."

"Joey, how long have these assaults been going on?"

"Since I was ten."

"Have you ever told anyone about them?"

"My mom and my sister, Rosemary."

"And?"

"Neither one of them believed me."

"Are they the only two people you've ever spoken to about this?" Brynne asked.

Joey nodded. "What happens now?"

"I'd like to have you examined by a medical professional," Brynne explained. "Unfortunately, because you're a minor I can't request one be conducted without parental consent."

"Can't I approve it since I'm the one it happened to?"

"No, I'm sorry. The approval must come from a consenting parent or guardian. Do you, by any chance, have any proof of your assault? Stained underwear, gown, anything like that?"

"I threw the bloody panties in a garbage can several days ago. I'm sure the sanitation man has picked up the dumpster by now."

"How about sheets or a blanket?"

"They've all been laundered. I have journals, though," Joey offered, then corrected herself. "Well, a journal." She wasn't about to turn over the one with the murder plots in it, or else she might be the one getting hauled off to jail and charged with conspiracy to commit murder. "I

wrote everything he's ever done to me, plus the threats against me if I ever told anyone."

"Would you be willing to give that journal to me?" Brynne asked.

"Yes, but it's at home."

"That's not a problem. I'll collect it when I visit your parents. Does anyone else know about your journal?"

"No."

"And you haven't spoken to anyone at all about your rape?"

"No."

"Not your mother, your sister, a best friend, maybe?"

"No, no one. But I know he did it, and Mac knows he did it. Isn't that good enough?"

"It is for me," Brynne answered.

"Who's Mac, Joey?" Lynda asked. "Didn't you tell Brynne and I that your father attacked you?"

"Mac is my father. That's what I call him now because I can't bring myself to call him daddy."

"Can't say that I blame you," Brynne replied. "What's his full name?" she asked, pen poised, ready to write it in her file.

"Macarthur Sheffield."

Brynne's pen paused just above the paper as she glanced up at Joey. "Macarthur Sheffield," she repeated.

"Do you know him, Brynne?" Lynda asked.

"There's probably not a living soul in Cornish who doesn't know him," Brynne answered. "You and I will discuss that further once we're finished with Joey."

"Does that mean you can't help me?" Joey asked sadly, feeling defeated. If Ms. Peacock knew who her father was, then she also knew how much money and influence he had in Cornish.

"Not at all," Brynne assured her. "But I will be honest with you, Joey. Once I move forward with my investigation, expect some bumps in the road. Men like your father don't take kindly to these types of allegations being charged against them, and I'm fairly sure your father will put up a fight. That doesn't mean I won't do my job, though."

Joey nodded. "I understand."

"Don't let any of that discourage you, Joey," Brynne said. "You did the right thing by telling the truth."

"Are you still going to speak with my parents?"

"Absolutely," Brynne stated with a nod. "It's the next thing I plan to do. I'll explain to them the nature of my visit and ask for their approval to have you physically examined."

"They'll never approve," Joey replied. "I've already told you my mother doesn't believe me, and my father will never allow it."

"If that's the case, then I'll be forced to petition the courts to issue a warrant demanding they comply. If it goes that far and they still don't conform, they could both face jail time for ignoring or failing to comply with a court order. The next step would be filing a petition to have you removed from the home."

Joey took a deep breath. "I understand. How soon will you be speaking with them?"

"As soon as I leave here. You can expect to hear from me again in the next couple of days."

That day never came because Mac had influential power in a community where money talked and threats to withdraw funding from several businesses and charities were taken seriously. One phone call from a sitting judge who was also one of Mac's golfing buddies, to the Director of Child Protective Services put an end to the investigation and Joey back to plotting her revenge kill.

Through that experience, she learned she was on her own in protecting herself, because no matter who tried to help her or how many complaints or phone calls were ever filed with social services, Mac would always interfere and end it before anyone could assist her and get her out of the horrible hell she lived in at Sheffield Manor.

Helen's hatred and wrath towards her increased after learning about the investigation into her husband's alleged sexual abuse of his daughter. Once the case was closed and there was no possibility of Ms. Peacock or Ms. Raineri ever coming to Sheffield Manor again, she'd spent more time in the punishment room than she did in any other room in the house.

And not only for a few hours at a time.

For days.

Chapter Sixteen

"We need to finish this," Helen said as she paced back and forth at the foot of her bed, angrily wringing her hands. "That conniving bitch almost caught us."

"But she didn't," Rosemary said. "And she won't. Not if I can help it."

"Well, you certainly didn't do a very good job tonight of keeping her away, did you?"

"How was I supposed to know she'd find the passageway?" Rosemary retorted. "You can't fault me for that. If you want to blame someone, blame daddy since he couldn't fight the urge to go into her room. You should've given him a stronger dose of whatever it is you're using to keep him sedated so he doesn't roam around all over the place, as you put it. And don't try to deny it, mother. You're slowly killing him by dosing him with whatever shit it is you're forcing him to take. After seeing him tonight, I can understand why you didn't want me or Robin to be around him. It's because you didn't want us to know what you're doing to him, so you concocted one of your pathetic stories about him needing sleep and rest because it's good for his mind. As if all those pills weren't enough, you stuck him in a room that's barely larger than a closet. I've seen dog kennels bigger than the room you've locked him away in." Rosemary paused for a moment to catch her breath, astonished by her audacity to speak so brazenly to her mother. Yet every word she'd spoken was the truth. She was appalled by the appearance of her father as she recalled the reason she'd been told he no longer had a nurse. Her mother was a hypocrite, carelessly tending to the needs of her father in a worse manner than his attending nurse would've ever dreamed of. "He may have appeared to be okay, wearing that dastardly jacket of his and smoking his pipe the way he used to, but he's far from being okay, mother. One look at him makes that quite obvious."

"I'll remind you to watch your tone with me," Helen scolded, shaking a crooked finger at Rosemary, pissed at her daughter's accusations. Rosemary wouldn't know the first damn thing about taking care of a man who couldn't distinguish between up and down, night and day, right or wrong. Some days she wanted to pick the bastard up by the seat of his pants and toss him out the attic window. Macarthur Sheffield was the last thing on her mind at the moment. There were more critical issues to address than Mac's sleeping habits and his choice of apparel, which he'd never be caught wearing again because she'd tossed the smoking jacket into the garbage the minute he took it off, along with his nasty pipe. She didn't know how he'd gotten ahold of them in the first place since she'd left them both in his old room, and he didn't have a key. Even if he did, what good would it do him when all he ever did was sleep? "I think we've waited long enough. It's time to finalize our plans."

"Exactly what plans would those be, mother?" Rosemary asked dryly.

Helen stopped pacing and turned to face her eldest daughter, her eyes glowing with anger.

"Something that should've been done years ago," Helen seethed through clenched teeth. "I want her dead and you're going to make sure that happens."

"What?" Rosemary cried with surprise, nearly bursting into laughter at the absurdity of her deranged mother's request. "You're joking, right?"

"Do I look or sound as if I'm joking?"

"Have you lost your mind like daddy has?" Rosemary replied loudly. "You certainly have if you think for one minute that I'm going to kill Joey. That is *not* going to happen."

"Do I need to remind you we made a deal?"

"Our deal was to get her to come home. I succeeded at that. Might I add, I did so under false pretenses. I *never* agreed to harm her, and I certainly didn't agree to be part of a murder plot."

"You'll do as you're told, or you'll find yourself as disinherited as Josephine. Money *is* the reason you agreed to this, isn't it, Rosemary? Afterall, having the best of everything has always been more important to you than anything else, including your husband and children."

Rosemary stared at her mother, mouth agape, disbelieving what she was asking her to do. Not once had she ever mentioned she wanted Joey dead. If she'd known killing her had been her intentions all along, she would've never agreed to get Joey to come back to the manor. All Helen had ever told her was that Mac wanted to see her again and that she and Joey needed to talk and put some unpleasant misunderstandings behind them. She'd known Joey would've never agreed to come back under those conditions and, according to her, what she needed to say was much too important to do by phone. Together they'd concocted a plan to tell Joey Mac was dead and hoped it would do the trick. It almost hadn't worked and wouldn't have if Joey hadn't changed her mind at the last minute about coming home for Mac's fake funeral. That particular detail had been kept from Robin for fear she wouldn't agree to help, which proved to be correct judging by the confrontation in the den earlier. "Why now, mother? After all these years, why are you so hell bent on destroying Joey?"

"Because she deserves it," Helen shouted.

"Why? What has she ever done to you that you think is so bad it can only be remedied by ending her life?"

Helen stood silently, glaring at Rosemary.

"Are you going to answer me or not?"

"She's been nothing but trouble ever since she came into this family," Helen hissed. "All the lies she's told, the problems she caused by bringing those investigators to the house, whoring around with that Abernathy boy. She's a tramp just like her…" Helen stopped abruptly.

"Just like her what, mother?"

"Nevermind," Helen said, shaking her head. "It isn't important. What matters now is doing what should've been done years ago. The sooner the better. I can't even stand the thought of her being in my house. She doesn't belong here. She never has."

"Mother, what in the hell are you talking about? She's your daughter, for God's sake."

"Forget about that and focus on what needs to be done and do it."

"I'm not killing her, mother. And I won't let you do it, either," Rosemary stated firmly, walking to the door.

"Oh, Rosemary?" Helen called sardonically. "Shall I schedule a sit-down with Dan and have a tete-a-tete with him about your, shall we say, indiscretion? It'd be a shame if he found out and divorced you, leaving you as penniless as a beggar, don't you think? No alimony, no inheritance from me and your father. Tsk, tsk, tsk. You might want to reconsider your answer."

"I fucked up one time in all the years I've been married to Dan," Rosemary yelled. "Once. But you keep that mistake dangling over my head like mistletoe in a doorway at Christmastime. Now it's my turn to remind you of something, mother. That was an indiscretion, as you so diplomatically put it, that you would've never known about had you not been so damned nosey, prying into my private life and hiring a detective to spy on me. Don't you dare tell me you were doing it for my own good, for my protection, because that's a damn lie. You did it so you would have leverage over me, something you could use against me in order to manipulate me into carrying out your disgusting plan to kill your own child."

Helen snickered. "As always, I did what I needed to do to get what I wanted."

"It always has to be about you, doesn't it? No one and nothing else matters in your world except for Helen Sheffield."

"You do have a choice, Rosemary," Helen replied. "At least I've given you that much."

Rosemary yanked the door open. "I never thought I'd say this, mother, but Joey is right. You really are an evil bitch."

* * * * *

Rosemary was wrong in assuming her desire to rid Joey from her life was a spur-of-the-moment thing. She'd been itching to do it since the first day she'd laid eyes on her. Even as an infant, she'd pondered the many ways she could rid her life of the unwanted nuisance. Drowning. Dropping her on her head. Smothering her with her pillow while she slept in her crib. The desire to end her life only grew stronger as she got older.

She'd been so disgusted by her that she left the majority of childcare in the hands of a nanny because she could barely stand to look at her, much less spend time with her pretending to be a loving mother or watching her play with the multitudes of toys rained upon her by her doting father. She found it all repulsive, and quite frankly, revolting.

Although Joey left home and moved away immediately after reaching legal age, her desire to see her dead had never lessened. She'd mailed scores of letters to her, begging her to come home so the two of them could discuss their differences and mend the broken bridges. Every single letter went unanswered, her phone calls were never returned, and the longer she waited, the deeper and stronger her desire grew. Of course, she hadn't meant a single word of anything she'd written, but she'd had to make it all sound believable in her exhausting efforts. Fifteen years of waiting was more than enough time and when she could wait no longer, she'd hatched a plan to get the wretched girl to return to Sheffield Manor so she could take care of what needed to be done. A task that should've happened many years before. Afterall, she wasn't getting any younger or healthier, and she'd be damned if she let that piece of trash outlive her. She knew she couldn't do it alone, so she'd enlisted the help of Rosemary and Robin, telling them only what they needed to know to play the roles they'd been assigned. They both knew their father was ill and getting worse with every day that passed, a situation she used to her advantage in order to enact and put into play the plan she'd so cleverly created. All they needed to do was get her to come home in order for her plan to be successful. Now that Rosemary had betrayed her by refusing to do what had been recommended of her, she'd simply have to do the deed herself because she certainly couldn't ask Robin. She was too much of a spineless weakling. She had no problem taking care of the task alone. In fact, the thought of watching the life slowly drain out of her while she strangled her to death was rather exhilarating, like a breath of fresh mountain air. Then again, perhaps she'd find a different method, a way in which death would be slow and painful so she could enjoy watching her suffer even longer.

What a delight that would be.

Chapter Seventeen

"Joey, I need to see you." Mason sounded unnerved and anxious when Joey answered her cell phone, not even giving her time to say hello.

"What time is it?" she asked groggily. Sometime after two a.m., when she'd last glanced at the clock, still sobbing, she'd drifted off to sleep. The shock of what she'd discovered about herself only hours before had taken an extreme toll on her emotionally. Even though she hadn't realized it at the time, it was also impacting her physically.

"Almost seven. How soon can you get dressed?"

"Mason, what's going on? Is everything okay?"

"We need to talk," Mason stated flatly. "As soon as possible."

"Okay," Joey said, getting out of bed and going to the closet, examining the sliding panel to ensure no one had tried to get back in. Fortunately, it didn't appear as though anyone had because the panel was still secured tightly against the wall exactly as she'd left it. "Go ahead. I'm listening."

"Not over the phone. Can you meet me?"

"I suppose so," she answered, her curiosity piqued. "Not right away, though. I have a couple of errands to run."

"Would those errands include visits to funeral homes?"

"Yes, but how did you know?"

"Nevermind that. Let's suffice it to say something was bugging me after we saw each other in the diner, so I did some checking around."

"And?"

"I'll explain everything when I see you."

"You want me to meet you at the diner?"

"No, somewhere private. Do you remember where Calloway Park is?"

"Yes." How could she forget the place? She and Mason had made a lot of plans in their youth while lying on a blanket along the grassy edge of the embankment, either staring out at the water or up at the sky.

"There's a gazebo there now, all the way in the back of the park by the pond. Meet me there in half an hour," he concluded, hanging up before she could respond.

Whatever he needed to talk to her about must be urgent if the tone of his voice was any indication. As if she wasn't already edgy enough after discovering the hidden passage and having an uninvited guest enter her room in the middle of the night, his demand to speak with her immediately only made her more uptight. What could he know that would prompt a phone call so early in the morning? *Go meet him and find out,* she thought.

Quickly showering, she changed into a pair of jeans and a black and red patterned flannel shirt, sufficient enough to keep her warm in the cool morning air.

"Where are you off to so early in the morning?" Rosemary asked as she came down the stairs.

"I need to go take care of a few things. I won't be gone long. A couple of hours or so."

"What kinds of things could you possibly need to take care of?" Rosemary asked snidely. "In a town you haven't been in for fifteen years?"

"Personal things," Joey answered.

"Do these personal things to which you refer have anything to do with Mason Abernathy?"

"Rosemary, that's none of your business."

216

"You really shouldn't get involved with him again," Rosemary stated with a shake of her head. "He's bad news. Didn't you learn that the first time around?"

"What the hell do you mean by that? Are those your words, or are you parroting something Helen told you?"

"I seem to recall that the two of you were supposed to be married. What happened, Joey? Didn't he ditch you and leave you at the altar, making you look like a fool?"

"You've got to be fucking kidding me," Joey stated, her anger rising toward the boiling point, a pressure cooker ready to blow its top. She'd had about all she could stand of her arrogant and judgmental elder sister. "Have you seriously forgotten that *I'm* the one who left, not Mason. I stood him up, not the other way around. If you've been brainwashed into believing something other than that, then you're a fool. I didn't leave to get away from *him*," Joey seethed. "I left to save myself. You would've known all this if you hadn't declined to be a bridesmaid, or even be a part of the marriage ceremony, period. As I remember it, you nor Helen wanted anything at all to do with the wedding because you were against it. Helen was, anyway. I'm sure you followed in her footsteps like a devoted little soldier should. Whatever Helen says, goes. Right, Rosemary?"

"Whatever," Rosemary replied, waving her off. "I do have a mind of my own, you know, and I am entitled to my own opinion."

"Because you know Mason so well?" Joey asked.

"Well enough to know he's no good."

"Why do you say that, Rosemary? Exactly what is it about him you find bad or no good? Is it because he owns a diner instead of a billion-dollar empire? Or that he lives in a regular house and not a mansion? Or is it because he doesn't drive a fifty-thousand-dollar car?"

"That's not what I meant, and you know it."

"Isn't it? In your eyes, I'm sure he's nothing more than a pauper, a poor boy from the wrong side of the tracks who found his financial meal ticket when he got involved with a rich girl. Just because he isn't the kind of man who'd ever be good enough for you because there isn't enough money involved for your satisfaction, doesn't mean he wasn't good enough for me or that he's a bad person. If I'd gone through with the marriage it would've been out of love for him, not for the love of riches. Can you say the same thing about Dan?"

"That's ridiculous," Rosemary protested. "You've always been different, Joey. In every way imaginable. You're nothing at all like me and Robin."

"You have no idea exactly how different I am," Joey stated, recalling the document she'd found in Mac's safe. "Besides, Helen certainly didn't help the situation, did she? Excluding me from everything the three of you did, buying you and Robin the best of clothes, expensive cars, sending you to the elitist of schools. I was never good enough to receive the same things you and Robin did, but I honestly couldn't care less. Personally speaking, I think the absence of all those things made me a better person, one who's learned to appreciate the simple things in life. It taught me that there are millions of things that are so much more important than money. I'll bet you never gave any of that an ounce of consideration growing up, did you? Did you ever ask yourself why I wasn't part of the familial clique? Or why there were so many differences made between me, you and Robin?"

"It's not my fault that you didn't want to be included. That's on you."

"Is that another one of Helen's excuses? Is that what she told you? Poor, uninformed and gullible Rosemary. You really don't have a clue, do you?"

"What would you like me to say, Joey? That I'm sorry? That I didn't know why you were excluded and can only go by what I'm told?"

Joey shook her head in disbelief. "In case you've forgotten, let me remind you that money has never meant a damn thing to me, and it certainly isn't as important to me as it is to you. If that's what you're basing Mason's worth on, I'd say that's pretty shitty, wouldn't you?"

"You're putting words in my mouth."

"No, I'm not. I'm simply deciphering your hidden code. You know, the one I can see right through? I've always been able to. Love is a hell of a lot more important than money, Rosemary. Or at least it is in my opinion."

"Are you saying you're still in love with him?"

"Now you're putting words in my mouth. I didn't say that at all. I was simply trying to make a point. Not that it's any of your business, but the answer to your question is no, I'm not still in love with him. I was as shocked to see him in the diner as he was to see me. Is that answer sufficient enough for you?"

"There's no reasoning with you," Rosemary said frustratingly. "Why don't you forget I even said anything."

"I intend to." Harshness had never been an emotion she was quick to display but considering everything she'd learned over the past few hours and wondering exactly how much Rosemary and Robin were aware of and how deeply they were involved in the profound deception she was caught in the middle of, she couldn't help but be angry. She was struggling with the fact that the two people she loved most in the world seemed to have betrayed her by lying and deceiving her. She wasn't ready to pass the final judgment on them quite yet, not until she found out everything she needed to know. However, if everything she suspected proved to be correct, forgiving them and moving on would take extreme effort, and the willingness to do so. She'd reserve that decision until she had all the facts. "Anything else before I leave?"

"Mother is planning a tea party this afternoon at six. She wants all of us to be there, so make sure you are," Rosemary ordered, turning around, and walking away.

"Aye, aye, Captain," Joey saluted mockingly, giving her the bird finger as she disappeared around the corner and out of sight.

* * * * *

From the second-floor landing of the west wing, he stood in the shadows just beyond the staircase, listening as the two women downstairs argued. He didn't know who the hell they were or why the hell they were in his house making such a ruckus, but he intended to go down there and tell them to shut the hell up because they were getting on his last damn nerve.

The tiny one with the short brown hair was feisty and full of fire, but the other one acted like a spoiled brat who needed her ass torn up and he might be the one to have to do it.

He moved closer to the railing to get a better look, wondering if the two women were about to fight like those lady wrestlers he saw on television sometimes. If that tiny one body-slammed the snooty one, he'd get a good laugh out of that because she'd be getting what she deserved.

Helen didn't know he was out of his room, so he needed to be cautious and keep an eye out for the dragon-lady. She'd be royally pissed if she caught him wandering around again unattended. That's what she gets for not locking his door, which she did quite often when she thought he'd fallen into a deep, drug-induced slumber. He'd learned a new trick she didn't know about, and he had no intentions of letting her in on his little secret. Just because she gave him a hand full of pills and a sip of water didn't necessarily mean he had to swallow them. And he hadn't. He did appease her by faking sleep though, but only long enough to hear Helen exit his room and close the door. Then he spat the pills into his hand and stuck them beneath his mattress with all the others. He was sick and tired of being a prisoner in his own house, not getting to go outside or explore the multitudes of rooms inside the large house. Helen constantly told him that bedrest was good for him and that's why he needed to sleep. Helen was nothing but a lying, conniving bitch who was trying to kill him and get him out of the way. He didn't know what she was up to, but whatever it was, it couldn't be good. Helen Sheffield had never done one good thing in her life, and it was doubtful she'd start now.

Glancing over his shoulder to make sure the dragon-lady wasn't standing there ready to drag him back to that awful room, he moved a tad closer to the banister, careful to stay out of sight. He wanted to watch them argue a bit longer to see if they were going to fight.

Something about the small girl was familiar to him, but he couldn't quite figure out why. His mind wasn't completely fuzzy since he hadn't taken all those pills. But attempting to remember something he knew he should, was a dire struggle for him and he usually failed to succeed. His eyes lit up when he heard the blonde woman call her

Joey, sparking a scintilla of his once photographic memory. "Angel," he whispered, trying to recall how long it'd been since he'd seen her, and how she'd gotten so much older during that time.

Hadn't he only recently seen her standing outside talking to that funny looking woman, the one with the Easter egg colored hair?

When was that? Yesterday? Last week? "Shit," he muttered, lightly pounding his temple, trying to make himself remember. He could pound all he wanted as hard as he chose to, but it was no use. Holy hell, he couldn't even recall what he'd done the day before, or why he'd come downstairs. Yet seeing her standing in the middle of the living room made him glad that he had. It was good to see her. He should go down there and say hi.

The slamming of a door startled him. He knew it had to be Helen, and he couldn't let her find him standing there. If she found out he wasn't taking his medications like he was supposed to, she'd lock the door every day and he'd never get out again. If she had her say about it, she'd let him die in there.

Turning toward the narrow stairs leading up to the attic, he shuffled away as fast as his aging legs would allow, holding onto the wooden handrail as he ascended, slipping quietly back inside his room.

* * * * *

Other than the diner, Calloway Park had been another of her favorite places to frequent. It was calm and peaceful there, a place where she could sit alone and think about the predicament she was in with Mac, her future life with Mason, and life in general. She always came there supplied with a bag of seeds. She'd loved feeding the birds and watching them dart about, chirping and tweeting as they snatched a morsel and flew off with it, only to come back moments later for seconds.

In the center of the park stood a bronze statue of Wilford Calloway, the town's founder, and sole donator to the construction of the park, having invested his own money to ensure that the local children had a safe place to play. The park was equipped with new swings, replacing the old, rusted ones she remembered. Slides had been added, as well as a merry-go-round and a large sand box, buckets and shovels not included. Benches surrounded the circular sidewalk in front of the statue, providing parents with a resting spot while their little ones enjoyed the playground. Whoever oversaw the maintenance of the park seriously needed to do a better job because the statue of Mr. Calloway was covered in white splats of bird shit. He deserved better respect than that, especially considering the amount of money he'd spent for the citizens of Cornish.

Joey followed the concrete walkway through the park until she reached the back section. The small pond she remembered had been replaced with an artificial lake, enjoyable only for the pleasure of watching ducks and geese gliding across the water's surface. A "NO SWIMMING AND NO FISHING" sign was posted on the water's edge, with a warning added to the bottom of the sign that violators would be prosecuted. On the right side of the lake was the gazebo Mason had mentioned, but he wasn't sitting there as he'd said.

Surely, he wouldn't have asked her to come there then not show up himself.

"Joey," she heard a familiar voice call. "Over here," he shouted, waving.

"You said to meet you at the gazebo," she said as she sat down across from Mason at a picnic table.

"I know, but someone was sitting there when I arrived, and we don't need to have a three-party conversation."

"If Cassidy finds out I'm meeting you here, I'm sure she'll give me another tongue lashing harsher than the last one."

"Cassidy?" Mason asked, frowning. "What does she have to do with anything?"

"She let me know in no uncertain terms to stay away from you because the two of you were a couple."

Mason threw his head back and laughed heartily. "In her dreams," he finally said. "Cassidy is delusional."

"Then you're not a couple?"

"Hell no. I went out on one date with her a couple of years ago and that cured me of asking her out a second time. Poor girl is about eight pints short of a gallon of milk, if you know what I mean," he said, spinning a finger in circles next to his ear.

"I think I do," Joey laughed. "Perhaps you should tell her that, though, since she seems to believe you are."

"She knows she isn't. There's no need to remind her."

"She sure seemed to know a lot about me and wasn't afraid to voice how she felt."

"Hey, don't look at me," Mason said in protest. "I certainly never spoke of you around her, but Cassidy does make it her business to know as much as she can about everyone and then gossips about what she thinks she knows. She's nosey, but harmless.

"What was so important you needed to see me immediately?" Joey asked, switching the conversation from Cassidy to the reason Mason had summoned her there.

"I pride myself on staying informed about what's going on in my community," Mason said, his tone turning as serious as it had on the phone. "After you left the diner, I got to thinking about what you told me about your dad dying and something about what you said didn't sit right with me."

"In what way?" Joey asked.

"I know about everybody in this town, and a majority of them are regular customers. When fifty of them are asked if they were aware of Mac's passing and not a single one did, I'd say that was statistically impossible. Afterall, your dad was, um, *is* a well-known and prominent figure in Cornish. Don't you think at least one of those people would've known?"

"I would think so."

"Strange, don't you think?"

"Yes," Joey agreed, nodding. "Which is exactly why I've done some checking of my own. So far, I've come up empty handed."

"Such as?"

"For starters, when I questioned Rosemary about Mac's arrangements, she went from telling me that none had been made to saying his body was at the medical examiner's office pending notification of her choice of funeral home. Both excuses were outright lies."

"You checked with the coroner?"

"Went there and spoke to him personally. He told me he knows Mac but wasn't currently, and had not been, in possession of his body. Today, I plan on making a trip to the two funeral homes in town."

"Don't waste your time."

"Are you saying I shouldn't go?"

"I'm saying that I'm ten steps ahead of you," Mason replied. "I've already spoken to directors from both of them, and neither one knew anything about funeral arrangements for Macarthur Sheffield. Nor was either contacted by any member of your family or the M.E.'s office."

"Why am I not surprised?"

"I went a step further than that, Joey."

"Meaning?"

"I went into the county clerk's office to see if a death certificate was available."

"And?"

"There wasn't. An application for one hasn't even been filed."

Joey shook her head. "Then he's not dead," she stated. "Which means every one of them lied to me."

"And if he isn't dead, why did your sister tell you he was, and have you come all the way here for the funeral of a man who's still alive?"

"I have a theory about that, but I can't say with certainty. Not yet anyway."

"Whatever reason Rosemary had it can't be a good one. I mean, what kind of sister tells such an abominable lie? Don't you find the whole thing rather peculiar?"

"Actually, Mason, I find it rather evil, and if Mac and Helen are *both* involved in this scheme, it isn't for good reasons, I can assure you of that."

"Care to elaborate?"

"Let's just say I've recently come across some extraordinarily stunning and shocking information. To be quite honest, I'm still reeling over it."

"What is it, Joey? You know you can talk to me."

Joey looked into his chestnut brown eyes, so soft and caring, recalling the numerous times she'd done the same thing so many years ago as she told him of her dreams and ambitions, sharing most of her secrets yet omitting her biggest one. Mason had always been kind, generous, and compassionate. She couldn't imagine any of that had changed because that's who he was, the type of person he'd always been, and she believed in her heart that none of that had changed. Mason Abernathy would always be a man of great character.

"Can I trust you?"

"Of course, you can, Joey. You know you can."

"I think this is the reason I've been lured home," she said, passing him a folded sheet of paper. "But for the life of me, I don't understand why."

"What the hell is this?" Mason exclaimed as he unfolded the document and glanced over it.

"I believe it's self-explanatory."

"Let me rephrase that," Mason said. "By reading it, I can see what it is. I'm asking if it's an actual, legal document?"

"If it isn't, Helen and Mac both went to a lot of trouble to keep it concealed. Why would they do that if it weren't genuine?"

"Where did you get this?" Mason asked, shaking the paper.

"I found it."

"Joey, you don't just *find* something like this. Knowing Mac and Helen, I'd say this isn't something they'd want to go public."

"It was in Mac's safe."

"You broke into his safe?" Mason asked wide-eyed, dropping his arm onto the table. "Joey, that wasn't a smart thing to do. What if Helen finds out?"

"She won't. The safe was ajar when I entered the library... through the secret passageway," she concluded, raising her brow to make her point.

Mason shook his head. "Did I hear you correctly? A secret passageway?"

"Yes, accessible through a sliding panel board inside the closet of the room I'm staying in. I followed it downstairs to Mac's library," she explained, intentionally leaving out details about secret doorways leading into the bedrooms of her and her sisters. That would be difficult to explain and not important right now.

"Why, in God's name, would anyone need something like that? It feels like I'm reading a script from one of those old, B-rated horror flicks, where secret passageways led down to the laboratory of a mad scientist."

"That's exactly what I was thinking as I followed the dark, musty corridors."

"I'm more concerned about why Mac thought it appropriate to have a hidden passage inside his house. What purpose did it serve, other than allowing him to roam around the house without anyone's knowledge? Which leads me right back to my original question. Why? What was he hiding?"

If you only knew, Joey thought. "All the years I lived in that house I never knew it existed. And I'm quite sure Rosemary nor Robin did, either."

Mason shook his head disbelievingly. "I'm not sure what to say. Not about that," he said, pointing to the folded document, "or about Mac's secret hideaway."

Joey stuffed the document back inside her purse. "Nor do I," she said. "But I intend to find out."

"Joey, you need to get out of that house right now. Go pack your things, and either check into a hotel or come stay with me. There's plenty of room in my house. I know it won't do me any good to tell you to go back to Indiana because I know once an idea is planted in your head, you won't rest until you get answers."

"As of now, I don't believe any of them know I'm onto their deceit and that they've all been lying to me. I'm going to see this through and stay put, act like everything's okay, and see how it all plays out."

"I don't think that's such a good idea. You're taking a huge gamble by doing that when you know they're up to no good. You could be putting yourself in harm's way."

"Maybe, but that's what I intend to do."

"Are you going to confront Helen over that document?"

Joey nodded. "When the time is right. She planned a tea get-together today at six and everyone will be there. That might be the perfect time to do it," Joey said, staring off into the distance. "In front of Rosemary and Robin so they can hear personally what a lying, conniving, deceitful woman Helen Sheffield truly is."

"And if they already know about it?"

"I can't imagine they do. With Rosemary's loose lips and Robin's inquisitiveness, one of them would've let it slip by now."

"Or they're both good actresses playing their parts perfectly. Have you thought about what might be at stake for them?"

"I suppose that's also possible," Joey agreed. "The only thing I can think of that would convince either of them to do something so hateful is money."

Mason grimaced. "Money's *that* *i*mportant to them? Important enough to make them do something like this to their own flesh and blood? To keep that kind of secret from you?"

"I believe so. And if they do have knowledge, then that's all the explanation I need for understanding why this has happened. Money talks, Mason. To people who idolize it, it speaks quite loudly and makes them vulnerable to doing something they normally wouldn't do. Either way, it'll be out in the open and they'll all know that I know about it now, too, and about what they've done."

"I hope you know what you're doing," Mason said with concern. "Don't put yourself into a situation that'll cause you to get hurt. I don't want to see that happen."

"Nor do I. I'll be careful," she assured him. "I promise."

"Still a hardhead, I see," Mason said with a shake of his head.

"Of course I am," Joey laughed.

"Do you have any plans for dinner?"

"Not unless Rosemary has cooked up another pot of whatever the hell it is that she makes in Helen's kitchen. Why?"

"Have dinner with me tonight."

"I don't know, Mason," Joey said. She had no interest in engaging in a conversation about the past or discussing the reasons she'd left, and he'd probably want to do exactly that. It could be that he'd been patiently waiting all these years for an explanation and saw dinner with her as an opportunity to get it. Some things were better left unsaid.

"Come on, Joey," Mason prodded. "It's an innocent meal between two old friends. We can eat, drink and be merry, and you can fill me in on how your tea party went."

Joey shook her head. "You're not going to give up, are you?"

"Nope."

"And you had the nerve to call me a hardhead?"

Mason smiled and gave a shrug. "What can I say?"

"In that case, I concede," Joey replied with a nod, hoping she wouldn't live to regret her decision. Because if he began pressuring her about things she didn't want to talk about, she'd only get pissed off and end up hurting his feelings, and she didn't want to do that.

"Great. You still like Italian?"

"Love it."

"Good. Meet me at Luigi's at eight."

"That place is still kicking?"

"It is, and they still serve the best lasagna in the world."

"Eight it is, then."

"See you tonight," Mason said, rising from the bench. "Please be cautious, Joey."

"I will. Thank you, Mason."

"For what?"

"Believing me, and for checking with the funeral homes. Everything, actually."

"Hey, what are friends for?" he asked, waving as he walked away. "Remember, eight o'clock, and don't be late."

With the visits to the funeral homes already taken care of, Joey had no other business in town to tend to, which meant she could either spend the next several hours driving around Cornish, admiring all the town's old architectural structures and reminiscing about her youth and growing up there, or she could return to the manor and wait the time out there. She had no desire to listen to Rosemary bitch about everything while waiting for Helen's tea party to commence or spending hours in her room doing nothing but staring at the walls. She may as well enjoy the town while she had the chance because when the current fiasco was over with, she would *never* return to her hometown, and especially not to Sheffield Manor.

A quiet drive through Cornish sounded nice and would give her the chance to prepare her mental state of mind for what lay ahead. It wasn't going to be easy by any stretch of the imagination, but it had to be done, even if it meant that Rosemary and Robin would be hurt by hearing the truth.

A few of the shops in town looked inviting, so she may as well spend some time browsing around. Hell, even going to the dentist and having a tooth filled would be more enjoyable than listening to her sister drivel on and on about nothing.

Six o'clock couldn't come fast enough. She was eager to address the situation, tell them all to go fuck themselves and get the hell out of Cornish.

Which is exactly what she intended to do as quickly as she could.

Chapter Eighteen

A visit to Sheffield Manor from social workers representing Child Protective Services did absolutely nothing to help free her from a life of misery or stop Macarthur Sheffield from his twisted and perverted attacks of lust upon his daughter. While it may be true that money can't buy everything, it damn sure bought Mac's way out of facing felony charges for sexual child abuse, therefore, keeping him from going to prison for the rest of his disgusting life. The accessibility of friends in high places and threatening to defund organizations and charities that those friends oversaw or held seats on the Board of Directors was beneficial to Mac insomuch as they were willing to turn their heads and look the other way, demanding that the investigation cease, and the file be destroyed without even hearing or reviewing the evidence. In making choices between doing the right thing and keeping the greenbacks flowing, continuing to line the pockets of the already filthy rich, the money would win, no matter the consequences for their greedy actions.

For many months following the initial complaint and dead-end investigation, Joey regretted ever having spoken with Brynne and Lynda. Both of her parents had refused to allow a medical examination and even though she wanted one, she'd fought a losing battle because she was a minor and minors had no say over such a decision, even when that decision pertained to their own body.

Helen's treatment toward her worsened after the allegations were brought to light, often referring to her as a liar, troublemaker, and vicious little whore, none of which were true. In Helen's eyes, all were accurate and equally unforgiveable. She'd upset Helen's apple cart, her perfect little world she'd carved out for herself in her very own private corner of the world. One in which she was a prominent and well-respected citizen, excellent hostess at her lavish parties that only the richest of the rich were invited to, and charitable donator to multiple organizations in the community. To have admitted that Joey's allegations were true or to have had such rubbish leak out into the community, would have tarnished her reputation, burst the bubble of the alternate world she resided in, and put her in the position of having others look down their noses at her, shunning her from societal gatherings, and being removed from their invitation lists for the most prosperous and prestigious galas in Cornish.

All those things were extremely important to Helen, and nothing came before them. Not even her children. When Joey had needed her mother the most, she'd turned her back on her, refusing to shield and protect her from the monster residing inside Sheffield Manor. To Helen, there was nothing to protect her from because every accusation she'd made was false.

Since Helen refused to side with her, Joey was forced to face the evil alone. She couldn't share what was happening to her with Robin because she was too young and wouldn't understand. She was desperate for someone to confide in, a person who she could rely on and who wouldn't judge her and blame her for what Mac was doing to her. She had plenty of friends, but none close enough to share that kind of secret with. There was only one person she could go to. Rosemary was her sister, they loved and respected each other, and she trusted her. Surely she'd understand what she was going through and offer her some degree of consolation, even confront Mac herself about his abuse. Unfortunately, that hadn't worked out the way she'd hoped it would.

Rosemary was on the phone talking to one of her girlfriends when she knocked on the door.

"What?" she called out.

"Can I come in?"

"If you have to," she replied cynically.

Unlike many teenaged girls who plastered their walls with posters of their idols or favorite movie stars, Rosemary's boasted expensive oil paintings and dozens of fancy, elaborate hats hanging on tacks, some with ribbons, others with feathers and beads. A vanity with track lighting held hundreds of dollars' worth of make-up and nail polishes, the blanket on her bed blue satin with white lace trim.

She was sprawled across the bed lying on her stomach, wrapping the phone cord around her finger while she talked and laughed with whoever was on the other end.

"What do you want?" she asked when Joey approached her.

"To talk."

"Can't you see I'm busy?" Rosemary asked, pointing to the receiver in her hand.

"I'm sorry to bother you. I'll come back later."

"Just say what you came to say."

"Not while you're on the phone. It's private."

"For crying out loud," she said, sitting up. Speaking into the phone, she said, "I'll call you back. My sister needs to talk."

Joey stared at the pink princess phone on the bedside table after Rosemary hung up. "Sorry," she said with a shrug.

"I hung up, so talk."

"Can I sit down?"

"Go ahead," she replied, rolling her eyes in exasperation.

"I need to tell you something then ask your advice about what to do."

Rosemary grunted. "I don't know what advice I could give you but go ahead. I'm listening."

"It's about Mac."

"You mean daddy," Rosemary corrected.

"Yes."

"What about him?"

Joey gazed at the floor, not sure how to say what she wanted to, knowing there was no easy way to articulate what she was feeling or what she was experiencing. "Not about him exactly. More like what he's been doing to me."

"Whatever that's supposed to mean."

Rosemary knew about the visit from the social workers, but not about the specific allegations. Helen had kept that part to herself, and when Rosemary questioned her about it, she'd told her that someone had reported her father for child abuse but that the charges were unfounded, and the case dismissed. Rosemary never raised the issue again, satisfied with her mother's explanation.

"He touches me, Rosemary."

"So what? He touches me and Robin, too. They're called hugs, Joey."

"What he does to me is way more than a hug."

Rosemary glared at her. "Where are you going with this, Joey? You'd better not say what I think you're going to say."

"He comes into my room at night and gets into bed with me."

"Shut up!" Rosemary demanded, holding up her hand to silence her. "I don't want to hear any more of your bullshit."

"I haven't told you anything yet."

"I've heard enough to know you're accusing daddy of inappropriate behavior. Isn't that what you were going to say?"

Joey nodded. "Because it's true, Rosie."

"Oh, good God! Give me a break!" Rosemary shouted. "You're his daughter. Daddies don't do disgusting things like that to their own kids. That's sick, Joey. Why in the hell would you say something so revolting?"

Joey was shocked and saddened at the way Rosemary had treated and spoken to her, destroying any hope she may have had of finally having an ally on her side. She'd gone to her sister in search of moral support and at least an inkling of understanding but was turned away in disgust because Rosemary refused to believe her, siding with her father instead of her, the victim. She learned a valuable lesson that day. Sometimes the ones we love and trust the most are the ones who betray us the worst.

"I thought I could talk to you," Joey replied, wiping away a tear as she stood up. "Obviously, I was wrong. I'll never bother you again."

"You're pathetic, you know that? No wonder you're treated differently than me and Robin. We don't go around spreading lies about our father molesting us. You seriously need some psychiatric help, Joey, and soon. Get out of my room and take your filthy bullshit lies somewhere else."

She'd practically thrown her out of her room that day, refusing to listen or believe. She'd tried to apologize the next day for speaking so harshly to her, but the damage had already been done. Never again would she attempt to tell Rosemary anything else about her situation, not even if she asked. Being ridiculed once was enough. Only gluttons for punishment went back for seconds.

Their relationship was never the same after that, and any closeness they'd once shared diminished because of that one conversation.

Two more years of suffering followed. Physically at the hands of her father and, mentally at the hands of Helen, thanks to her never-ending debasement and name-calling.

Thoughts of running away were constantly on her mind. On three separate occasions, she'd followed through, only to be tracked down by local law enforcement officers, many of who were Mac's friends. Each time she'd gotten away, she was returned to the lion's den, only to be dealt the severest of punishment with each act of defiance. One phone call from Macarthur Sheffield was all it took for him to get what he wanted, and there were always those willing to comply with his demands. Why? Because money talks, bullshit walks.

She'd been made to sit in the cold, dark punishment room for such extended periods that she lost track of the days and the time. Food trays with bread and water were brought to her once a day. Bathing was suspended for the period she spent inside the room. She was forced to sleep on the hard floor with no pillow or blanket. Helen refused to even provide her with clean changes of clothes. The room contained a toilet, but no sink or tub, so she couldn't even wash her hands. Her desire to get away only strengthened each time Helen locked her inside the room, causing her deep-seated despise for Helen and Mac to intensify.

Days locked away from everyone else were her days of peace and solitude because Mac never bothered her when she was being punished. He hated the attic room and wouldn't step foot inside of it. Perhaps it was because he didn't like seeing "his little angel" being mistreated, or maybe he recalled being put in there himself as a kid and didn't like being reminded of what he'd gone through. Whichever it was, she didn't care because it kept her away from him and out of his reach.

At fifteen, she'd made a vow to herself that she'd never allow Mac to violate her again, no matter what she had to do to stop him.

As far as she knew, there were no firearms in the house, but there were other items she could use as weapons. All she needed to do was find one and take possession of it. If protecting herself resulted in Mac's death, she'd swear it was self-defense for all the years of abuse she'd been subjected to and would stand firm on those facts, even if Helen or Rosemary denied her allegations. If that didn't work, she'd kindly refer law enforcement to Brynne Peacock and Lynda Raineri, both of whom she was certain would corroborate her allegations.

It wasn't difficult locating a weapon. A visit to the kitchen and the theft of a butcher's knife from the wooden block on the countertop was all it took. If she were ever questioned about the whereabouts of the missing cutlery, she'd deny knowing anything about it and would keep it well hidden inside her bedroom to ensure it wasn't discovered if Helen decided to search her room.

Every night from that point forward, she slept with the knife under her pillow and her bedroom door locked, knowing if Mac wanted in, he'd find a way and no door would stop him. He had no respect for her or her privacy, so why should she respect his house rules? The time had come for the rules to change in her favor and the game to be played according to her standards. Mac wasn't going to be happy with the change of plans, and she hadn't given a rat's ass.

Killing Mac was the only option she had left because he'd given her no other choice, nor was she any longer afraid to confront him. Enough was enough. She was eager to put her head into the lion's mouth and find out if he were a tame kitten or if he'd bite her head off and crush it between his teeth.

One month after securing her weapon and sleeping with it in arm's reach, Mac gave her the chance she'd desperately been waiting for. The moment to prove her bravery. Not only to him, but to herself.

She awoke to find him standing over her bed, glaring down at her as he masturbated, moaning and huffing as he stroked himself in the dimly lit room. Swiftly, she yanked the knife from beneath the pillow and rose to her knees, the razor-sharp blade aimed only inches from his throat.

Mac's eyes widened in surprise when he saw the five-inch blade, its stainless-steel reflecting shiny specks of light from the bedside lamp. Never had she stood up to her attacker, and the adrenaline that rushed through her body as she finally confronted him after years of suffrage was exhilarating.

"Go ahead and try it, you son of a bitch," Joey spat, her unblinking eyes burning with rage. "If you ever lay a finger on me again, I'll slit your throat and laugh while you bleed to death," she seethed.

"Calm down, my sweet little angel," Mac said, tucking his manhood inside his pants and taking a step away from the bed. "Daddy means you no harm. I only wanted to come in and check on you to make sure you were okay."

"When did checking on me include jacking off while watching me sleep? And don't you ever call me that name again. My name is Joey, not angel, and I'm damn sure not yours."

"Take it easy. No need to get violent."

Joey slashed out at him with the knife as she clambered out of bed. "Don't make me kill you," she warned, taking a step toward him as she thrust the knife blade at him. "Now get the hell out of my room and don't you ever come back in here. I swear to God if you do, I'll cut your dick off and shove it down your throat."

Mac shuffled backwards all the way to and out the door, never taking his eyes off her, a gesture Joey perceived as him taking her threat seriously, which was good because she'd meant every word.

"You're too old for me now anyway," he grumbled as he closed the door. "Little whore," she heard him mutter.

Once he was out of the room she began to tremble and cry. Not out of fear, but relief. Had she finally slain the monster that'd been taunting her for the past five years? Would she finally be able to sleep at night without him making surprise and unwanted visits? All she could do was hope so and continue to keep the knife handy. Just in case she was wrong.

Regardless of whether Mac had continued his midnight assaults on her, she knew she would never be safe if she continued to reside at Sheffield Manor. The only thing that would bring her the peace she longed for was to get out and as far away from Mac as she could. She started spending less and less time there by enlisting in after-school programs, even if she had no interest in them. At least time spent there would shorten any time spent at home. Then she surprised her friends and rich sisters by taking on part-time jobs, questioned about why she chose to work and earn an income when she could simply ask her father for it. Her friends could never know the truth about the reasons behind her choices, so she'd given them a simple answer. "Because I want to make my own money and earn my own way," she told them. Rosemary grunted and made faces at the mere thought of having to do such an atrocious and unspeakable thing. Robin was too immature to understand exactly how wealthy she was; therefore, planning or even talking about a future career meant nothing to her. All she was interested in at the time was being a famous pop star although she couldn't sing worth a shit. But who was she to burst her bubble? Let her enjoy being a kid while she could. Adult life would come soon enough, then she could make those kinds of decisions.

Too young to work full time, Nat, the owner of the diner, had given her a part-time position working a couple of hours in the afternoons and on Saturdays. When she wasn't working at the diner, she was either serving popcorn and sodas at the theater concession stand or babysitting for parents outside her mother's societal circle.

She'd only been working at the diner for a couple of weeks when a group of teenage boys came in, all wearing red and black Lettermen's sweaters, the colors of the football team at Cornish High School, the same school she attended. She didn't know any of them and none looked familiar. Although the sweaters represented sportsmanship, they didn't exhibit the stereotypical behavior most jocks did. They were all extremely kind and respectful. One of them caught her eye, making her blush when he smiled at her and winked. He was handsome, charming, and sophisticated, even though he wasn't from a family anyone would consider to be elite.

"What's your name?" he asked as she stood by their table waiting to take their orders.

"Josephine," she answered. "But my friends call me Joey."

"Then I'll call you Joey as well," he said, extending his hand. "I'd like to be your friend. My name is Mason Abernathy."

"Hi, Mason, nice to meet you."

That casual meeting turned into a steady relationship that lasted for more than two years.

He was already a senior in high school when they began dating, with no plans to go to college. Instead, he wanted to stay in Cornish and help his dad run their family's hardware store. She, on the other hand, couldn't wait to leave and get away from Mac and Helen. Eighteen couldn't come fast enough.

The more time she spent with Mason, the less she wanted to leave, imagining a life with him by her side, living happily in a small house with a white picket fence and a couple of kids and a dog running around the yard. When she was with him, she didn't think about Mac or what he'd done to her. Mason made her feel good about herself and gave her hope for a brighter future outside the walls of Sheffield Manor. Through Mason, she learned what true love was, and how gentle and enjoyable lovemaking was supposed to be. For days following their first sexual encounter, she'd felt horrible and guilty for allowing him to believe he'd taken her virginity. Yet telling him a harmless lie was so much easier than telling him the truth.

Mac nor Helen had ever approved of Mason. According to them, he came from the poor side of town and was nothing short of a beggar who was using her to make himself rich and weasel himself into the family of a prominent millionaire. What they didn't know or care to learn was the fact that Mason had no interest in money or community status. Other things were more important to him, like providing and caring for his parents, assisting friends when they needed help, and giving to those who were less fortunate than him. They were all acts of kindness that neither Mac nor Helen would know the first thing about because they only cared about themselves.

Four months before her eighteenth birthday, Mason informed her he had a special dinner date planned for the two of them and she should dress up because he'd be taking her to a restaurant with a strict dress code where no jeans or informal wear were allowed. She'd thought his request strange because he'd never discussed her choice of attire, regardless of where they went. And she couldn't think of a single public restaurant in town that operated under such strict conditions. Mason nor his father were members of any elite clubs in Cornish, so he couldn't be taking her to any such place. Because she loved him, she adhered to his request, donning a red satin, spaghetti-strap dress with a white bolero jacket and red and white heels.

The restaurant turned out to be a picnic blanket and basket dinner at Calloway Park, both laughing as Mason popped the tabs off the tops of soda cans, passing one to her. "Cheers," he said, taking a large gulp of his. "You look stunningly beautiful tonight, Joey," he said, brushing a strand of blonde hair away from her face.

"Thanks," she said. "You're not so bad yourself."

"Do you have any idea how much I love you?" he asked.

"As much as I love you?"

"Probably more," he said, leaning in and kissing her softly on the side of the mouth. "You are everything to me, my whole world, and I'd like to spend the rest of my life with you."

"Mason?" Joey asked nervously. "What are you doing?"

"I would love to marry you, Joey," he answered, pulling a small black box from his pants pocket. Opening it, he revealed a small, pear-shaped diamond. "Josephine Renee Sheffield, will you be my wife?"

Joey stared at the ring for several moments, her heart pounding with joy and excitement.

"Well?" Mason asked.

"Yes!" she exclaimed, hugging him tightly. "Yes, I'll marry you. I'd be honored to be Ms. Mason Abernathy."

Once the ring was on her finger and they were both fully committed to each other, they began planning their future. Where to live, how often they'd indulge in date nights, what movies to watch. For months following their engagement, they couldn't seem to get enough of each other and relished in the joy and pleasure of their time spent together and imagining what married life would be like.

She was elated over her upcoming nuptials, and as badly as she'd wanted to share her good news with her sisters, she knew she couldn't for fear that one or both of them would run straight to Helen or Mac and blurt it out to them. The news would undoubtedly piss them both off, albeit for different reasons.

Joey feared what they may say or do to Mason over his proposal, but mostly she feared they'd destroy her happiness and prevent her from marrying him. That was a risk she wasn't willing to take.

They were to be married the day of her eighteenth birthday. She would then be of legal age and wouldn't require parental consent. Since Mac and Helen had both been against her relationship with Mason from the beginning, she was elated to be spared that legality, despising the thought of having to ask either of them for anything. All plans had been finalized, verbal invitations extended to their closest friends, church reserved, dress bought, cake chosen and paid for.

She'd awakened that morning feeling nervous and anxious, unsure if she'd made the right decision. She loved Mason dearly, but if she married him, she'd have to stay in Cornish where there would always be the possibility of running into Helen or Mac and she knew she'd never be completely happy while living under those circumstances. The whole point was to get away from them, not to remain in a proximity where she might continue to be the object of their hatred and ire. On the very day that should've brought her sheer joy, Helen and Mac had inadvertently managed to steal her happiness away simply by making her reconsider all her choices and the consequences that would ensue.

It broke her heart to think about leaving Mason, but she couldn't stay there, and she knew Mason would never leave. He was too devoted to his parents and his position at his father's hardware store to walk away and leave them on their own.

She'd been forced to make the most difficult decision of her life. In the predawn hours on what would've been her wedding day, she packed a suitcase full of clothes, took the envelope of money she'd been saving and slipped away quietly into the darkness, toward an exit from Cornish where she could leave all the terrible memories behind and work toward a better future, hopefully one that would help her erase from her mind all the painful suffering she'd endured.

While guests were gathering at the church to witness the marriage between her and Mason, she was on a bus bound for Tuscaloosa, thinking about Mason, wondering how he was going to deal with her leaving so abruptly, and without saying goodbye.

The day would come when she could tell him everything, explain to him why she'd made the decisions she had, and hope that he could, in time, understand and forgive her for everything.

She'd done what she'd thought she needed to do in order to make her first step towards healing, and that step was to put as many miles as she could between her and Cornish, telling herself to never look back and to never return to Sheffield Manor, no matter what.

Fifteen years later, she broke that promise to herself by returning to the one place she'd vowed she'd never go to again, brought there by deceit, greed and unadulterated hatred so Helen could finally get even with the one child she saw as a stain upon the Sheffield name.

Chapter Nineteen

"Can I come in?" Rosemary asked, peeking her head inside the door. Robin lived in a townhouse on the outskirts of Cornish but had agreed to stay at the manor during Joey's visit so she'd be available to help fulfill Helen's wishes. Rosemary would've never imagined that her mother's plans to lure Joey home was actually the hatching of a diabolical plot to murder her. But it was, and it was crucial that she share the information with her sister.

Robin was standing inside the walk-in closet when Rosemary entered, changing into a pair of tight, black jeans and a tie-dyed tee-shirt with the same rainbow colors as her hair. "Looks like you already have," Robin teased, slipping into a pair of black loafers. "What's up?"

"Robin, we have a problem. Our willingness to participate in mother's scheme has put us in an awkward position. We're in way over our heads."

"How so?"

"Mother just revealed to me the *real* reason she wanted Joey back here, and you won't believe what she's asked me to do. Ordered me to do is a better way of putting it."

"Are you about to spring another surprise on me like the one about daddy being dead?"

"This is worse," Rosemary said, plopping down on the side of the bed. "Much, much worse."

"How could anything be worse than lying to Joey, telling her daddy had died and asking her to come home for his funeral? I feel bad enough about doing that to her."

"Then you're going to hate what I'm about to tell you."

"You know, Rosemary, when I agreed to help you and mother, I did so innocently, thinking you'd make up some dumb, lame excuse for getting Joey to come home. I believed the two of you when you said mother wanted her here so she could talk to her and apologize and bury the hatchet. And for daddy to be able to see her one last time. Was any of that true?"

"Partly," Rosemary admitted. "The part about daddy and talking, anyway. Can you honestly see mother ever apologizing to anyone for anything?"

"No," Robin answered, shaking her head. "According to her, she's never wrong, even when she is. Go ahead and enlighten me. Tell me what mother wants you to do."

Rosemary glanced at the closed door, wondering if Helen was standing outside eavesdropping, listening to every word she and Robin were saying. Unlike Robin's old bedroom, this one wasn't bugged, so the only way she'd be able to hear them was if she had her ear pressed to the door. Helen had insisted on planting listening devices in Robin's room, knowing Joey would never agree to stay in hers, and had tasked her with ensuring the dirty deed was completed prior to Joey's arrival. She wanted to be able to keep tabs on Joey and listen in on all her conversations. That's how she'd known where to find Robin when Helen sent her upstairs to retrieve her. She'd been convinced Robin was on the verge of telling Joey what was going on and why she was there. Robin had gotten a sharp tongue-lashing because of that conversation, but after telling her mother she was only going to tell Joey how sick their father had gotten and nothing more, Helen eased off and dismissed it.

Helen tasked her with the duty of finding and hiring a technological professional to install the bug. Knowing nothing about how to accomplish the task, she had no idea where to turn or who to go to in order to fulfill Helen's demands. An electronics store in town sold Do-It-Yourself kits with installation instructions, but she wasn't electronically savvy enough to figure out where to put it or how to hide the microphone, so buying one would've been a waste of money.

Knowing her father had multitudes of friends on the police force, she placed a call to the Cornish Police Department and, after asking generalized questions, was transferred to an officer whose specialty was surveillance, which included the installation of wire taps.

"Do you mind if I ask why you feel it necessary to install a wire in your home?"

"It's for my father," she lied. "You see, he suffers from dementia and my mother wants the device in his room so she can keep an eye on him."

"Baby monitors work just as well in situations such as yours."

"That's what I told her, but she's insisting on a device he can't see."

"Um hmm." The officer sounded suspicious, as if he weren't buying a word she was saying.

"Allow me to explain," she told him, hoping she could make up a believable excuse. "The worst thing to do with a dementia patient is to alter an environment they've grown accustomed to. The slightest of changes in an otherwise normal pattern can cause outbursts of anger and uncontrollable behavior. Hence, not wanting to place a visible monitor where he can see it because he'll know it doesn't belong there, and it would further confuse him. Mother doesn't want that to happen. She's also afraid he'll break the monitor out of frustration, and she'd end up having to continuously replace them. I'm sure you can see why that would be defeating the purpose."

"I see," he replied. "What's your name?"

"Rosemary Van Allen."

"Your father's name?"

"Macarthur Sheffield."

Silence, then, "Mac has dementia?"

"I'm afraid so."

"Gee, I'm sorry to hear that. I didn't know."

"Few people do. We prefer it that way out of respect for my father."

"I understand."

"Do you have any suggestions about how I can proceed with this?"

The officer answered with a loud exhale through the phone. "The police department can't get involved with your request, not without a court order."

"I was afraid of that. What else can I do?"

After a few moments, the officer replied, "Do you have a pen and paper handy?"

"Yes."

"Write this down," he said, advising her which store was the best choice to purchase the proper kit and the best brand to buy. "Call me back once you have it. I'll stop by and show you how to install it."

"That sounds great. Thanks." *It really is beneficial to belong to a family with money, notoriety and influence,* she thought as she hung up.

When he came to the house two days later, Rosemary thought the device was to be installed in Joey's room, and had Helen not come upstairs to check on the progress, it would've been.

"Good heavens," Helen exclaimed as she entered the room. "What on earth are you doing?"

The officer looked perplexed by her outburst, turning to Rosemary and shrugging.

"This is *not* the room I want the gadget installed in," she barked. Turning to Rosemary, she continued. "You incompetent twit. Can't you do anything right? It's the room next door, Robin's old room."

Without responding to her mother's verbal humiliation, she led the officer to the proper location, and within fifteen minutes, the device was operable and ready for use.

Not until after he left did Rosemary confront her mother. "Did you really feel it necessary to embarrass me like that?"

"It's your own fault for being so stupid."

"You said you wanted it in Joey's room, then have the audacity to call me stupid when I attempted to do exactly that?"

"I meant the room I knew she'd be staying in, not the one she had while living here."

"How was I supposed to know that? You never told me."

"You should've asked."

"How can you be so sure Joey won't stay in her old room?"

"Because unlike you, I know what I'm talking about when I speak." *It is, afterall, where all those dreadful things took place. No way would Joey be willing to spend a single night in that room.*

"She wants me to kill Joey," she said in a faint voice.

"WHAT?!" Robin shrieked. "I thought daddy was the one who's out of his mind. Mother is as well."

"Shh," Rosemary said, putting a finger to her lips. "Keep your voice down. I don't want her to know I'm telling you this."

"Rosemary, please tell me you're not going through with it."

"Of course not," Rosemary protested. "But mother is insisting, threatening to tell Dan about the affair I had over two years ago."

Robin shook her head. "Mother and her manipulative powers. She prides herself with that attribute, you know?"

"Tell me about it."

"What are you going to do?"

"I don't know what to do, Robin. If I don't follow through with her wishes, she'll keep her word and tell Dan everything. Then he'll divorce me and fight for custody of the girls. I'll lose my kids, my house, my car... everything."

"Are those your words, or mother's?"

"Both, I think. She made it a point to make that extremely clear to me."

"So what if she tells Dan? He won't believe her."

"He would once she showed him the proof."

"What proof?"

"A report from a private detective."

"Are you fucking kidding me?" Robin exclaimed. "She had you tailed?"

Rosemary nodded. "She has photos, too."

"Have you seen them or are you taking her at her word?"

"I've seen them."

"They're not of you... well, you know?"

"In bed with him? No. Kissing and hugging him? Yes. More than enough evidence to prove to Dan I was unfaithful."

"If it comes to that, tell him it's an old friend you ran in to and were embracing because you were happy to see each other."

"That might would work if not for the pictures of us kissing. It'd be hard to explain that."

"It's worth a try," Robin said, her eyes widening as she suddenly had a thought. "Shit."

"What?"

"If she knows about your affair, what are the chances she knows about me and my girlfriend?"

Rosemary shrugged. "No clue. Unfortunately, I wouldn't put anything past her."

"Who's to say she hasn't spied on me as well? Seems like something she'd do to ensure we're towing the line and worthy of our inheritances."

"Could be. I can't think of a legitimate reason she would have for watching us. Or me, anyway. And what do you care if she knows about you? It's none of her business."

"I don't. Still, hiring private investigators to spy on her own kids is an extremely low move, even by mother's standards, but not surprising."

"True."

Robin shook her head in disbelief. "If it's any consolation, I think she's wrong."

"About?"

"Dan. He worships you, Rosemary. You and those two beautiful daughters of yours. If I know Dan the way I think I do, I don't believe he'd divorce you. He may be upset over your infidelity, but in time, I believe he'd forgive you. Don't let mother manipulate you into thinking otherwise. Call her bluff."

"What do you mean?"

"Stand your ground, beat her to the punch. Tell Dan and get it over with. Take away her leverage."

"Boy, would that ever piss her off."

"Yes, it would, but it'd give you the upper hand. Let her know you will not be intimidated by her extortion and vicious threats."

"I honestly don't think I have the heart to tell Dan. Just thinking about the pain it'll cause him is enough to make me nauseous."

"Don't wait and allow mother to be the one who tells him. Hearing it from someone else would hurt him worse. It needs to come from you."

"That's easy for you to say. Holding your tongue has never been a problem for you, but I don't know if I have the courage to do it."

"Who are you kidding? You're the biggest bitch I know," Robin said with a chuckle. "Besides, you never know what you're capable of until you apply yourself, Rosie. Don't let her get to you like this, and for God's sake, don't let her scare you into committing a murder. Especially when the one she wants murdered is our sister. You'll spend the rest of your life in prison for doing her dirty work. God forbid, Helen Sheffield should ever get her own hands dirty."

Rosemary sighed heavily. "I'm afraid to tell her no, Robin. I'm scared of what she might do or say. What choice is she leaving me?"

"Let's say you honor her request and go through with it. Then what? How do you think you're going to cope with realizing you're the one responsible for Joey's death?"

"I wouldn't be able to live with myself knowing I slaughtered my own flesh and blood to please that vile woman. Again, what choice do I have?"

"Are you fucking kidding me, Rosie?" Robin stated, her voice rising again. "The choice is that you don't kill your sister and you tell mother to kindly go fuck herself."

"Maybe I should go to the police and tell them what she wants me to do."

"Why, so you can embarrass yourself by being unable to answer all the questions they're sure to ask? They'll want proof of the conspiracy, and you don't have any. Word of mouth isn't good enough to make an allegation accusing someone of plotting a murder. By doing that, you'd be sure to suffer the hateful wrath of Helen when she vehemently denies it. You and I both know she will. She'll say she doesn't know what you're talking about and feign surprise at the mere thought you could think such a thing."

"You're probably right," Rosemary replied, nodding. "I wish with all my heart that I'd never agreed to any of this. If only I could turn back time."

"But you can't, so you have to deal with the here and now. Whatever solution you come up with, I hope it doesn't include offing our sister."

"I'll figure something out. In the meantime, I'll do whatever I have to do to avoid mother and prevent her from pressuring me."

"I know this is probably a stupid question, but is daddy aware of anything that's going on concerning mother?"

"Daddy," Rosemary breathed. "Now there's a whole different situation."

Robin furrowed her brow. "What do you mean by that?"

"When was the last time you saw him?"

"It's been a while. Every time I ask if I can visit him, mother says no and makes up one lame excuse after another why I can't. Anything to prevent me from seeing him."

"There's a reason for that, one I recently only learned myself."

"And?"

"She's killing him, Robin," Rosemary said sadly. "With all those pills she's constantly shoving down his throat to make him sleep. I don't believe any of them were prescribed to him. I think mother took it upon herself to medicate him with narcotics she deems necessary to care for him, not what was prescribed by his doctor. He looks and smells awful. I don't think she's even bathing him. Adding insult to injury, she moved him from his second-floor room into the attic."

"Not into the…?"

"Yes. He barely has enough room in there to move around. Not that it matters since he's sedated most of the time. He doesn't even have a bed. She's making him sleep on a cot. When I said something about it, she told me it was for his safety because it was lower than his bed and he wouldn't get hurt if he fell off of it."

"That evil bitch," Robin spat. "We should call social services and report her for elderly abuse. That would get him removed from her care and placed in a hospital where he can get the medical attention he needs."

"That suggestion is definitely something to contemplate," Rosemary agreed. "I would've never considered doing that if I hadn't seen the condition he's in."

"You think mother's doing it on purpose? Do you seriously believe she's intentionally trying to kill him?"

"Yes."

"Why?"

"To get rid of him. She doesn't want to be bothered with him anymore because he's too much of a responsibility."

"That call should be made immediately. The sooner the better before she *does* kill him. How's his state of mind these days?"

"Terrible and continuously deteriorating. It's only a matter of time before he completely loses his memory."

"All the more reason for him to be placed in a medical facility. They're trained to deal with patients like him and they damn sure won't try to murder him."

"Mother never has been one to be attentive to the needs of others, not even to us. Remember?"

"How could I possibly forget?" Robin answered with a frown. "You should sit down with Joey and tell her everything. Why you lied, why she's here, the entire truth about daddy. For God's sake, whatever you do, don't tell her mother wants her dead."

"She would never forgive any of us if I told her what we've done. We hardly ever see her as it is, and I can guarantee you if she learns the truth about all this, we'll never see her again."

"Let me give you something else to think about," Robin said. "Joey's not stupid. I think we can both agree on that. Keeping that in mind, don't you think she might already be getting a little suspicious at this point? Afterall, she *is* here for a funeral that hasn't been planned yet. She's already confronted you over that and you got all tongue-tied trying to give her a sensible answer. That alone likely triggered a modicum of doubt. Knowing Joey, she's already either called or gone to see the medical examiner and the funeral directors. If she has, then she already knows we've been dishonest with her. If I had to take a guess,

I'd say she doesn't have much trust in any of us right now."

Rosemary considered Robin's theory momentarily. "Do you really think she'd do that? Go around checking, I mean?"

"Yes, I do."

Rosemary stood from the bed. "Then whatever I need to do, I'd better do it quickly. Mother has that stupid tea party planned for this afternoon. It wouldn't surprise me one bit if Joey came home, packed her suitcase, and left. To be honest with you, I wouldn't blame her one damn bit if she did."

Chapter Twenty

The tea party was set up in the parlor, one of the many rooms Joey and her sisters had been forbidden to play in or entertain friends there during their younger years. Joey was surprised to see that Helen had chosen it to host her soiree, allowing the same people to come in that she'd denied entrance to for the entire length of time they'd all lived there.

All four walls were adorned with maroon and black, paisley-print tapestries, giving the area an even gloomier than usual ambience beneath the dim lighting of the overhead chandelier. Joey noticed that several of the bulbs had burned out and manor staff had failed to immediately replace them with fresh ones. Helen obviously wasn't the hostess of get-togethers and Bridge parties as she once had been. Otherwise, such carelessness would've never been permitted, and the staff member who allowed it to happen would've been fired on the spot for such gross incompetence. It was apparent the lighting fixture hadn't seen a decent dusting in quite some time, evidenced by the multitudes of stringy cobwebs dangling from the tear-drop shaped crystals.

In the center of the room was a square, four-place setting solid oak dining table. Next to it, a sterling silver serving cart held four individual pots of tea, cups, and saucers.

"Josephine, you'll sit here," Helen ordered, motioning to her right. "Robin, you're on the other side. Rosemary, you take the opposite end."

No staff was present to assist with the distribution of the pots and cups, meaning there wouldn't be anyone hovering over them, waiting to fill their empty cups faster than they could return them to their saucers. Joey thought it strange that Helen had opted to do the serving herself since she'd always had a servant for everything. It wouldn't have surprised her in the least to learn she also had a servant for wiping her ass after taking a shit.

The lack of household servitude made Joey wonder if Helen no longer employed anyone. With the dilapidation of the fountain, exterior of the house, foliage, and flowers, it was quite clear that no maintenance had been performed anywhere on the grounds for a long time. What was Helen planning on doing? Taking her inheritance and abandoning the large home for something smaller, leaving the much-needed repairs for the next owner? Did she have her eyes set on a beachfront condominium in Florida she was planning to retire to? She might as well forget about it because it would never happen. In fact, Helen would soon be receiving a huge, disappointing surprise.

"Rosemary, I've brewed green tea for you," she said, handing the pot to Robin. "Pass that to your sister."

"Chai for you," she said, handing Robin her own personal tea pot.

"For you, Josephine, I've brewed a special tea. It's a new favorite of mine. I hope you enjoy it."

Joey placed the teapot on the table in front of her, forgoing pouring a cup. Thin wisps of steam emitted from the small spout and smelled similar to licorice. It was enticing, but she wasn't ready to join in on the party just yet.

"Go on, drink up," Helen said, her right pinky finger in the air as she sipped from her own porcelain cup. "You'll like it, I promise," she said, expressing what Joey saw as an arrogant sneer.

"Is anyone else coming?" Joey asked.

"No one else was invited," Helen replied snidely, placing her cup gingerly on the saucer. "Were you expecting someone else?"

"No, I wasn't," Joey answered coolly, knowing full well that Helen was making a patronizing reference to Mason. "I only wanted to make sure no one else was going to be here, because there's something I need to say and once I get started, I don't want to be interrupted."

"What on earth could you possibly have to talk about that you feel would be so important that an intrusion would be ghastly?" Helen asked, taking another sip of her peppermint tea.

"Well, Helen," Joey began.

"Joey," Rosemary reprimanded. "You should show mother some respect."

"Respect is earned, Rosemary," Joey replied, turning to look at her. "Not given."

"You could at least call her mother and not use her first name."

"There's absolutely no reason for me to call her anything other than Helen, but I'll get to that in a minute," Joey said, noticing a slight tremor had developed in Helen's hand, forcing her to put her cup down lest she break one of her cardinal rules by spilling it and making a mess all over her precious antique table. "Now, where was I? Oh yes," she said, folding her elbows atop the table, a habit Helen despised and had also forbidden. Helen glared at her but didn't speak.

The pendulum on the large Grandfather clock in the corner by the shuttered window swung back and forth, ticking away the seconds as the three of them waited, eyes glued on her, to hear the declaration she was on the brink of making.

"Before I get to the juicy pulp of this entire ordeal, I'd first like to say that I know why you were so adamant about getting me to come back here," Joey stated. "And it wasn't for a funeral because I know for a fact that Mac isn't dead. Before any of you begin to contradict that, you should know I've already paid visits to the coroner, funeral homes, and clerk's office. There's not even a death certificate on file. Furthermore, no one I spoke with knew anything about Mac's death."

Joey glanced around the table to see their reactions as she informed them of the truths she'd uncovered. None of them made eye contact with her. All were more focused on their teacups and its contents than they were of meeting her gaze.

"Anyone? No one? Good, then I'll continue. Unless one of you three thought it funny to play a practical joke on me, he's made at least one visit to my room since I've been here. I clearly smelled his disgusting cologne and that sickening cherry tobacco he always smoked. If none of you are guilty of the charges I just spoke of, then not only is Mac still alive, but he's also still living inside this house. Let's put all that on the back burner for now and move on to more important things," she remarked, turning to Helen. "Would you like the pleasure of telling them the truth about me, or shall I do the honors for you?"

"Tell us what?" Robin prodded.

"I have no earthly idea what you're referring to," Helen replied without looking up.

"No? Is that your final answer?"

"Joey, what the hell's going on?" Rosemary wanted to know. "What are you getting at?"

"This," she exclaimed, slamming the unfolded document she'd found in Mac's safe face up on the table. "Now's your chance, Helen. Going once, going twice…"

"Stop this nonsense!" Helen shouted, recognizing the piece of paper. "You'll cease this disgusting talk this instant, or else. Do you hear me?"

"Or else what, Helen? What could you possibly do or say to me that could be any worse than the lie I've been living for thirty-three years?"

"Mother, what's she talking about?" Rosemary asked.

"Nothing important, as usual."

"Joey, what is that?" Robin prodded, pointing to the paper beneath Joey's hand.

"It's a birth certificate," Joey stated, her eyes locked on Helen.

"What's the big deal about that?" Robin asked. "I'm sure we all have one."

"I'll guarantee you neither of you have one like this. Since Helen won't tell you, I will," Joey stated, picking up the document. "After I tell you about it, perhaps you'll both better understand why I was always the black sheep of the family, the one who suffered the brunt of Helen's wrath, the one who could never do anything right or be believed when she revealed the abuse she was suffering at the hands of her father, the one who was always accused of being a liar, a rotten bitch and a whore."

"STOP IT!" Helen screamed, slapping the table, her cold blue eyes transfixed on Joey, aimed and ready to fire ice daggers.

"I won't stop until Robin and Rosemary hear everything!" Joey yelled back. "They deserve to know exactly what an evil and hateful woman you really are and how you've also lied to them all these years. Hell, who am I kidding? We all lived a lie. One great big, elaborate lie."

"Mother, can you explain to us what she's referring to?" Rosemary demanded to know.

Helen sat stiff in her chair, her eyes barely more than slits, the look of a rabid animal ready to attack.

"Helen isn't my birth mother," Joey proclaimed. "Isn't that right, Helen?"

"What?" Robin asked, her voice rising in pitch. "This is a joke, right?" she laughed.

"I assure you it isn't," Joey stated sharply. "In fact, I don't find it funny at all. It's clearly stated right here in black and white," she said, waving the certificate. "Name of child is Josephine Renee Sheffield. That's me, by the way. Said child has the same birth date as me, but the birth mother is listed as April Baggett, not Helen Sheffield."

"Oh, my God," Robin breathed. "Then you're adopted?"

"I don't think so," Joey said. "Mac *is* my real father. His name is listed on the certificate as well."

"Holy shit," Rosemary exclaimed, covering her mouth.

"That means he fathered an illegitimate child. Me. With another woman. April. Yet somehow, I ended up here as an infant and was raised as Helen's natural daughter."

Rosemary and Robin were fascinated by what they were hearing, their eyes wide with amusement, mouths agape as they learned that Joey was only their half-sister and not the whole sister they'd both been raised up to believe.

"Tell me, Helen. How did I end up here? Did you threaten April? Pay her off to keep her quiet? Or did you simply steal me away from her without an ounce of remorse? Seems logical to me that would be your sick, twisted way of ensuring that Mac's infidelities were never made public. God forbid your precious name should ever be dragged through the mud in such a dirty manner."

"You shut your filthy mouth right now!" Helen hissed through clenched teeth. "You should be grateful you were raised in a house full of luxuries and entitlements instead of living in housing projects or run-down shacks, which is surely where you would've ended up had you stayed with that piece of trash woman who gave birth to you."

"Dear God, mother," Rosemary gasped. "Are you admitting that Joey's telling the truth? How could you keep something like that from us?"

"It was for your own good," Helen argued. "I saw no need trying to explain what your father had done. It was between the two of us and no one else's business."

"For our own good, huh?" Joey shouted. "And you think I should be thankful for luxuries and entitlements I never received? Do I need to remind you that you ostracized me from any family functions? You made sure I wasn't a part of any activities involving you, Rosemary, and Robin. And I'm aware that you lied to them over the years by telling them the reason I wasn't included was because I didn't want to be. You are one evil fucking bitch, Helen."

"Joey," Rosemary was reprimanding her yet again.

"Shut up, Rosemary," Joey said. "You might want to hear what I have to say next since it involves you more than you're willing to admit."

"Oh, boy," Robin said quietly. "What next?"

"You know what, Helen? I would've gladly given up what you referred to as luxuries if it meant living a wholesome, happy life. I would've rather lived in a cardboard box and eaten scraps out of garbage cans than to have been sexually molested by my own father for more than five years and being *RAPED BY HIM AT THIRTEEN*!" she screamed. "Is that your idea of living a luxurious life, Helen? Is it?"

Rosemary and Robin were both stunned into silence as they listened to Joey proclaiming the sins against their father.

"And don't sit there acting like you're innocent and don't know what I'm talking about. I came to you and told you about it, hoping and praying you'd do something to help me. Instead, you sent me away. You called me a liar and told me to stop making up stories. And I came to you," Joey said, pointing an accusatory finger at Rosemary. "Like Helen, you laughed and told me to stop telling lies about your dear daddy."

"Dear God," Robin sighed. "What kind of disgusting shit went on in this house?"

"Do you really want to know, Robin? Would you like me to tell you how I was treated?"

"Please do," Robin nodded. "I'd like to hear it."

"When social workers came here to follow up on a complaint about me, Mac and Helen sent them on their way, telling them I was an embellisher to facts and should be ignored. Mac paid off the judge and the investigators to shut down the case."

"That's bribery," Robin said. "Isn't that against the law?"

"You honestly think that mattered to Helen or Mac? Their honor was at stake. They did what they had to do to protect it." Turning her attention back to Helen, she continued. "Did you know I carried three pairs of bloody underwear to school in my backpack just so I could dispose of them there because I was too afraid they'd be discovered here, and I'd have to answer a bunch of questions I wasn't prepared to answer?"

"Mother, you told me those social workers came here to investigate a complaint of child abuse and it was unfounded. You *never* said a thing about the allegation being sexual. You lied to me," Rosemary said, her tone distant. She was absorbing all the new-to-her information like a sponge.

"You sound surprised, Rosemary," Joey stated, glancing at her sister. "Lying comes as easily to her as sucking a bottle does to an infant. Our lives are built on nothing but lies. Isn't that right, Helen?" Joey asked, turning back to face her.

"You knew Joey was telling the truth all along and you did nothing about it," Rosemary said as she stared into her tea as though she were speaking to the cup instead of her mother.

"Shut up, Josephine," Helen warned her.

"No, I won't shut up. I did that for too long, and what did it get me? Attack after attack. Mac slipping into my room at night through what I now know was a secret passageway. At the time I didn't know that because I didn't even know it existed. But I did wonder how he kept getting into my room when I locked my door at night."

"A secret passageway?" Robin asked, her voice filled with surprise. "Tell me you're kidding."

"I'm not. Every single one of our rooms is accessible through the passageway inside the interior walls, compliments of sliding wooden panels on lubricated runners so they don't make any noise when they're moved. I know both of you have denied that Mac ever did anything inappropriate to you, but I'd sure like to know why he felt it necessary to have those doors. How many nights did he slip in unknowingly and stand over us, leering at us as if we were some type of freak show on display? Unfortunately for me, the leering developed into something much worse."

Robin grew quiet as she listened to Joey describing the panels, appearing to be in deep thought about an idea that'd just come to her.

"Rosemary, did you know about any of this?"

"The passageway, yes. The rest, no," she answered. "This is all news to me. Go on, Joey. I'd like to hear more."

"You need to be quiet, Josephine," Helen warned.

"Both social workers gave me, you, and Mac the chance to either prove or disprove my allegations by offering to perform a complete medical examination on me, which would've proven beyond a reasonable doubt that I was brutally raped. What did you tell them, Helen? Go ahead, tell Rosemary and Robin what you said to them about me."

Helen was growing angrier by the second. Her lips were drawn into a snarl as she exhaled through her nose, a dragon on the verge of blasting flumes of fire and smoke.

"Nevermind," Joey said, waving her off and turning to face Rosemary and Robin. "She refused to allow the examination, going as far as telling Ms. Peacock that the exam wouldn't prove a thing because I was already sexually active and would most likely end up pregnant before turning sixteen." Turning back to Helen, she said, "You didn't know I knew that little tidbit of information, did you, Helen? Here's a surprise for you. I know about that and about a hell of a lot of other things. Shall I go on?"

Helen bolted from her chair. It tumbled over backwards and crashed to the floor. She slapped Joey hard across the face, startling her and her sisters. "Shut up!" she hissed. "You're nothing but a trashy, worthless whore," she seethed. "I was right about one thing. You are exactly like your mother. You always have been and you always will be. You're an ungrateful, wretched bitch."

"Mother!" Rosemary shouted, rising from her chair. "Stop it this instant!"

"It's okay, Rosemary," Joey said, massaging her stinging cheek. "Helen just verified everything I told you. Why else would she be so obstinate about shutting me up?"

"All those distasteful lies you told about your father, bringing shame and disgrace to this family. I should've thrown you out on your ass years ago."

"Yet they weren't lies, were they, mother?" Rosemary asked.

"You have no idea how much I wish you had," Joey retorted. "What I wouldn't give to be able to erase from my mind the years of torture I endured from Mac. Thanks for the memories, Helen," Joey said sarcastically. "May you rot in hell."

"I have so many questions but don't even know where to start," Rosemary said, slinking back into her chair. "I remember you bringing a baby home, mother. Now that I think about it, I don't recall you ever looking pregnant. It's possible that I was too young to understand why you didn't have a growing belly. Most four-year-old kids wouldn't."

"And Mac never came into your room?" Joey asked. "Not even once?"

"Not that I can remember, and I'm sure I wouldn't forget something like that."

"It's easy to forget when you don't want to remember," Robin said in a near whisper. "I thought I was dreaming."

"Robin?" Joey prompted. "What are you trying to say?"

Her eyes were filled with tears when she raised her head, one escaping and running down her cheek. "I hadn't thought of it in years," she stated.

"It seemed like a dream, so I didn't dwell on it, nor did I ever mention it for the same reason."

"Did Mac come into your room, Robin?"

"Yes," she replied. "Many times."

"What did he do to you?" Joey asked, her voice growing harsh with anger. "Did he touch you inappropriately, Robin? Did he make you touch him?"

"No," Robin said. "He just stood over my bed, staring down at me while I slept. I guess I must've woken up frequently if I saw him more than once. Like I said, I was young and thought I'd had bad dreams."

"See what you've done?" Helen spat. "Because of your cockamamie babbling about untruths, you've now got Robin believing the same thing happened to her. I hope you're happy with yourself for what you've done."

"Congratulations, Helen," Joey said icily. "You have officially lost your fucking mind if you think any of this is my fault. While we're on the subject, there's something you should know," she said, turning to Rosemary. "I feel awful for betraying Julia like this, but you need to keep her away from

Mac. I caught her yesterday talking to my old doll, Molly, and what she was telling her was quite disturbing. When I pressed the issue with her, she let me know Mac has done the same thing to her. You have a choice to make, Rosemary. Is your daughter more important to you than money, or are you going to ignore her pleas for help and let the same thing that happened to me happen to her?"

Rosemary glanced at Helen, then at Joey, but said nothing.

"Let me make something perfectly clear to you, Rosemary. If you refuse to listen to your daughter and continue to subject her to Mac's abuse, I will personally turn you in to child protective services myself and tell them what's happening to her. In doing so, at least I can provide her with the protection that was denied to me. Do you understand? I will not leave here until I know Julia is safe. I mean that."

"Hogwash," Helen chided, pouring another cup of tea. "Julia is a duplicate of her mother in every way possible, including the embellishment of stories to make them believable when, in fact, they're not true. Exactly like the one you just relayed."

"Are you calling my daughter a liar?," Rosemary asked. "Unfortunately, Julia did say something to me about it, but I dismissed it because I didn't believe her. Much in the same way I didn't believe Joey. Now that I know it was all true, I'd like to state for the record that if he ever touches my daughter again, I'll fucking kill him with my bare hands. And as long as he remains here, my daughters will not be returning."

Did Rosemary realize that her statement confirmed Mac was still alive and residing at Sheffield Manor? Amazing how anger is capable of bringing out the truth.

"For what it's worth, Joey, I am deeply and truly sorry that I didn't believe you or do anything to help you when you needed me to."

"Protect Julia," Joey stated flatly. "That's your redemption."

"I will. That's a promise."

"God Almighty," Helen exclaimed with disgust. "Like mother, like daughter. I shouldn't have expected anything less."

"You have quite the nerve to accuse someone else of lying," Rosemary replied. Her mother was still pissed at her for refusing to follow through on an order, hence the harsh and hateful accusations being hurled her way. "Considering what Joey has told us, I'd say you're the real liar here with a ton of explaining to do. I think I can speak for us all when I say you owe us that much. All our lives you've poisoned our minds with garbage about Joey, trying to turn us against her, hoping we'd hate her as much as you did. Everything's coming together now. Why you always treated her differently, why you excluded her from our outings, why she repeatedly got sent to the attic. You couldn't stand the sight of her because she was a constant reminder of what daddy did to you. Even though she was innocent of everything you accused her of, you still chose to ostracize her and justify your actions with lies about what a bad child she was and how desperately she needed to learn her place in this family. She wasn't bad, though, was she mother? She simply didn't fit in. Because in your eyes, she was an outsider and not truly a Sheffield. Did I miss anything?"

Helen sighed deeply and shook her head. "I suppose you're right," she said calmly. "An explanation is certainly in order, but it'll take a considerable amount of time to tell you everything. Can we all have a cup of tea together first and enjoy the calm before the storm? Is that asking too much?"

Joey poured a cupful from her pot and gulped it down in two swallows while Helen watched. Not only did it smell like licorice, but it also tasted like it. There was a hint of a bitter aftertaste, yet not enough to prevent it from being enjoyable.

Pouring a second cup, the teapot suddenly felt like it weighed a hundred pounds. Unable to hold on to it, she dropped it, shattering the fine porcelain, spilling its contents over the tabletop.

"Joey?" Rosemary was calling her name, her voice muffled and far away. "Are you okay?"

Her mouth was as dry as cotton. Her tongue stuck to the roof of her mouth when she tried speaking.

"Joey?" Robin's voice was coming from inside a tunnel somewhere in the house.

Joey rose from her chair, holding onto the edge of the table to keep from falling over. "You *bish*," she slurred, swaying unsteadily before collapsing onto the floor.

"Dear God, mother," Rosemary cried, leaping from her chair and kneeling beside Joey. "What have you done?"

"What you didn't have the courage to do," Helen answered.

"You drugged her!" Robin yelled accusingly. "Why would you do that to her?"

"Because she deserves to die," Helen answered, placing her teacup down and scooting her chair away from the table. "The two of you pick her up from the floor and take her to the wine cellar. A bed has already been prepared to lay her on. Now stop dilly dallying and do as you're told."

"What are you going to do to her?" Robin asked.

"I'm going to give her what she deserves," Helen replied. "For the record, Rosemary, as far as explanations go, I don't owe you a fucking thing," she stated before turning and walking away.

"Rosemary, we can't let her do this," Robin whispered. "We have to stop her."

"I know," Rosemary said. "For now, let's take her downstairs like mother said, so she doesn't get suspicious about us plotting against her or else we may end up in the same situation as Joey."

"What are we going to do?"

"Right now, I don't have an answer. Maybe if we put our heads together, we'll think of something. Don't worry, Robin. I'm not going to let mother kill our sister. If she tries, she'll have to go through me first to do it."

* * * * *

"You stupid, stupid old fool!" Helen screamed as she slammed the door to his room. He had no idea why she was yelling at him. He hadn't left his room since overhearing those two women arguing in the living room. Nor had he been rummaging through the boxes in his favorite place. He also hadn't gone into any of the other forbidden rooms in the west wing, so why was he in trouble?

"What?" he asked, sitting up on the side of his cot as he stared at her through confused and watery eyes. "What did I do?"

"What good would it do for me to try to explain it to you when you'd never understand a single word I said with that malfunctioning brain of yours?"

she scolded, berating him as usual. He deserved her wrath sometimes. Like when he misbehaved and defied her orders. But times like now when he couldn't even remember his name, all he could do was frown and listen to her rant. "Even with that sponge brain of yours, you still managed to revert back to your old habits."

"Huh? Wha…"

"Oh, shut up, you blithering idiot," she hissed, shoving him forcefully back onto his pillow. "Tomorrow, you won't recall anything I'm about to say, but I'm going to say it, anyway. What you did to Josephine was something I cared nothing about, but if you ever touch Julia or Jackie again, you won't have to worry about growing any loonier because I'll destroy you before you can," she said, patting him on the shoulder as though she'd just told him she'd made a special batch of cookies instead of threatening to execute him.

"Who's Julia?" he asked, wiping saliva from his chin with the back of his hand. "And Jackie?"

There wasn't a day that went by that she didn't grow weary of him, disgusted by his child-like behavior one day and clarity the next, never knowing what to expect from him one day to another. On his clear-headed days, he acted out on foolish ideas such as what she'd learned about his behavior with Julia. But on cloudy-headed days, he couldn't even remember to wipe his ass, much less what he'd done the day, or even minutes, before. Caring for him was the equivalent of tending to a newborn baby again. She was repulsed by it all, in the same way she found his overall appearance reprehensible. She could hardly wait until he keeled over and she no longer had to monitor his every move or baby and medicate him to ensure he didn't burn the house down or fall out of a window. Rarely did she have the luxury of devoting any time to herself, loathing him for denying her such a humble indulgence. She still had needs, too, and things she enjoyed doing, such as watching her soap operas on television, reading a good mystery novel, or solving a daily crossword puzzle. All those enjoyments had become a thing of the past since most of her attention had become focused on him. She fantasized about his death quite frequently. If the bastard didn't hurry up and die naturally, she'd be forced to take matters into her own hands and solve the problem herself.

The sooner he was out of her life, the quicker she could return to doing what made her happy. Hopefully, that time was near.

"Here," she said, passing him a hand full of pills. "Take your medicine. You need to get some sleep and relax your brain. I'll come back later to check in on you. For now I have some issues to take care of."

* * * * *

She should've known he wouldn't be able to stay away from Joey. He never had been able to. Even with his unwell and declining mind, he'd found his way to her, like a sinking ship following the guiding beacon from a lighthouse until it reached safe shore. One of thousands of reasons Helen hated her so much was the unbreakable grip she had on Mac without even realizing it. To him, she was the equivalent of a childhood toy that he simply couldn't depart with, no matter how many times he tried giving it up. To Joey, Mac was nothing more than a despicable, wicked man who she'd grown to loathe over the years. The knowledge of knowing about all the dastardly things he'd done to her during her childhood brought Helen immense pleasure, a near-ecstatic euphoria.

Joey bore a slight resemblance to her father, enough to pass for his daughter without anyone asking questions, but she'd inherited a greater amount of her mother's traits, making it easy for Helen to hate her because she was a constant reminder of Mac's unfaithfulness, a love affair that'd occurred right under her roof and under her nose.

April Baggett had been an employee at the manor, hired as the gardener and landscaper. She was a lovely young woman, there was no doubt about that. Small and petite, olive-colored skin, and eyes the shade of violets, with extensive knowledge of, and the love for, maintaining a perfect flower garden, producing roses that Helen had entered in multiple contests at her Garden Club functions.

Mac soon developed a fondness for her, continually finding reasons to be around her by asking for her assistance with mundane duties, all of which he could've easily done alone. No excuse was too flimsy for Macarthur Sheffield if it resulted in spending time with April.

All the attention he gave her and the infatuation he displayed whenever he was near her, she found impressive. Afterall, what young woman struggling to make it on her own wouldn't see a gold-digging opportunity whenever a rich, handsome, middle-aged man exhibited an attraction for them? She thought if she could get her hooks into him and make him leave his wife and children, she could have Mac and all of his money to herself. She couldn't have been more wrong.

They'd been carrying on for months before Helen gained knowledge of their affair, brought to her attention by the maid who'd walked in on them while in the act. She may not have informed Helen of the illicit affair had Mac not stormed downstairs immediately following the incident, promptly firing her on the spot for not knocking before entering the room. When she'd confronted Mac in the maid's presence about how ludicrous it was to terminate her over something so foolish, the maid blurted, "I'll tell you why, Ms. Sheffield. I just caught your husband screwing your gardener. That's why he's firing me."

She had every intention of terminating April as well. But Mac told her she'd do no such thing because she was pregnant with his child. Initially, she'd thought the statement to be nothing more than his way of ensuring that she remained employed so he could continue to see her regularly. However, after a few months had passed and April's belly began growing into a small, rounded bump, she knew he'd been telling the truth. Shocked at the pregnancy and furious over his betrayal, she decided to play along, keeping April employed. Not because she needed the money with a child on the way, but to keep an eye on her and deal with the issue properly when the time came to do it. There was no way in hell she'd ever allow Mac's whore to flaunt her illegitimate bastard child all over Cornish, a town where everyone knew her and Mac, claiming that Macarthur Sheffield was the father. She'd be the laughingstock of the entire county, and she'd rather die than allow that to happen. How could she keep that from occurring? By hatching a plan to ensure it didn't.

From April's sixth month of pregnancy on, Helen chose not to be seen in public to avoid any suspicious stares or gossip when she suddenly appeared with a new infant in her care without developing an expanding belly to confirm a second pregnancy.

Two weeks before April was due to give birth, she'd paid her a visit at her apartment and gave her a firm ultimatum.

"Ms. Sheffield," she said with surprise as she opened the door to see her standing there. "What brings you to this part of town?"

Had she not had business there, she wouldn't have been caught dead in such a poor, filthy neighborhood. However, one must do what they had to do when an urgent matter needed attention.

"May I come in?"

"Of course," April replied, opening the door wider and showing her into the living room.

The small apartment was clean and well-maintained, items for the baby already assembled and ready for use. Helen sneered disdainfully at the swing and crib, pitying the fact they'd never be used. She certainly wouldn't be taking them, and April would have no use for them.

"Have a seat," April said.

"I'd rather not," Helen replied, scowling at April's cheap and worn furniture, disgusting pieces she wouldn't allow inside her garden shed, much less her home. She supposed the design on the fabric was intended to be representative of a rustic or Southwestern design, imprinted with a water mill and flowing stream, but she found it to be a despicable travesty. "What I came to say won't take long."

"Can I get you anything? Water or tea?"

"No. Sit down, April, and listen to me carefully."

April lowered herself onto the sofa, guarding her large belly as she sat.

"What I'm about to offer you is a choice. Take my advice and choose wisely," she stated authoritatively, looking down her nose at April. "When that child you're carrying is born, you will turn him or her over to me immediately. By immediately, I mean the child shall not leave the hospital in your care. Failure to do so will not be pleasant, I assure you of that. You will be duly compensated for the exchange. You'll receive more money than you've ever dreamed of. Enough to leave Cornish and go somewhere far away and never, under any circumstances, return here. You will have no contact with the child, and you will relinquish all parental rights to me. As far as this town and its residents are concerned, you were nothing more than a surrogate carrying a child that I couldn't."

"Are you crazy?" April protested, rising from her seat, prompting Helen's protector, a definite yes-man who was undoubtedly willing to do whatever Helen Sheffield told him to do if the price was right, to take a step forward, proving he'd accompanied her to keep her from harm. "I'm not giving up my child," she exclaimed, hugging her belly as though she were afraid Helen would slice her open and take the baby right then.

"Ah, but you will. You see, social services don't take kindly to druggie mothers tending to newborns. One phone call to them and they'll come and remove the child and place it in foster care."

"I don't do drugs," April protested. "I've never been addicted to anything illegal."

"Is that so? You may not be now, but you will be when I'm finished with you. Not in the literal sense, but it'll certainly appear as if you're not only a junkie, but a dealer as well. Trust me when I tell you I have the power to make that happen."

"Lady, you're a fucking lunatic," April shouted.

"The question here, April, is not whether I'm the crazy one, but whether you are. Are you honestly willing to take that chance with me, knowing who I am? Have you any idea exactly what I'm capable of and the influence I have in this town? Or the power I possess? The people I know who would jump to my aid with the snap of a finger?"

The yes-man took a small leap from the floor, glowering at April as he did.

"See what I mean?" Helen asked. "He's only one. I have many more like him."

"I don't give a shit about your stupid money or your power," April cried. "You can go to hell as far as I'm concerned. You're not getting my child."

"We'll see about that," she threatened. "Deadly accidents do happen. Right, Bruno?"

Bruno nodded.

"Quite often, so I've been told. That unborn child *will* be placed into my care."

"Are you seriously threatening to kill me, or have me killed so you can get your way?"

"I wouldn't call it a threat. More like a suggestion."

"Then I'll report you to the police."

Helen laughed heartily. "You do that. Have I mentioned that the Sheffield's make large donations to the policeman's charity ball every year? Or that the Police Chief and Sheriff are close friends of my husband's? It'd be your word against ours, and who do you think they'll believe? Prominent citizens of the town, or a gold-digging piece of trash like you?"

"Does Macarthur know you're doing this?"

"Sweetheart," Helen said condescendingly. "Who do you think sent me here?" He hadn't a smidgen of an idea what she was up to, and she had no plans to inform him about it.

All he'd need to know when the time came was that April reconsidered raising a child on her own and had decided, in the best interest of the child, to sign custody over to his or her biological father in order to be raised with a family where the child's needs could be met accordingly.

It wasn't necessary for him to know exactly how the child came to live at Sheffield Manor, only that it had.

"I can't believe this," April said, shaking her head and leaning back against the sofa. Macarthur had told her he loved her and would help her financially with his child. It was all a lie. She felt stupid for believing him, and for being used. "You're extorting me then telling me there's nothing I can do about it."

"Call it what you like. In case you haven't figured it out yet, you're boxed in a corner with no way out. You made a horrible mistake crossing me, and I'll make sure you pay greatly for your transgression."

"I'll pack my things and run away somewhere that you'll never find me."

"No, you won't. If you so much as attempt to run, I'll be notified immediately of your actions. At which time I'll give the order to execute my requests. Do I make myself clear?"

"You're having me watched?"

"Surveillance sounds so much better, doesn't it, Bruno?"

Another nod of agreement.

"You're deranged, lady," April cried. "A bona fide crazed maniac."

"Since you're no longer employed and on maternity leave, there's no reason for you to go anywhere other than a visit to your doctor or making a run to the grocery store. Each time you leave, I'll know about it. I'll be kept abreast about where you're going, who you're with, how long you're gone, and when you return home. Use your head, April, and choose wisely. Don't do anything stupid that you'll regret. Are we clear?"

April stared at her through tear-filled eyes, her bottom lip quivering as she grasped Helen's words. "You'll have to kill me then, because I'm not giving you my baby."

Helen laughed mockingly. "Your way it is, then" she said as she turned toward the door. "And might I add, an extremely stupid choice," she said before walking out.

The need to execute any of her ultimatums never arose. Nature took care of the problem for her when April died of complications from the anesthesia used during an emergency Caesarean section, never getting to see her newborn daughter.

Because Mac was the biological father, custody of the child was given to him without argument or interference from the courts. Whether April had any family was unknown since no one protested the court's decision to place the child in the care of her natural father.

Rosemary was only four and elated when she came home with a new infant. She hadn't been old enough to understand or ask where the baby came from. She was simply happy to have a little sister.

In the beginning, having Joey in the house hadn't been as hard emotionally as she'd expected it to be. Afterall, she was an innocent baby who didn't get to handpick her parents. Still, she couldn't stand being around her, refusing to hold or cuddle her. She absolutely couldn't do that, knowing she'd been conceived during an act of betrayal, and to look at her or spend time with her was a constant reminder of that. It wasn't until she grew older that Helen developed a strong dislike for the child. She bore a striking resemblance to her mother, with light olive skin and the same violet-colored eyes. Over time, the dislike transitioned into a deep-seated hatred as she watched how Mac groveled over her, picking her up and hugging her, playing with her while they laughed, neither of which he'd done with Rosemary. It was a daily struggle pretending to be the mother she wasn't because she was incapable of expressing a love she didn't possess, and the only civil way she could deal with such emotions was to avoid her as much as she could by leaving her necessary daily care in the hands of a professional nanny, and by focusing her attention on Rosemary.

Refusing to allow Joey to be the sole recipient of her father's undivided attention, she allowed herself to get pregnant again. Not because she'd wanted another child, but because she wanted the chance to give Mac what he'd always wanted. A son. She believed it'd distract him from his unnatural attraction to Joey. Alas, Robin came along, destroying any chance of ever fulfilling Mac's desires. Robin's birth did nothing to divert him, and like Rosemary, went ignored by her father. After suffering five consecutive miscarriages, she relented to the sobering truth that she'd never bear another child, which only gave Mac further reason to focus all his attention on his bastard child.

Then she began noticing that Mac's attraction to the child wasn't so much fatherly as it was lustful. Deep desire reflected in his eyes, as though Joey was a prize he was forbidden to enjoy in the way he wanted to.

Until he began to act on those desires, a move she could use to her advantage. She wanted the illegitimate bitch out of the picture and out of her house, and what better way to achieve that goal than to let Mac manage the problem for her. Although she was fully aware of his pedophilic desires for Joey, he was warned that if he felt those same desires for Rosemary or Robin and acted upon them, she'd personally castrate him and wear his balls around her neck as a trophy. Fortunately for him, he'd never touched either.

She knew about his frequent nightly visits to Joey's room. She'd chosen to ignore the issue and do nothing to stop what was happening, calling Joey a liar when she approached her and told her about it. She'd underestimated Mac's patience because she'd been positive he'd execute his severest act on her much sooner than he had. She'd become impatient with him for making her wait so long to do what needed to be done.

Secretly, she'd hoped the rape would kill her, either from injuries or shock. Unfortunately, she'd survived it, which had then resulted in a big-mouth teacher sticking her nose where it didn't belong and initiating an investigation on her and Mac for child abuse. In instances such as that, money talks if it speaks to the right person. Or in their case, the right people. They'd both denied the allegations to the social workers, and she'd told one of them that Joey was already sexually active and couldn't be believed because she didn't want to take a chance on having her removed from the home. If that happened, Joey would never be allowed to return, and she'd never have the opportunity to see her deepest desire fulfilled. She wanted her dead so their lives would be ridded of her permanently.

Joey changed drastically following the incident and avoided being around her or Mac every chance she could, practically living in her bedroom or staying in Robin's room talking or listening to music. When she wasn't there, she was either at one of those dreadful jobs of hers or with that peon Abernathy boy.

When Joey turned eighteen, she'd packed her things and left without saying a word to anyone. Because she stayed in contact with Rosemary and Robin, she always knew where she was. Although she was out of the house and out of her sight, that wasn't satisfactory enough for her. She wanted Joey to pay for all the hurt and shame she'd brought to the Sheffield name, and there was only one solution for that.

When she learned she'd settled down in some pissant town in Indiana, she began sending apologetic cards and letters to get her to come back, but none of them were ever acknowledged. She didn't even know if Joey had taken the time to open the envelopes and read the contents, or if she'd simply thrown them in the trash after reading the return address. There were numerous occasions when she'd also tried calling her only to get her voice mail or her calls went unanswered altogether. That only pissed her off further, making her even more determined to sate her desire. How dare she ignore pleas from her own mother who'd taken the time to write and beg her to come home so they could talk and make amends?

When Mac became ill and it was clear his health was steadily and rapidly declining, she saw his sickness as yet another advantage point to be used in her favor. Surely Joey would come home one last time to say goodbye to her father. It was a longshot because Joey despised him, but maybe she'd put her feelings aside for the benefit of her father's health. Her letters must've also gone unopened because she never came home, leaving her with only one remaining option. Telling her he'd died and beg her to come home for his funeral.

Knowing Joey would never answer a call from her, she'd asked Rosemary and Robin for their assistance. Even though she'd persuaded Rosemary to phone Joey, she didn't tell either of them the *real* reason she wanted Joey back. If she had, neither one would've agreed to help. Only Rosemary knew of the lie about Mac's death and had protested against it until she'd been forced to use extortion tactics against her by threatening to tell her husband about her affair with her Pilate's instructor.

Regardless of the measures that had to be taken, they'd resulted in accomplishment. Joey had finally returned home. And it'd be the last time she ever stepped foot inside Sheffield Manor because she had no intentions of letting her leave.

Joey belonged to her now, and she couldn't be happier.

She could've quickly eliminated the problem by overdosing her to the point of death, but that would've been too easy. Her initial plan was to watch while Rosemary satisfied her desires, but since she'd betrayed her by refusing to participate, she'd simply have to do it herself.

She couldn't wait to watch her take her last breath. To watch the light go out of her eyes when her heart stopped beating.

At last, after so many years of waiting, her wish was finally going to come true.

Chapter Twenty-One

Mason checked his watch for what seemed like the hundredth time, drumming his fingers impatiently on the table. The waiter had already come over twice to check the status of his pending guest's arrival, and Mason expected the third time would happen any second since he hadn't ordered anything yet. He didn't understand the waiter's impatience unless there was another couple waiting in the wings for the booth he was occupying, and all he was doing was taking up space. As usual, the restaurant was buzzing with a line of people waiting to be seated. He supposed the waiter's repeated trips to his table was his way of telling him that if he wasn't going to eat, then he needed to get the hell out and make room for those who were.

Joey was more than fifteen minutes late for their dinner date, and she hadn't called or texted to let him know she was either running behind or not coming. He wouldn't be surprised if the latter were accurate since she'd stood him up once many years before. On their wedding day. Who's to say she hadn't done it again?

He wondered if she knew how hard it'd been seeing her at the diner after so many years of being away. Could she have known that the diner belonged to him, and had intentionally stopped in hoping to see him there? It was possible one of her sisters could've told her if she'd kept in close contact with them, and there was no reason to believe she hadn't since they'd always been close. If that were true, why would she want to see him? Was there something she wanted or needed to say to him? Apologize perhaps? Didn't she know the day she'd walked out on him was the same day she'd broken his heart and it still hadn't mended? Joey Sheffield was the reason he'd never married. He knew he'd never love another woman as much as he loved her. He'd only be failing his potential partner and himself if he pretended that he could. He'd gone out on plenty of dates over the years to have fun and enjoy the company of another human being, and even though some women he'd dated were beautiful and intriguing, he had no interest whatsoever in committing to a long-lasting relationship. Not a man to lead anyone to think otherwise, he'd always made that perfectly clear, usually ending any chance of a second date.

Was it possible after all this time, he still held on to a glimmer of hope that they'd finally be the couple they were meant to be? Seeing her again only reignited the flame he thought had burned out long ago. If that light continued to glow inside him now, it was safe to say that it'd never been completely extinguished.

No woman on earth would ever be capable of stealing his heart the way Joey had. Unfortunately, not only had she robbed him of it, but she'd run away with it tucked inside her pocket, never returning it to its rightful owner, leaving a massive hole inside his chest.

When he saw her in the diner, he'd considered avoiding her and not speaking to her at all, but that kind of behavior wasn't in his nature, and he could never forgive himself if he'd given up the opportunity to talk to her. She'd looked as surprised to see him as he had been to see her, proving he'd been wrong about assuming her visit had been intentional.

She hadn't changed much in the time she'd been gone. Her long blonde hair was now shoulder-length and light brown, having no effect at all on her beauty. Her new hair color only accentuated her violet eyes. Seeing her again caused a stir of emotion inside him he hadn't felt since the day she'd left him behind without even as much as a farewell note.

Once more, he looked at his watch. Another five minutes had lapsed while he reminiscenced about their past, and she still hadn't shown up or called. Disheartened, he dropped a ten-dollar bill on the table to compensate the waiter for his patience and understanding.

As he headed for the door, his cell phone rang. Quickly answering it, he said, "Joey, where are you?"

"Is this Mason Abernathy?" an unfamiliar female voice asked.

"Yes."

"Mason, my name is Ellen Jacobs. I'm a friend and co-worker of Joey's."

Mason stepped out onto the sidewalk, away from the noise of the restaurant so he could hear her more clearly. "Okay."

"I'm sorry to bother you, but I think Joey might be in some kind of trouble."

"What makes you think that?" Mason asked, his pulse quickening. Hadn't he told Joey that same afternoon to be careful when approaching her family with that birth certificate? Had she followed through with the confrontation and as a result, either Helen or one of her sisters had retaliated in a way that put her life in danger or had injured her? Was it possible she hadn't stood him up at all, but didn't show up because she couldn't?

"Well," Ellen explained. "She called me earlier this afternoon and told me some things were going on there with her family and she had an important matter she needed to discuss with them. She mentioned something about her mother hosting a tea party and she was going to use that as an opportunity to address them all at once."

"Did she say anything else, something that makes you think she may be in trouble?"

"No, only that it might not have gone over so well. She asked me to call her around six to check on her and make sure things were okay, and that if I couldn't get through to her, I should call you and tell you about it. I've been calling her for the past two hours and she isn't answering my calls or texts."

"She didn't show up for our eight o'clock dinner date, either," Mason said.

"Do you think she's okay? I've had a bad feeling about this trip ever since she told me about it."

"I wouldn't put anything past her family," Mason said, unlocking his car door and sliding in. "There's only one way to find out."

"What are you going to do?"

"Drive out there personally and see for myself what the hell is going on."

"Can you please keep me informed?"

"I'll do my best," Mason said, disconnecting the call and exiting the parking lot, squealing his tires on the pavement as he headed toward Sheffield Manor.

* * * * *

He hadn't been to the manor in several years. After Joey left, there was no reason to return. Even when he'd gone there to see Joey, he'd never been treated as a guest, but as an outsider, a nuisance wasting the precious time of millionaires who couldn't be bothered by indigents. In the eyes of Macarthur and Helen Sheffield, he never had been good enough for their daughter and could never provide her with the finest things that money could buy. They never understood why Joey didn't feel the same way they did and why she continued to waste her time on such an unbecoming and poor deviant. Apparently, he knew Joey much better than they did because she didn't share their love for money, status, or exuberance. In fact, after they'd been dating for a few months and he'd learned how rich her father was, he'd been surprised that she'd chosen to earn her money by working instead of depending on the family's wealth. That's when she'd told him in no uncertain terms that she didn't want a dime of her father's filthy money, preferring to make it her own way. He'd always felt there was more to the story than what Joey told him, that something had happened somewhere along the way to make her feel the way she did. If it had, she'd never talked about it with him. Surely she would have if she thought it was important enough to be discussed.

From the moment he'd entered the manor and every time thereafter when he visited, he'd felt uncomfortable. It wasn't because it was the only mansion he'd ever been inside of or the largest home he'd ever seen. It wasn't even because of Joey's cold and distant parents. It was much more than that. There was something mysterious and sinister about the mansion, as if it harbored dark and malevolent secrets that could never become known. If homes had souls, Sheffield Manor's would be dreadfully vile and bleak. He never understood why he felt that way, and still couldn't explain it after all these years.

As he drove through the front entrance gate onto the paved driveway, that gnawing feeling overcame him again, stronger than he'd ever felt it before. Maybe it was due to the condition of the house and surrounding grounds that gave it such an eerie quality. Upkeep was extremely lacking.

The obvious absence of maintenance and lawn care made it appear as though it were about to be cast on a television show for America's scariest or most haunted homes. Hands down, Sheffield Manor would take home the winning trophy. The place gave him the creeps.

Outside lights illuminated the front yard clearly enough for him to see the ruin that'd befallen what was once an immaculate and well-kept mansion, and one of the most envied properties in Bristol County. Never having seen an aerial view of the grounds, he could only imagine that the layout was like a maze with mice working their way through twists and turns, around walls and obstacles until they located the prized piece of cheese at the end of the trail, a small reward for their hard labor. Why he envisioned such an image was a mystery to him, but he thought it was because of the stone walls built around the perimeter of the property, completely boxing the house and grounds inside its borders, separating it from the outside world. The wall's massive spires extended beyond the roof, the sharp apexes resembling arrows that were waiting to be fired at the darkened sky. Beyond the walls lay hundreds of acres of untouched woods that were probably teeming with wildlife that were too frightened to even consider trespassing on Sheffield property. No doubt they, too, sensed the malign force that emanated from the area.

Three cars were parked in the driveway, one behind the other. Mason parked behind Joey's car, turned off the engine and made his way to the front door.

Chapter Twenty-Two

"Is she dead?" Robin asked anxiously, picking up Joey's feet as Rosemary lifted her upper body from the floor.

"No," Rosemary answered.

"What did mother drug her with?"

"I have no idea. But whatever it was, it's strong."

"What if it's something she's allergic to? Couldn't that kill her?"

"I doubt it's anything that serious. Remember what I told you earlier about daddy?"

"About what mother's doing to him?"

"Yes. Whatever she uses to keep him sedated is likely the same thing she put in Joey's tea."

"Which means it only knocked her out."

"Right. For how long, who knows? That depends on what she gave her and how much."

"Why did mother do this, Rosemary? Why does she hate Joey enough to want her dead?"

"That's a question I've been asking myself for a long time. We got our answer tonight."

"We have to stop this," Robin said. "I don't care if we don't have the same mother, she's still our sister."

"You think I don't know that?" Rosemary said, winded from carrying an unconscious Joey from the living room, through the kitchen, and to the cellar door.

"We should call the police," Robin suggested.

"And tell them what? That our mother is plotting the murder of her daughter?"

"Joey's not her daughter, remember?"

"Of course, I remember. But no one else in Cornish knows that, and if we called and made that kind of allegation against Helen Sheffield, we'd be laughed right off the phone."

"Shouldn't we at least try?"

"No. We'll take care of this ourselves."

Robin held onto Joey's legs as she reached behind her to open the cellar door. "We can't do this," she said, groping the wall in search of a light switch. "It's dark down there and smells awful."

Rosemary looked down at Joey slumped in her arms, then at Robin who was still crying not only for Joey, but because she'd allowed herself to become involved in a heinous act that she'd wanted no part of in the first place. She knew how Helen operated, never taking the blame for anything, even when she *was* to blame. Scapegoats were always the victims where Helen Sheffield was concerned because there would always be someone willing to do her dirty work for her, and it usually involved money. God forgive her, but she was just as guilty as any of the other goons Helen had used and discarded. She was in this mess over fear of losing her inheritance. If they got law enforcement involved and they made a trip to the house, Helen would claim innocence and blame the entire ordeal on her and Robin and would allow them to take the fall for a plan she'd hatched and initiated in her own deranged mind.

"You're absolutely right," Rosemary said. "Close the door."

"Where are we going?"

"Not into that damn cellar, that's for sure."

"Mother's going to be pissed when she finds out Joey's not down there."

"Let her be pissed," Rosemary panted. "I'll deal with her. It's past time someone stood up to her. It might as well be me since I got us into this mess."

"She's heavier than she looks," Robin said, struggling to keep a grip on Joey.

"Tell me about it," Rosemary replied, opening the door to a small suite down the hall from the kitchen.

"We're putting her in the maid's quarters?"

"It's the best place I can think of right now. Since there's no staff on duty, she'll be safe in here until she wakes up."

"Whenever that might be."

"You stay here and keep her quiet. Lock the door behind me and don't open it unless I tell you to."

"Where are you going?"

"To deal with mother."

"Be careful, Rosemary. I'm afraid of what she might do."

As she closed Robin inside the room and made her way back toward the living room, the doorbell rang. Before she could make it to the door, Helen answered it.

"Ms. Sheffield," she heard a man's voice say. "I'm Mason Abernathy."

"I know who you are," Helen said coldly. "What do you want?"

"I'd like to speak with Joey, if I may."

"Whatever makes you think she's here?"

"She's staying here while she's in town, isn't she? At least, that's what she told me. And that's her car parked over there in the driveway."

"So it is. And?"

"And she was supposed to meet me for dinner tonight, but she didn't show up or call. I was concerned, so I came to check on her."

"She isn't here right now. Have you considered that she may have found a more suitable companion to go out with."

"Her car's here, but she isn't?"

"Are you insinuating that I'm lying about her not being here?"

"No, ma'am, it's just..."

"Will there be anything else?" Helen snapped, cutting him off.

Before Helen slammed the door in his face, he glimpsed Rosemary standing in the hallway next to the kitchen, listening to their conversation. Behind her mother's back, she used her hands to flash the number nine, then a one and another one, pointing behind her and mouthing "Joey."

Rosemary didn't need to be verbal for him to understand what she was telling him to do.

Ellen had been right.

Joey was in trouble.

Chapter Twenty-Three

Helen turned from the door to see Rosemary standing at the kitchen entryway, her arms crossed in a questioning stance. "What did Mason want?" she asked.

"Nothing of any importance," Helen answered as she walked toward her.

"Sounded important to me. I would've sworn I heard him asking about Joey," Rosemary replied, leaning back against the butcher block island in the center of the kitchen.

"So what if he was?"

"He knows she's here. You lied to him and said she wasn't. He won't take your word for it and simply walk away. It isn't as though her car being parked in the driveway isn't a dead giveaway."

"He can't get in here unless I allow him through the door and that won't be happening."

"What if he calls the police?"

"Let him. He can't prove a damn thing," Helen stated. "Enough about that piece of human filth. Have you and Robin done as you were told?"

"Yes," Rosemary lied. "She's still unconscious, though."

"That makes no difference to me. Perchance it'll be better for her that way."

"Tell me something, mother," Rosemary said, stepping away from the block and standing in front of Helen. "What exactly are you planning on doing to Joey?"

"I think I've already made that perfectly clear, or do you lack the skill of comprehending the English language?"

Ignoring the debasement, Rosemary answered, "Yes, but you haven't told me or Robin how you plan on pulling this off. Joey does have friends back in Indiana who will surely notice if she goes missing, and they'll report it if she doesn't return home, which will then prompt an investigation into her disappearance. No doubt that would lead them here, or did you not give that any consideration? Second, she's been spending time with Mason, and he knows she's staying here, so that's another matter to contend with. Let's just say you do kill her, what are you going to do with her body? What method will you be using to destroy her? Are you going to dissolve her in hydrochloric acid? Chop her into a million little pieces and feed them to the wildlife out there?" she asked, thumbing towards the woods behind the estate. "Sounds to me like you've been so gung-ho about killing her you've failed to think things through. Or is it that you simply don't care, as long as you're able to complete your objective?"

"How I deal with it is none of your concern," Helen stated flatly.

"Oh, that's where you're wrong, mother. It is of grave concern to me because you involved me in your wicked scheme to bring Joey home by lying to me about the reason behind it. I'm concerned that Robin and I will take the blame for your sick actions because you'll never admit to your own involvement. You'd rather let both of us rot in prison than admit your own guilt."

"That's rubbish."

"No, it isn't. Do you know what's really bothering me the most about this whole ordeal, mother? I can't seem to figure out why, after all these years of Joey being gone and out of your life, you've waited until now to exact your revenge on her.

And for what? Not being your blood daughter even though that isn't her fault? There are so many other ways for you to ostracize her from your life, so why choose death? I don't understand that."

"Are you turning against me, Rosemary?" Helen asked, her mouth curled into a vicious sneer. "Might I remind you what you have at stake should you do that?"

"Do whatever you feel you need to do because I don't care anymore. You can tell Dan about my affair, you can disinherit me, or trash talk me all over town like you do anyone else who goes up against you. This is where it ends, mother. I'm through playing your warped and malevolent game and I won't let you kill Joey."

"What do you suppose you can do to stop me?" Helen laughed. "You're nothing but a sniveling weakling. You always have been."

"That might've once been true, but I'm warning you, if you try to cross me to harm Joey, I'll make you live to regret it, if it's the last thing I do."

In anger, Helen snatched a butcher knife from the wooden block on the counter and slashed out at

Rosemary with it. Her swift movement happened so fast that Rosemary didn't have time to recoil from the unexpected attack.

Hot pain washed over her as the long blade penetrated through her shirt and into the soft flesh of the right side of her abdomen, promptly followed by the flow of warm liquid against her skin.

Rosemary clasped her hand over the wound, the wetness oozing through her fingers and dripping onto the floor. Blood from the injury flowered across her white blouse, continuing to spread until the entire front of her shirt turned crimson.

"What have you done?" she asked weakly, buckling onto her knees.

"Try stopping me now, you ungrateful bitch," Helen seethed. "You or no one else is going to stop me from doing what I have to do."

As Rosemary lay on the cold floor watching her blood streak across the while tile and into the grout, Helen disappeared from view, undoubtedly in search of her target.

"Keep her safe, Robin," Rosemary muttered before passing out.

* * * * *

"Joey," Robin breathed, lightly tapping her cheek. "Joey, wake up."

Joey moaned but didn't open her eyes.

"Joey," Robin called again, vigorously shaking her. "Wake up. We've got to get you out of here."

Whatever Helen had given her was potent and long-lasting. Nothing she'd tried so far had aroused Joey from her drug-induced sleep. Not splashing cold water on her face or laying a wet washcloth across her forehead. If she didn't wake up soon, she'd have to drag her from the room, out of the house and into safety.

From the room where she kept watch over Joey, she'd heard Helen and Rosemary arguing, but she couldn't make out what they were saying. Helen was fuming about something Rosemary had either done or said and was reprimanding her for it. Had she told her they hadn't put Joey in the cellar as she'd commanded them to? Or that together, she and Robin were not going to allow her to kill Joey? It was only a matter of time before she discovered they'd hidden Joey away from her and she came looking for her. She'd tear down every door in the house if that's what it took to locate Joey. She had to get her to safety before that could happen. If they stayed where they were, they were sitting ducks waiting to be slaughtered.

"Joey, come on," Robin said, pulling her upright. Her head lolled from side to side against the weight but had no effect on rousing her. Her eyes flitted but didn't open.

Robin hated the thought of doing what she was about to do, but it was the only other thing she could think of that might stir Joey enough to at least get her out of that room and to a different location. "Please forgive me," Robin said, drawing back her hand and slapping Joey forcefully across the face, leaving a red mark on her cheek. "Joey!"

Her eyes slowly opened to thin slits. "Wah-win," Joey slurred, trying to say Robin's name. "Wha's wong?"

"Joey, can you sit up?" Robin asked, growing more anxious with each second that passed, expecting her mother to bust through the door and whisk Joey away in order to finish her deadly deed.

"I twy," she answered, barely lifting her head off the pillow. "Hep me."

Robin placed one of Joey's arms around her neck, holding onto it as she pulled her to an upright position. "We need to get out of this room, Joey. I'm sure Mother's already looking for us."

"Bich," Joey moaned.

"Bitch is right. She drugged you. She wants to kill you, Joey, but we're not going to let that happen," she said, pulling Joey to her feet. "Lean on me. I'll help you walk."

Robin gently eased the door open, peeking up and down the hallway to make sure Helen wasn't there. A door leading to the patio was only a few feet away, but she'd have to pass by the hall entrance leading into the kitchen to get to it, praying Helen wasn't hiding inside the archway waiting for them to pass and seize her chance to capture Joey. If she could make it there without getting caught, she could hide Joey in the garden shed and leave her there until she sobered up enough to walk on her own.

Less than a foot from the exit, Helen stepped out of the kitchen and stood rigidly in front of her, blocking her way.

"Going somewhere, Robin?" Helen asked bitterly, wielding the bloody knife. "You might want to reconsider that choice since it didn't work out too well for Rosemary."

Chapter Twenty-Four

Mason stood on the front porch staring blankly at the closed door Helen had slammed in his face, thinking about the desperate message Rosemary had given him. He could call the police, but their response time might not be quick enough to help, or even save, Joey. She needed his aid now, and his only option was to find a way inside the house. After checking the doorknob and finding it locked, he simultaneously pressed the doorbell and pounded repeatedly on the door, hoping it would annoy Helen to where she'd have to open the door, then he could push his way past her and demand to know where Joey was.

He could pretend to be a human ramrod and burst through the door like the cops did on T.V. shows, but if he attempted such a dangerous move, he'd fracture his shoulder because his bones were no match for the thick wood and deadbolts. If he injured himself to the point of helplessness, what good would he be to Joey then? Windows were impassable, all of them protected by cast iron security grates with sharp, pointed spikes.

Climbing the stone walls was impossible without a ladder, and questionable even if he had one because of their height. If he had access to a pistol or rifle, he could shoot the lock out and get through the door that way. Unfortunately, he was a terrible marksman with no firearms training and with that kind of luck on his side, the bullet would ricochet off the metal and shoot him instead.

If ever a gardener was needed, it's now, he thought as he stared at the overgrown, chest-high, rose bushes. He couldn't go around the ones closest to the wall because several of their branches extended up and over the tops on both sides of the home. The only way to get into the backyard was to go *through* them. He'd never wished for a jacket or long-sleeved shirt so badly in his life. Battling the multitudes of thorns would be painful as hell, but he had to do it. Joey's life depended on the choice he made, and he couldn't let an obstacle like rose thorns prevent him from getting to her. What were a few puncture wounds compared to death? If Joey died, he'd never have a second chance at the possibility of having her in his life again. That thought alone was enough to encourage and propel him to save the woman he'd never stopped loving.

With his arms up to shield his face, he pushed through into the bramble thicket, thorns instantly digging into his bare skin, pricking and pulling at the fabric of his shirt and trousers. "Son of a bitch," he muttered when one of the wild branches escaped his grip and swung backwards, striking him across the forehead and embedding a broken-off thorn above his left eye.

No time to worry about removing it now. Forget about the pain and focus on getting to Joey in time.

Motion-sensitive lights flashed on as he entered the back area of the house, flooding him in a bright white glow, revealing dark red, vein-like trails from multiple thorn-inflicted wounds streaming down both arms. Blood oozed from the brow injury as he plucked the thorn from his skin and tossed it onto the ground.

Abutted against the back wall of the property was a medium-sized aluminum shed that he assumed stored gardening tools. Whatever implements were in there apparently hadn't been used in years, if the condition of the grove of overgrown hedges was any sign. He remembered Joey giving him a tour of her father's garden maze, begging her to get him out of the unending labyrinth of zigs and zags, twists and turns, because he was afraid they'd get lost and never find their way out. Joey laughed at him, promising him she knew the layout like the back of her hand. The maze had once been where the overgrowth was now, overrun by the abundance of wild weeds and lack of maintenance, never to be walked through again.

To his left was a canopy-covered patio, the wooden Adirondack style furniture rotting and falling apart. The water of the in-ground pool was teeming with green algae and other debris, perfect swimming conditions for frogs, tadpoles, and snakes. As a teenager while dating Joey, he'd swam in the pool on numerous occasions. He shuttered at the thought of falling into the grimy, bacteria-infested water. He recalled there was an entry door to the house accessible via the patio. He began making his way in that direction, stopping short when he heard a woman's voice.

Through the glass, he saw Helen standing in the hallway with her back to him, unaware of his presence. Over her shoulder, he could see Robin straining to keep an unconscious Joey propped up and out of reach of their mother, who was blocking their path, refusing to let them exit through the patio door. Rosemary was nowhere in sight. If she was inside, why wasn't she doing anything to help them? Surely she must know they were in danger. Unless she couldn't help because she was injured herself, unable to assist Robin and Joey.

Then he saw the knife Helen was holding, the silver blade wet with fresh blood. Since Joey and Robin were both in view, the blood could only belong to Rosemary, meaning she was in serious trouble and was either severely injured or dead. There was, however, one other person inside Sheffield Manor that the blood could belong to. Or had Helen killed him along with Rosemary, and the blood on the knife was from both victims instead of one? He had to find a way inside and stop Helen from causing any harm to Robin or Joey. There was no way he could get through the door without drawing attention because the only thing that came to mind was hurling one of the heavy patio chairs through the glass, dashing through the opening and subduing Helen before she could kill anyone else.

Robin's face was twisted with fright as she stared horrifyingly at her mother. She couldn't run away, not without leaving Joey behind. To do so would leave Joey vulnerable to Helen's attack.

Helen spun around when Mason knocked loudly on the glass door, staring at him as he waved innocently. "Ms. Sheffield, can you please open the door?" he called out. "I really need to speak with Joey."

"Go away, you despicable fool. You have no business here," she said, turning away from the door and refocusing her attention on Robin. "How dare you betray me?" she seethed, taking a step forward. "I gave you an order, and you deliberately defied me."

"Back off, mother," Robin warned. "Please don't make me have to do something I'll be sorry for later."

Helen threw her head back and laughed wildly. "You?" she mocked. "The weakest one of all? That's a mighty big threat coming from such a small person," she said, taking another step forward as she brandished the knife.

"Mother, stop!" Robin screamed, fighting to keep a grip on Joey as she moved backwards, away from her mother.

"Hand her over to me, Robin. Do as you're told, and you walk away unscathed. Continue to defy me, and you'll suffer the same consequences as Rosemary has."

"I won't!" Robin yelled through tears. "You're not going to kill Joey!"

"This is your last warning," Helen cautioned her, moving in closer as she tightly gripped the knife handle. "Hand her over. Punishment must be dispersed. *NOW!*" she demanded, lurching forward, the knife blade raised in a position to strike.

Behind her, the sound of shattering glass crashing onto the bare floor startled her. She spun around in time to see Mason rushing through the smashed door, his face and arms covered in dried blood. In a flash, he grabbed onto her wrist, squeezing and twisting until she released her grip and dropped the knife to the floor. Mason quickly retrieved it and tossed it into the algae infested swimming pool through the gaping doorway.

"Where's Rosemary?" he panted, shoving Helen aside as he made his way toward Robin.

Helen made a swift dash for Mason, unfazed by his personal attack on her, determined not to let him interfere and take Joey away.

Mason shoved her backwards again, surprised by her resilience and agility at her age.

"NO!" she screamed, leaping onto his back like a feral cat, pulling his hair and clawing at his face and neck. "You can't have her!" she yelled in his ear, tearing at the collar of his shirt. "She's mine!"

"Crazy bitch!" Mason shouted, ramming backwards into the wall trying to shake her loose, but she held tight. Reaching over his head, Mason grabbed a hand full of her hair, tugging hard and forward as he flipped her over his shoulder, her hair still clutched in his hand. "I've never struck a lady in my life," he fumed through clenched teeth, balling his right hand into a fist. "You, madam, are no lady," he said, punching her hard enough to stun her, yet not hard enough to cause serious bodily harm. Going to prison for her murder was the last thing he needed or wanted. She simply wasn't worth it.

Helen fell to the floor, dazed, and angered that once more, she'd be denied the chance to fulfill a years-long yearning, fully aware that another opportunity to destroy Joey would never come.

And that was unacceptable.

She wouldn't allow anyone to interfere with finalizing her goal. She was ready to, and would, take down anyone who stood in her way.

"I don't know," Robin answered. "She told me to stay inside the room with Joey and keep the door locked."

"Go find her," he said, scooping Joey into his arms. "I think she's hurt."

"You're ruining everything!" Helen shrieked. "This is none of your business! You'll pay for this. I'll see to it!"

"Shut the fuck up, you deranged old bitch. Haven't you caused enough trouble?" Mason stated angrily, hastily making his way into the kitchen when he heard Robin's cry.

Rosemary was lying on her side on the kitchen floor, clutching onto her stomach, her hands and shirt drenched with bright, red blood.

"Rosemary!" she exclaimed, falling to her knees beside her sister. "Oh, my God! What has she done to you?"

"Don't worry about me," Rosemary gasped, barely able to speak. "Get Joey out of here."

"I'm not leaving you," Robin protested.

"You have to. You must save Joey."

"No," Robin said, rising from the floor. "I'm calling an ambulance."

"Put that phone away," Helen demanded, appearing in the side entrance to the kitchen that she'd used to block Robin from leaving. "You're not calling anyone, and no one's going anywhere," she said, brandishing a pistol and pointing the barrel directly at Robin. "You heard me. Hang up."

"Mother, what's gotten into you? Why are you doing this? You tried to kill Rosemary, you want

Joey dead, and now, you're threatening to kill me? You've gone stark raving mad."

"It wasn't supposed to be this complicated," Helen said, moving into the kitchen, only feet away from the four of them. "I had the perfect plan all worked out. Because of your betrayal, I now have to resort to other measures. Remember, Robin, this is *your* fault." With her thumb, she pulled back the hammer, the loud click echoing off the tiled walls.

"Mason?" Joey asked groggily, opening her eyes. "What are you doing here? And why are you holding me in your arms?"

"Well, well, well," Helen laughed evilly. "Did that worthless bitch finally wake up? I thought she was going to sleep forever. Guess I gave her a wee bit too much sedative."

"Joey, can you stand?" Mason asked, looking down at her.

"I'm not sure, but I'll try."

Her legs wobbled beneath her as her feet touched the floor. Her head was still spinning and felt like it was as big as a hot-air balloon. "I'm a little unsteady, but okay," she assured him, holding onto Mason's arm to keep from falling. "What's happening?"

"Mother's lost her damn mind," Robin said. "She stabbed Rosemary, and now she's going to shoot us all."

"Not all of us," Mason replied. "She can't do that, not with that peashooter she's holding," he said, moving Joey behind him. "One shot, maybe. If she's lucky, she *might* hit one of us, which will then give the others the opportunity to overtake her. So, Helen, which one of us is it going to be?"

"Don't you dare come any closer," Helen commanded. "That whore behind you is the only one I'm interested in."

"You'll have to go through me to get to her," Mason stated firmly. "I don't intend to hand her over to you, you sick, twisted bitch."

Helen pulled the trigger and fired. The bullet whizzed past Mason's ear and struck the wall behind him. Shards of white ceramic crumbled onto the Formica and scattered across the countertop.

Cocking the gun again and taking aim, the sudden booming sound of a man's deep voice echoed throughout the kitchen, startling them all and turning their attention to the entrance that Helen had used only moments before.

"*HELLLENNN*!" he shouted.

* * * * *

His mind was impeccably clear tonight. It was in the most excellent working condition he could recall since becoming ill. So sharp, in fact, that when Helen came into his room, he'd heard everything she'd said and comprehended every word perfectly, except for the part about Julia and Jackie. He had no idea what she'd been referring to. Both were his granddaughters, he knew that much, but he'd never done a thing to harm either of them. Not that he could remember, anyway. If what Helen had said was true, he supposed he had. Then again, not a word that came out of that hateful bitch's mouth could ever be believed. For all he knew, she could be making accusations against him in order to have an excuse to slap the piss out of him again, even if the pretext was a fictitious, made-up one. With her, who knew? He should be given an acting award for his performance tonight in making Helen believe he was having a rough evening, when in fact, he felt better than he had in a long damn time. Probably because he hadn't been overdosing himself with all those nameless pills Helen insisted he take every day, telling him they were all for his own good. No, they weren't. They were only good for one thing. To keep him out of Helen's hair so she didn't have to be bothered with him.

He was gloriously thankful that, at least for the moment, when he needed his mind to be in mint condition, the thick fog had lifted, the clouds dissipated, and he hoped and prayed to God that he could retain a strong and coherent level of lucidness long enough to do what must be done. He'd been given an assignment and he couldn't fail. If he did, Helen would continue her reign of terror against him, and he could no longer deal with her excessive abuse. Enough was enough. It had to stop. The only way to see it through and complete it was to do so while he was aware of what he was thinking and what he was doing.

He wanted to believe that God Himself had planted the deed in his head, but he supposed it could've just as easily been Satan because not even *he* wanted to stake a claim on that wicked woman. All he knew was that one minute the thought wasn't there, then the next minute it was. No different than getting a sudden urge to go out to an ice cream parlor and buy a chocolate cone or vanilla milkshake. Another period of such remarkable clarity may never come again. He knew the time to complete his operation was now and he must act quickly before he forgot what it was he was supposed to do.

The pills she'd given him were now scattered on the floor because he'd only pretended to take them while she watched, cleverly hiding them beneath his tongue the way he'd taught himself to do. The second she'd left the room, he spat them out, knowing if he ingested them, they'd instantly knock him out and he didn't want to sleep. Helen was up to no good, and he *knew* it. She'd been in too much of a rush to medicate and leave him, as if she had something extremely important she needed to do, and he wanted to know exactly what she was planning.

He was sick and tired of the way she treated him and talked down to him, constantly calling him ugly, hateful names, even striking him. He knew he wasn't well, but that didn't give her the right to treat him in such a harsh manner or be so condescending and mean to him simply because he was sick. Every day got worse where Helen was concerned, and he'd rather die than spend another day under her care. She'd already moved him to a different location twice, and he wasn't willing to let the third move be to the cemetery, not at her expense. At least in the last room he'd been in, he'd had a window to look out of so he could enjoy the warmth and brightness of the sunshine. The room he was in now had a small window, but it was painted black, and he couldn't see a damn thing out of it. There was also no heat or air, making his living conditions worse than that of unwanted kennel dogs.

He must deal with Helen for the last time to ensure she'd never batter or drug him again. Come tomorrow, chances were he wouldn't even remember who he was or why he needed to do anything about his wretched wife. If that happened without being able to fulfill his mission, he'd continue to be subjected to her unending mistreatment until it ended with her putting him in his grave. Death was imminent for him just as it was for every living soul on earth, but he'll be damned if his would be at the hands of Helen instead of his maker.

He was in his favorite place, looking at photos, able to put names to the faces, when he heard a loud commotion downstairs that sounded like glass breaking. He stood quietly as he tried to figure out if Helen had broken a dish or a mirror. If she did, then the vulgar words would begin any second. When they never came, he knew whatever was happening had nothing to do with dinnerware.

Curious, he exited the attic and made his way down the west side hallway, stopping at the top of the stairs and glancing down. Whatever was going on must be taking place in the kitchen because the living room was empty.

Slowly descending the stairs, making sure no one was nearby to detain him, he was suddenly alarmed when he heard a woman scream, "Rosemary!" He knew that name, and he recognized the voice that'd called out. They were his daughters. Something was wrong. He could tell by the shrillness and fear in Robin's voice when she'd called out to her sister.

They were in the kitchen as he'd suspected, and whatever Helen had intended to do, it was happening now, and it didn't sound good.

At the bottom of the stairs, he turned right, enroute to where he knew he needed to go. Carefully easing the library door open, he made his way to the desk, recalling that it held a secret drawer, and inside that, a unique surprise he'd been saving precisely for Helen, understanding he'd be forced to use it when the time came. And that time had arrived.

From a red cherry wood box engraved with the Sheffield family crest, he retrieved the one thing he knew he'd need to deal with his demented and wicked wife, put it in his pants pocket, then headed down the hallway toward the back of the house where he'd cut through the parlor and into the east side hallway, putting him near the archway of the kitchen entrance.

He'd be so quiet that no one would hear him coming.

He couldn't wait to see the look on Helen's face when she beheld the surprise he was bringing her.

The excitement he felt nearly made him piss his pants.

Again.

* * * * *

There are many things that improve with age. Whiskey. Wine. Cheese. Even some people succeed at shedding their adolescent awkwardness and oddities and grow into comely adults.

That was not the case with MacArthur Sheffield.

Time had not been his friend.

In his youth and throughout middle age, he was considered to be strikingly handsome, an unfeigned ladies' man. There was no longer any trace of the once sophisticated and polished man that women at one time lusted over. Women who were willing to jeopardize their own marriages and reputations for the opportunity to sleep with the richest man in Bristol County. Age and illness had reduced him to nothing more than a fraction of the man he used to be. Mac no longer stood tall. Osteoarthritis had taken its toll on his spine, diminishing his height by at least three inches. Unable to stand erect, his hunched figure loomed in the doorway, glowering angrily at Helen.

Greasy white strands of disheveled hair hung limply in his face. Spittle glistened in the silver growth of chin stubble. Once used as a weapon against her, he couldn't even control his dick well enough now to keep from pissing his pants, evidenced by the dark, overlapping stains covering the front of his crotch. He was unkempt and unclean, a man lacking the personal care and medical attention that he obviously required and was being deprived of. The stench of his body, a combination of urine, sweat, and shit, was so strong that it permeated throughout the entire area.

Joey stared wide-eyed at the old man who'd made her childhood and teen years a living hell, wondering how a person as vibrant and strong as he'd once been, could deteriorate into a person who she barely recognized. Was this the monster that she'd feared would spring at her from the closet or the dark hallways of the secret passage hidden inside the walls? All her life, he'd brought more trepidation and panic to her than any make-believe movie monster ever could. Yet even with all the horrible things he'd done to her for all those years, what she felt now wasn't apprehension. It was pity.

She hadn't seen or spoken to him since leaving Cornish, and any time Rosemary or Robin had attempted to discuss him, she'd silenced them, uninterested in hearing anything that had to do with Macarthur Sheffield. Therefore, it came as no surprise that she hadn't been aware of his declining mental illness.

Everything Helen Sheffield touched died. Not even her husband and children were exempt from her love and desire for ruin and destruction. It was apparent by Mac's appearance that she was inattentive to his care, and much too heartless to hire a medical professional who specialized in the nursing of dementia and Alzheimer's patients. She'd seen homeless men in the hospital parking lot begging for money who didn't look as uncared for as Mac did. Karma can be a funny thing. What goes around, truly does come around. Sometimes. Yet it was sad to think that of all the things Mac could've lost as a payback from the universe for his years of sexual and physical abuse, it'd taken nothing of material value, but something much more valuable.

His mind and mental stability.

"Macarthur!" Helen scolded loudly. "What are you doing out of your room? I thought I told you to stay put."

"What are you up to, Helen?" he asked, cognizant of what he needed to say, yet struggling to speak.

"That's none of your concern," Helen snapped.

"You're trying to kill my little angel," he garbled, his throat filling with phlegm. "Robin and Rosemary, too. I can't allow you to do that, you evil, wicked woman."

Helen took a step backwards as he advanced through the archway and entered the kitchen. He was extremely angry. Before his illness took control of his mind and body, she'd known what he was capable of when mad. With his mental faculties no longer stable, he'd be more apt to lash out violently against those who'd hurt him. Or do something much worse than cause an injury. Without the ability to think rationally, his actions could prove unpredictable, and that's what frightened her the most. His ire was focused solely on her. Whatever retaliation he was planning, she was guaranteed to be the victim. "Do as you're told!" she snapped authoritatively. "Return to your room this instant!"

"I won't," he protested. "I'm through taking orders from you. Tired of you keeping me locked away in that cold, dark room all day and night, never allowing me to come out. Sick of you mistreating me, making fun of me, calling me names, and hitting me. You need to pay for all your sins, Helen. You are a miserable, vulgar woman."

From the pocket of his tan trousers, Macarthur Sheffield pulled out the pistol he'd taken from the box inside the hidden drawer of his desk. With a shaking hand, he aimed it at his wife.

Helen gasped when she saw the shiny black barrel pointed at her chest. "Macarthur! You stop this foolish nonsense this instant!" she demanded. "Put that gun away before you hurt someone. You don't know what you're doing!" she demanded. In her shock and panic at his sudden, threatening appearance, she'd momentarily forgotten she was holding a weapon of her own. Confronted with the likelihood that she was staring her own mortality square in the face, she raised the barrel and pointed it at Macarthur.

"That's where you're wrong, Helen. I know exactly what I'm doing. It's amazing how well I can think and what I can remember when I refuse to take that poison you force down my throat every day. Do you think I don't know you've been trying to kill me? And for what? To get all my money?" he laughed huskily, coughing up phlegm and spitting it on the floor. "Because you're sick of me and no longer want to be bothered with me? The bottom line is, Helen, the reason you've done all these things isn't important. What matters is that you must be stopped," he said, ignoring her weapon as he fired a shot. "You're not going to hurt anyone else."

Helen dropped her gun, stumbling backwards into the butcher-block table as she clutched her chest. Blood gushed through her fingers, streaming down the front of her yellow silk blouse.

Robin screamed when her mother fell to the floor in a bloody heap beside Rosemary. "Daddy, *NOOOOOOOO!*"

"You're the one who doesn't deserve to live," Macarthur said, placing the barrel of the gun beneath his chin. Before pulling the trigger, he said, "And I don't want to anymore."

The sound of Robin's shrill screams reverberated through the kitchen as Mac fell backwards into the hallway, the clanking of the gun's metal striking loudly against the stone floor.

"Don't look," Mason told Joey, burying her face into his chest. "Come on, let's get you to the couch."

"Rosemary?" Joey said weakly, lying back on a throw pillow.

"Stay here. I'm going to check on her and Robin," he said.

It was difficult to look at the violent carnage Mac left behind. The coppery smell of fresh blood encompassed the entire kitchen. Mason struggled to keep from vomiting, covering his nose and mouth with a dish towel to prevent inhaling the disgusting odor. It wasn't necessary to check on Mac. He couldn't have survived a gunshot wound that blew his brains and pieces of skull over the hallway wall and floor.

Rosemary's pulse was weak, but she was still alive. Robin remained on the floor, holding her mother's head in her lap, gently stroking her hair. Her clothes were saturated in Helen's blood.

"Robin, you need to let go of her and come with me," he said, reaching out to help her from the floor.

"No," she said, pulling away. "I'm not leaving her."

"She's gone, Robin. The police and ambulance are on their way. We need to help Rosemary."

Robin glanced up at him, confusion distorting her face. "Rosemary?" she asked blankly, as though hearing her name for the first time.

"She's been stabbed, Robin. Remember? She's injured and we need to do what we can to help her until the paramedics arrive. Do you understand?"

Robin nodded, gently removing Helen's head from her lap and placing it carefully on the floor before crawling to Rosemary's side. "Rosie?" she called, taking her sister's hand in hers. "Everything's going to be okay. Help is on the way," she soothed before fresh tears began to flow as she looked over at her dead mother and the body of her father lying motionless on the floor.

Sirens wailed in the distance as Mason returned to the couch and took a seat beside Joey. "How are you feeling?" he asked, putting an arm around her shoulder.

"Still sleepy," she replied groggily. "But better than I did. Whatever Helen put in my tea is finally beginning to wear off."

"Rosemary's hurt," he told her. "She has a stab wound to her abdomen. She's lost a lot of blood, but I think she'll pull through."

"Helen stabbed her?"

"Looks like," Mason replied. "What the hell would've made your mom snap to the point of trying to kill you and Rosemary?"

"It's a long story, Mason."

"One I hope you'll find the time to tell me."

"Eventually."

"Does any of this have to do with that birth certificate you showed me this afternoon?"

"Yes, and so much more."

"Can't wait to hear about it," he remarked dryly. "Should be interesting."

"What happened to your face?" she asked, gently touching the wound above his eye. "And your arms?"

"I had a fight with the roses."

"The roses?" Joey asked, confused by his answer.

"The ones around this house that direly need a gardener."

"I don't understand," Joey said, shaking her head. "How did you get injured by flowers?"

"Because I had to go through them."

"Why would you do that?" she asked, leaning forward, and turning to look at him.

Mason shrugged. "Helen wouldn't let me in the front door, and I couldn't get through any of the windows. Going through the brambles was the only way I could get to you."

A light smile crossed Joey's face. "You did that for me?"

"Of course, I did," he answered, taking hold of her hand. "I'd move heaven and earth for you if I needed to, Joey. You should know that."

The blare of sirens coming up the access road was getting closer. Their vehicles would be pulling up to the house any second. "Joey, I'm sure the officers will have a lot of questions for you to answer. Do you think you're capable?"

"I'll do my best."

"You need to let the medics examine you as well. There's no telling what kind of poison she gave you, and they need to know that you've been drugged. The hospital can run a drug screen in case you need a dose of antitoxin to counteract it. You understand, right?"

"Yes," she answered. "You can relax, Mason. She didn't poison me. If she had, I'd already be dead."

"We don't know that for sure."

"I do."

"How so?"

Joey smiled. "I'm a nurse."

"You're a..." Mason started, realizing this was a part of Joey's life he knew nothing about. "I'd say we have a lot to talk about when you're able. I'd like to hear more about that."

"You're on," Joey replied. "After I sober up, of course."

"Huh," Mason said absently. "How about them apples?" Shaking his head in amazement, he said, "A nurse. Imagine that."

Sirens halted as the ambulance and police cars arrived at Sheffield Manor. A succession of car doors slamming was instantly followed by a loud banging at the front door.

"Cornish Police Department!" a man's loud voice called. "Open up!"

Chapter Twenty-Five

Rosemary's hospital room was filled with wall-to-wall bouquets of flowers, potted plants, and Get-Well cards from multitudes of friends. Her room smelled like a floral shop. Dan and Robin were sitting at her bedside when Joey and Mason entered the room.

"Joey," Rosemary cried hoarsely. "I didn't think I'd ever see you again."

"Why would you think that?" Joey asked, bending over to hug her.

"I think you know why."

"We don't need to discuss it right now, Rosemary. Wait until you're well."

"I am so, so sorry," she said, a tear rolling from the corner of her eye. "For everything. I should've never let mother talk me into something so heinous."

"Me, either," Robin echoed. "We had no idea what she was really up to, or that it'd end this way."

Their words sounded sincere enough. Yet it was possible they were as fake as the reason they'd used to persuade her to come back to Sheffield Manor. Were they both sorry to have been involved in such a horrendously devious plot for no other reason than to please their insidious mother, or were they sorry because their plan hadn't worked out quite as planned, leaving them both exposed to their own individual involvement? Asking herself these questions made her wonder if she'd made the right decision by doing what she'd done, a small matter of business she'd taken care of on the same afternoon she'd spoken to the coroner and realized the reason she was back in Cornish may not have been as it seemed. It'd been done in private and in secret because no one, not even Helen Sheffield, knew what she'd had in her possession for the past two years, to be enacted when the time came to do so. What they'd all done to her couldn't have been a more perfect time to set it all in motion.

"I know I said we'd discuss it when you're better," Joey began. "But since you brought it up, I do need to ask the two of you one question and I hope you can both give me answers. Is that okay?"

"Yes," Rosemary answered to Robin's nod.

"Let me reiterate one thing first. We all know exactly how manipulative and powerful Helen could be. Can we agree on that?"

"Yes," they both answered.

"With that in mind, what did she hold over the both of you to get you to agree to do what you did? I ask that because I don't believe either of you would've agreed to help her unless something you thought was important was involved. What was it? Did she have some not-so-pleasing information on you that could be used against you to shame or embarrass you? Did she threaten to cut you out of Mac's will if you refused to help her? Whatever it was must've been quite powerful, or at least that's what I think. Rosemary?"

Rosemary was caught off guard by the question, unable to answer immediately because she'd not yet told Dan about her affair, and she certainly couldn't bring it up now in a room full of people. That was a conversation that needed to take place in private when she and Dan were alone. "Both for me," Rosemary finally answered, glancing over at

Dan. "I'll tell you everything later, honey. Now isn't the time."

Joey continued. "In your case, it was because of compromising information and money. Is that what you're saying?"

Rosemary nodded.

"Robin, how about you?"

"Certainly not because she had any derogatory information on me, because she didn't. Even if she did, who was there to tell? I'm not married or in a committed relationship. As far as I know, she wasn't aware that I have a girlfriend, but she did threaten to disinherit me and evict me from my apartment if I didn't cooperate."

"Then it's safe to say that yours boiled down to money as well, right?"

Robin shrugged. "I suppose that's true."

"That's all I really wanted to know. It's been bothering me, wondering how she got you to get involved in her scheme. Now that I know, let's all forget about it, okay?" Joey said, taking a seat on the side of the bed. "What's done is done. As far as I'm concerned, it's over." Their answers only confirmed she'd made the right decision, erasing any doubts she might've had prior to hearing their explanations.

Absently, Rosemary stated, "I should've known. I don't know why I didn't see it. I suppose I was so overcome with grief about daddy's deterioration that I failed to see what was happening to mother. Or maybe I did see it and just didn't want to admit to it."

"Should've known what?" Joey asked. "What didn't you see?"

"That mother was just as mentally unwell as daddy. I suspected something was off with her when she started firing all her staff, refusing to maintain the grounds, selling furniture and jewelry. Every room in the west wing is completely empty, Joey. She got rid of everything. There's not even a bed sheet left."

"Why would she do that?" Joey wondered. "It couldn't have been because she needed the money.

"I questioned her about it and got the same answer I did with anything else I've ever asked her."

"That it's none of your business what she does?" Joey asked.

Rosemary nodded. "Since she wouldn't give me a straightforward answer, I surmised that her erratic behavior was caused by stress from having to tend to daddy."

"She could've hired a nurse," Joey offered. "She didn't have to take on all that responsibility alone."

"He had a nurse," Rosemary said. "An excellent one. Mother fired her without warning and without an explanation."

Joey thought about that for a moment. "Maybe her intentions all along were to get rid of him," she said. "Mac was convinced she'd been trying to kill him. At least that's what he accused her of before he shot her. It's possible that he knew something you didn't."

"Maybe," Rosemary agreed.

"I guess we'll never know now," Robin said.

"Something you just said piqued my curiosity, Rosemary. As kids, we were never allowed to enter any of the rooms in the west wing. I conjured up all kinds of scenarios about why we were forbidden to go in any of them. At one point, I convinced myself that Helen was hiding dead bodies in them. As an adult, were you finally permitted to go in the rooms?"

"Yes," Rosemary said. "I can assure you there were no dead bodies."

"What was so special about them that Helen felt it necessary to keep them locked?"

"There wasn't anything special about them at all," Rosemary confirmed. "Nothing but fancy, expensive bedroom furniture that she didn't want us to ruin. Those were her words, not mine."

Joey sighed. "I find that rather disappointing," she said. "I liked my theory of dead bodies better. It's much more exciting than boring furniture."

Rosemary stared dismally at Joey. "I never intended for you to get hurt," she said. "In the end, when Robin and I realized what mother's intentions truly were, we tried to stop her. We did everything we could to protect you."

"I can vouch for that," Mason said, eliciting a strange look from Joey. "I would've explained everything to you last night, but you were still in la-la land, so I let you sleep instead."

"I'm surprised the doctor let you go home," Robin stated. "I figured he'd admit you for the night to keep an eye on you. Was the doctor able to determine what mother poisoned you with?"

"It wasn't poison," Joey replied. "It was Alprazolam, an extremely potent sedative. According to the doctor who treated me, there was enough of it in my system to take down a horse. He wanted to keep me overnight for observation, but Mason promised him he'd take me home with him and watch over me," she said, turning to Mason and offering him a smile. "And he did. I slept it off, so no harm done."

"I'm glad you're okay, Joey," Rosemary said. "I truly am."

"Thanks, same here. How bad is your injury?"

"Deep, but no internal damage," Dan answered. "Doc said she was lucky that no internal organs were damaged. It took twenty stitches to close the wound. She'll be sore for a few days, but she can go home tomorrow."

"That's good news," Joey replied. "Look, I know this is a shitty time to bring this up, but arrangements need to be made for Mac and Helen. I've decided to stick around for a couple more days to help with that. If it's okay with the two of you, that is."

"Seriously?" Robin said. "Do you even need to ask?"

"Thanks, Joey," Rosemary said. "You really don't need to do that, but it's kind of you to offer. You don't owe us anything, especially after what we've done."

You're right, I don't, she thought, thankful she'd never been influenced by the love of, and greed for, money. Nor the desire to have the best of everything that money could buy. But to not offer would make her as much of a shitty person as they were. "Think nothing of it."

"I'd like that," Rosemary said. "I'm delighted that you haven't disowned us both. You're more than welcome to stay with me and Dan while you remain. We have plenty of room and I know Julia and Jackie would love having their Aunt Joey around."

"She'll be staying with me while she's here," Mason interjected, keeping Joey from having to decline Rosemary's offer. "Even if the manor was suitable for living in, I don't think she'd want to be there."

"Who would?" Robin stated.

"Speaking of the manor, add that to the list of decisions that need to be made," Joey said. "I have no say in anything since I was disinherited years ago." *It's my turn to be a bitch now. Turnabout is fair play, and you'll find out soon enough who controls the playing field.* "You'll need to choose whether to keep or sell it."

"What?" Robin shrieked. "You were taken out of daddy's will?"

"Another detail Helen failed to mention," Joey said snidely. "Color me shocked."

"We'll divide it evenly amongst the three of us, Joey," Rosemary assured her. "You're just as much their daughter as we are, and it isn't fair for you to be left out."

"I don't want it," Joey said, shaking her head. "Let me be clear about something. I don't want anything from the estate. No money. Nothing from inside the house. Or anything else there may be. I want no part of it."

"Why? It's yours."

"No, it isn't. The two of you can either split my share or donate it to a respectable charity. I think you both know why I refuse to accept it."

"We do now," Robin said.

"Joey, you do believe we were never told mother wasn't your real mother, don't you?"

"Yes. Her and Mac both went to great lengths to keep that fact hidden. Hence, the birth certificate being hidden in a safe. That's not something Helen would've ever wanted anyone to know about, especially those in her social circle. She was too vain to allow that to happen."

"The offer still stands," Rosemary said. "If you change your mind about staying with Dan and I."

"I won't," Joey replied, rising from the bed. "Call me once you're released. I'll come to your house, and we can take care of the business that needs to be dealt with and make phone calls that need to be made. I'm sure there are a lot of legal details to be overseen, what with Mac's wills and all. We'll get it done, so don't worry."

"Thanks, Joey. I really appreciate that," Rosemary said.

"Ditto," Robin said. "Hey, Joey. I don't know if this is the appropriate time to bring it up, but I'd still like to see that tattoo of yours before you leave to go home."

"In that case, I suppose now is as good a time as any," Joey replied, lifting her shirt and lowering the waist of her pants. "Since you probably won't get another chance to see it."

And she wouldn't. Once Rosemary and Robin were made aware of their financial futures, they'd probably never see or speak to each other again.

In the center of her lower back was a black heart with one word inked in red across the center.

SURVIVOR.

"Powerful word," Robin said.

"And true," Joey replied. "See you both tomorrow then?"

"Tomorrow."

How hard it'd been to tell them they'd been forgiven. They'd both been involved in a cunning conspiracy to get her back home to the house where she'd suffered the most horrible sexual abuse imaginable, into the sticky web of a spiteful woman who was eviler and more despicable than the man who'd raped her. Their willingness to collaborate with Helen had damn near ended her life. And they'd agreed to it because of a boundless love for money, and in obedience to a mother who'd never genuinely cared for or loved either one of them.

None of their transgressions were forgivable. Even if they were her sisters.

"Mason," Joey said once they left Rosemary's room. "What do you say we stop and grab a bite to eat and take it back to your place? I think it's time I told you some things. Secrets I should've shared with you years ago, but I don't think I can tell you on an empty stomach."

Chapter Twenty-Six

"Son of a bitch," Mason exclaimed, dropping the uneaten portion of his hamburger onto its paper wrapper. "No wonder you left."

"I wanted so badly to tell you back then what was going on, but I couldn't bring myself to do it."

"Why not?"

"You have to remember, Mason, I lived in a house full of people who never believed a word I said. A part of me didn't think you'd believe me, either. Have you any idea how difficult it was, and still is, to discuss an issue like that, especially when the perpetrator was my own father?"

"You could've trusted me," he told her. "I would've protected you."

"I know that now, but back then, my mind wasn't as clear or mature as it is today. I suppose I can also add that I thought you wouldn't love or respect me anymore."

"Oh, Joey," Mason said softly. "There's nothing you could've done or said that would've made me stop loving you," he added, picking at the few

French fries left in the box. "I never stopped loving you, you know?"

"Nor I you. But I couldn't stay, and I knew you wouldn't leave."

"You could've at least said goodbye."

"Which would've only made it harder for me to go. I truly am sorry that I hurt you, but my heart was broken, too. It took me a long time, with the help of hours and hours of therapy, to get past all of it. I was doing exceptionally well until I got the call from Rosemary."

"Telling you about Mac?"

"Yes. All the years it'd taken me to get to a good place in my life were washed away in a split second with that one phone call."

"There are no words in the human vocabulary that could express how sorry I am to know what you went through," Mason said, taking her hand in his. "Was all this going on the whole time we were together?"

"The molestation had stopped by then, but I still locked my door at night and slept with a knife under my pillow. I can't tell you how many nights I lay awake trying to figure out how he was getting into my room without me hearing him. Now I know."

"The secret passageway," Mason stated flatly.

Joey nodded.

Mason shook his head. "All I have to say is that you sure are one forgiving person."

"Am I?" Joey teased, furrowing her brow.

"If my brother or sister did something like that to me, I don't know if I'd ever speak to them again. Yet you forgave Robin and Rosemary for what they did to you even though they nearly got you killed."

"Did I?" Joey asked, tilting her head slightly and grinning.

"Didn't you?" Mason asked curiously.

"Let's suffice it to say that Robin should be thankful she has a job and Rosemary has a wealthy husband."

"That sounds intimidating," Mason teased. "Care to share?"

"Mason Abernathy, I thought you'd never ask," Joey answered with a wink. "First, let's get this mess cleaned up. This will be a conversation that needs to be moved to the couch with a cup of coffee in hand."

Joey sat at one end of the sofa with her legs drawn up beneath her. Mason sat at the opposite end facing her.

"I can't wait to hear this," he prompted. "Whenever you're ready."

"It all started about two years ago when I received a letter in the mail from an attorney here in Cornish. When I saw the return address, I started to throw it in the trash because I thought it was some kind of plea letter from one of Mac's attorneys begging me to come home. I got curious and thought, what the hell, open it and see what it is. So I did."

Mason's eyes were focused intently on Joey as he anticipated what was coming next. "And?"

"It was definitely from one of Mac's attorneys, but it wasn't what I thought it was. Enclosed with the letter was a Power of Attorney, making me sole executor of his estate and his will. Mac knew he was sick and that it was only a matter of time before his dementia took complete control of his mind. He didn't want Helen to be the one with the say about who got what, so he instructed his attorney to give me complete and exclusive power over his money and assets."

"Holy shit," Mason exclaimed. "I'll bet that pissed Helen off."

"It probably would've if she'd known about it."

"She's his wife. Doesn't that automatically include her in any decisions that are made?"

"Not the way Mac set it all up," Joey replied, blowing into her cup. "You see, Mac had his attorney draw up two wills, one real and one fake. Guess which one Helen possessed?"

"I'm guessing it wasn't the real one."

"Your guess would be accurate. Instructions were given to the attorney to carry through on the actual will without Helen's knowledge, so she was none the wiser about what Mac had done. And she wouldn't have known about it until Mac's death, when she attended the reading of the will."

"She would've exploded," Mason said.

"Yes, I do believe she would have."

"What did you do? About the will, I mean."

"I accepted the responsibility, signed the Power of Attorney in front of two witnesses, had it notarized and returned it with a copy of my photo I.D. Not because I wanted anything he had. What I said to Rosemary and Robin about that was true. I don't and never did want any of his money. I agreed to it to keep Helen from inheriting anything. I guess you could say that was my way of getting even with her for all the hateful things she'd ever done and said to me."

"The ultimate payback."

"Something like that. The sad part about all this, Mason, is that I would've made sure Rosemary and Robin both got their inheritances. I would've never cheated them out of it. Why do you think I asked what I did today at the hospital?"

"You wanted to know if they did what they did for money," Mason answered.

"Exactly. And when I got their answer, it made me glad that I did what I did."

"This is the part I've been waiting for. What did you do?"

"Remember the day I was in the diner?"

"How could I forget?" he replied, smiling.

"After I left there, I went to see the medical examiner. After talking to him and learning what I learned, I knew something wasn't right about the whole ordeal because Rosemary had told so many lies, and nothing was making sense to me. I had no idea what it could be, and certainly never dreamed that either of them would've gone to the lengths they did to put their plan in motion. What I do know is that I had an extremely uncomfortable feeling about everything. Before going back to the manor that day, I stopped in to see the attorney to discuss Mac's will. I didn't tell him Mac had died, and he didn't ask. All I said was that I was in town for a family visit and wanted to check in while I was there. It was that very day that I made the changes I did, but I told the attorney there was a possibility I could be making more changes and would keep him apprised of my decision."

"What kinds of changes?"

"In case I learned that Rosemary and Robin were innocent and only Helen was involved, I intended to put them back in the will."

"Turns out they weren't innocent."

"No, they weren't. That's why I didn't make any other changes. I had to verify their reasons before making my final decision."

"Go on," Mason prodded. "I've a feeling the best is still yet to come."

"Depends on how you look at it," Joey smiled. "When the time comes for the will to be read, Rosemary and Robin are going to be beyond pissed, while numerous and various charities around the world are going to be extremely happy. I instructed the attorney to conduct an estate sale and give all proceeds of that to multiple children's cancer networks. Any profits from the sale of the manor are to go to no-kill shelters for animals. Of course, at the time I made those changes, neither Mac nor Helen were dead, and I didn't know that making the determinations would come so soon. I had to make swift decisions on how to disperse it."

"Let me get this straight," Mason said, placing his cup down on the coffee table. "Rosemary nor Robin are getting anything?"

"Not a penny," Joey said, finishing her coffee. "Nothing from inside the house or from any of the sales. They get absolutely nothing of value. It was the least I could do considering that money was more important to them than I was. I wanted to make sure they never make that mistake again."

"That's what you meant when you said, 'put them back in the will'"?

"Yes."

"I thought you meant Helen or Mac had removed their names."

"No, I did. That's what I went into his office to discuss with him."

"What did he have to say about it?"

"What can he say?" Joey shrugged. "It isn't his money, and he has absolutely no say over the contents of the will. His job as the attorney is to carry out the wishes of the executor."

Mason took a deep breath and let it out slowly. "You do know when they learn about this, there's a possibility they'll never speak to you again."

Joey nodded. "I figured as much, but it's a chance I'm willing to take. They're my sisters and I love them dearly, but what they did to me was inexcusable. They know they were wrong, and so do I. It's certainly their prerogative to decide whether to disown me, but that doesn't make me regret my decision."

"Out of curiosity, how much are we talking here?"

"Between the price that the house might bring, which could be way below market value since two people died there, Mac's stocks and holdings, all assets not including the estate sale, roughly about half a billion."

Mason let out a loud whistle. "Holy shit," he exclaimed. "And you gave it *all* away?"

"Every last dime of it. I told you, I have no interest in it."

"You devious little angel," Mason laughed.

"That's an oxymoron, you know?"

"But it's true. You got the last laugh."

"In a manner of speaking, yes. But nothing about what they did was funny."

"No," Mason said, shaking his head. "It wasn't. The way you were talking to them in the hospital made me believe you were being sincere about forgiving them and moving on."

"It's not like I could spring it on them right there," Joey exclaimed. "Where's the surprise in that?"

"I have to admit, Joey. That was an impressive move. Bravo to you."

"I really didn't want to and had no intentions of doing it. The way I see it is that they gave me no other choice. They revealed their true colors by agreeing to put me in harm's way for no reason other than money."

"Do you believe they honestly didn't know Helen wasn't your birth mother?"

"I do believe that. The looks on their faces when I announced it told me they were as shocked to learn about it as I was. Helen prided herself on her public persona, her standing in Cornish and the respect she received from the residents. She would've never wanted something like that to get out. That's too scandalous for her liking."

"It must've been hell living in that house."

"For a long time, it was. In hindsight, knowing what I know now, I realize why I was always treated differently than Rosie or Robin."

"How so?"

"In every way imaginable. They both got new cars when they turned sixteen, but I never got one at all. Helen chauffeured them all over town and bought them name-brand clothes, but always excluded me on those trips. They attended private academies while I attended public school. I spent more time in the punishment room than anyone else because, according to Helen, I was the bad seed who always needed to be disciplined."

"The punishment room?" Mason asked. "What the hell is that?"

"Exactly what it sounds like," Joey replied. "A small, dark room in the attic where Helen sent me for disciplinary measures."

"In an attic?" Mason asked angrily.

"Yes. With no lights, no heat or air, nothing to keep myself occupied. Sometimes I'd sit in there for hours at a time waiting to be let out."

"What kind of sick fuck puts a kid in the attic?"

"Helen Sheffield. She believed the quiet, alone time was good for the soul and should've been used to think about why I was in there and what measures I could take to ensure it didn't happen again. It did. Over and over and over. The funny thing is, I never knew why the hell I got put in there. It didn't matter to her whether I'd done anything wrong or not. I think she did it because she hated me and enjoyed seeing me suffer."

"What a sadistic bitch."

"No arguments there."

Mason sighed heavily and shook his head, disturbed by the abuse Joey had suffered at the hands of her parents. "All that horrid treatment you were subjected to is awful, but I believe something good came out of it."

"What's that?"

"Have you ever considered that's why you're not obsessed with money? Because you never had it thrown at you like your sisters did, so you didn't know the difference between having it and not having it? And the reason you're such a kind, caring and loving person is because you know what it's like to be mistreated, so you don't treat others with contempt?"

"I have, actually. I'm extremely thankful for that because I honestly do believe it made me a much better person than I would've been otherwise. I simply cannot imagine putting money before someone I love. Nothing is that important."

"You always were different, Joey. From the first moment I saw you, I knew that. It's one of the many things that attracted me to you. You didn't act like most spoiled, rich kids do."

"Because I wasn't," Joey laughed. "I wanted to earn my own money and not depend on or expect handouts from my parents. I'd like to think it's a trait I inherited from my real mother. Guess I'll never know."

"Did you mean it when you told Rosemary you'd stay long enough to help with the funerals?"

"Yes," Joey nodded. "I'll go see the attorney tomorrow to notify him of Mac and Helen's deaths and tell him not to execute the reading of the will until after I'm long gone from here."

"What I wouldn't give to be a fly on the wall when that meeting goes down."

"I can't imagine it'll be pleasant, but they can only blame themselves for the outcome."

"I'm glad you're who you are, Joey. I wouldn't have it any other way," he said, leaning forward to brush a strand of hair away from her eye. "I'm so happy you'll be staying a few more days, but I sure am going to miss you when you leave. I've kind of gotten used to seeing you again."

"I'll miss you, too, but you know I can't stay."

"I know, and I understand why now."

"I'm not that far away, Mason. You could drive to Indiana and visit me. You're welcome to do that anytime you want."

"One of these days, I might take you up on that offer. For now, would it be okay if I kissed you?"

"I'd like that."

It was so good to feel his soft lips touch hers again, to feel the warmth of his skin, the gentleness of his touch, and the strength of his affection. "Make love to me, Mason," she whispered softly in his ear, fondly remembering the first time they'd shown their deep love for each other, in the soft green grass on the embankment at Calloway Park, all those years ago.

Chapter Twenty-Seven

"Hey, babe," Mason called from the kitchen when Joey entered their one-bedroom apartment.

"What's that delicious smell?" she asked, giving him a quick kiss.

"Lasagna," he answered. "Hope you're hungry."

She hadn't been feeling well for the past several days, vomiting frequently and hadn't had much of an appetite. Every time she ate, the food didn't stay down long. The only thing she'd been able to nibble on was saltine crackers. Concerned about her health, he'd encouraged her to see her doctor. Much to her chagrin and protests for not wanting to go, she'd finally buckled and agreed. Why were medical professionals always the worst at seeking medical attention, yet had no qualms about preaching to others the importance of their own health?

"I wasn't until I walked in and smelled the food."

"A letter came for you today from that attorney in Cornish," Mason told her, pointing at the coffee table. "I had to sign for it so you might want to open it and see what it is."

"That's odd," Joey said, picking up the envelope and glancing at the return address. "This isn't the same attorney I met with about Mac's will. Maybe this lawyer is representing Robin and Rosemary in a lawsuit against me," she said with a shrug.

"And they waited nearly a year to do it?"

"They probably grew weary of stewing in their juices and decided to do something about it," she laughed, carefully unsealing the envelope so as not to rip the contents. "Tough luck. All the money is gone."

"I'm sure Rosemary will get a decent settlement once their divorce is final," Mason offered. "Between alimony and child support, she should get enough to get by on. If not, guess she'll have to partake in that drastic word she has no experience in," he laughed.

"Working a job," Joey said with a nod. "I did let Robin keep the apartment. I couldn't live with myself if I knew I left her homeless."

The letter couldn't be about the mansion. It'd sold to a self-proclaimed paranormal investigator who intended to profit off the deaths that'd occurred there, leaving the home as is and making no repairs, hoping the ambience of the appearance would add to his claim that the house was haunted, hoping his droves of gullible customers would fall for his bullshit.

Little did he know there were definitely ghosts inside Sheffield Manor, but not the kind that groaned and rattled chains.

Joey gasped and covered her mouth as she read the letter.

Dear Ms. Sheffield:

My name is Dwayne Bridges, an attorney in Cornish, Alabama.

My services were retained by Macarthur Sheffield, a client who is now deceased, and named you, his daughter, Josephine Renee Sheffield, as sole benefactor in his will that is on file with this office. The amount of $10,000,000.00 is being held in trust at First National Bank of Cornish, to be withdrawn and surrendered to you upon verification of identity.

Please contact this office at your earliest possible convenience so that we can arrange to finalize your settlement.

Kindest Regards,

414

"Mason, you're not going to believe it," she said excitedly, rushing into the kitchen and shaking the letter at him. "Read this."

Mason glanced up from the correspondence, his eyes wide with surprise. "Is this genuine?"

"Looks legit to me," Joey answered. "A phone call will verify whether it is or not," she said, punching the number into the keypad of her cell phone.

Mason stood silently as he listened to Joey speaking with someone at the attorney's office, anxiously awaiting to find out what was going on.

"It's definitely real," Joey confirmed as she disconnected the call. "Seems Mac had a separate will besides the other one that I was executor of and hired a separate attorney to represent him for this one."

"And once again, you're the sole beneficiary?"

Joey nodded. "Ten million dollars," she exclaimed.

"Mac sure didn't want Helen getting her hands on his money, did he?"

"Apparently not."

"Is it just me, or is almost a year a long time to wait in notifying a benefactor about an inheritance? Mac and Helen have been gone for eight months and you're only now receiving a notification letter?"

"Mr. Bridges said he's been trying to locate me for several months. Coincidentally, he had lunch with the first attorney and asked him if he'd ever done any legal work for Mac. That's how he found out how to get ahold of me. If not for that lunch, I may have never known about this."

"Mac didn't give them an address when he drew up the will?"

"I doubt he had it since I made it perfectly clear to Rosemary and Robin they were not to disclose that to him. In hindsight, I suppose it's possible they could've since they gave it to Helen after I asked them not to. If he had it, he didn't divulge it to the attorney because the address they had on file for me was the manor, which makes me wonder exactly how long this will has existed."

"No telling. Guess we need to decide which charity to give that money to," Mason teased, removing a large pan from the oven.

"I'm not so sure I want to do that," Joey said, chewing her lip thoughtfully.

"Seriously? You're keeping it?"

"I have an idea in mind."

"Oh, yeah? Like what?"

"I want you to have it," she answered. "I'm giving it to you."

"What?" Mason shrieked. "I don't want your money, Joey."

"It's not *my* money," she replied. "It's *ours*. We are married, you know?"

"I do, but my answer is the same."

"Hear me out, will you?"

"You know I will," he said. "Do you want white or red wine with your dinner?" he asked as he opened the refrigerator.

"Water, please."

"You're turning down wine?" he frowned teasingly. "Is the world ending?"

Joey didn't answer. "I want you to take this money and build a diner, a mockup of the one back in Cornish, complete with red booths and stools, jukebox, the works. This is enough money to pay cash for it. Then you'll own it outright. It's the least I can do since you sold the one back home and moved here to be with me."

"Joey, I can't do that," Mason protested. "It wouldn't be right."

"Give me one good reason why not."

"It's not my money to spend."

"Okay then," she nodded. "It's my money and I want to spend it on you."

"Why is this so important to you?"

"Several reasons," she answered. "I loved that diner. I have a lot of good memories from the time I spent there. It's where I met you."

"Both times," Mason reminded her.

"True. But there are other reasons as well. I want to be able to take our son or daughter there someday and show them where I met their father. I know it won't be the real diner, but it'll be close enough if it looks the same."

"I understand that. Then you can tell him or her how cool their dad was back then, sporting around town in his Letterman's jacket."

"With the pictures to prove it," Joey added. "I'd also like to buy a house. Nothing fancy, but bigger than this apartment, with a couple of extra bedrooms."

"I thought you liked it here."

"I do," she answered. "But I think it's time we upsized."

"If that's what you want, then we'll start looking."

"Great. I'm glad you agree."

"Do we have to make a trip to Cornish to get the money?"

"Nope. I'll do the same thing I did when I agreed to be executor of Mac's initial will. Mr. Bridges said he'll verify it with what the other attorney has on file, and if the signatures and identification match, a cashier's check will be in the mail."

"And he can vouch for you since you visited him in his office while you were in Cornish."

"Right."

"That settles it then," Mason said, giving her a quick kiss on the forehead. "Guess we'd better start looking soon."

"Yep."

"That look on your face tells me there's something else," Mason said. "You have that 'wait, there's more' expression."

"Do I?"

"Um hum, and I know what it is."

"Do you now?"

"You're waiting for me to ask you what the doctor said, so please allow me to do that now," Mason said, grinning.

"You think you're so smart, don't you?"

"Kind of. Seriously, though, what did he say. Is it the flu?"

"Nope."

"A stomach virus?"

"Nope."

"Okay, I give up. What is it, then?"

"Well," Joey said. "In about eight months I'll need to take some time off work and if you have the diner, I won't have to worry about missing a few paychecks."

"With ten million bucks, I don't think you need to worry about money."

"A substantial portion of that will be used to purchase your diner and our house, but whatever is left over, we'll put into our savings. That way, it'll be there when we need it."

"I can live with that," Mason said, scooping spoonfuls of lasagna onto their dinner plates. "Why are you taking time off? Are we going somewhere?"

"You could say that."

"On a trip?"

"A short one."

"Where to?"

"The hospital."

Mason's face lit up as he suddenly comprehended what Joey was hinting at. "Hold on, hold on," he stuttered, dropping the serving spoon into the pan and taking Joey gently by the shoulders. "You don't want any wine with your dinner, you've been throwing up a lot, in eight months you're taking off work, you referred to our son or daughter. Are you... are you?"

Joey nodded eagerly. "You're going to be a daddy."

Mason picked her up and hugged her, spinning her around in circles. "Joey," he said, putting her back down and cupping her face in his hands. "I love you so much. You're going to be a wonderful mother."

"And you will be a terrific daddy. Can we eat now? I'm starving."

"Yes, yes," Mason said gleefully, pulling her chair away from the table. "Sit down and enjoy. You *are* eating for two now."

The happiness she'd strived all her life to find had finally been fulfilled. The love of her life was now her husband who'd given up his home and business in Cornish to spend his life with her. Together, out of a deep and passionate love for each other, they'd created another life that contained a part of them both and would be loved beyond measure and raised to appreciate the simple and important things in life.

After so many years of hurt, heartache and regrets, Joey Sheffield Abernathy was, at last, a happy and contented woman. With optimism, she looked forward to the future and what it held for her, Mason, and their growing family, promising herself that she'd leave the past where it belonged. Behind her.

Glenda Norwood Petz (July 29, 1959) is an American author born in Pahokee, Florida. She now resides in Clarksville, Indiana with her husband. Ms. Petz is also the author of the fiction novel, Hurricane, winner of the 2021 Best Suspense by AudioBookReviewer.com.

To learn more about this author, visit her website at:

https://glendanorwoodpetz.com

Follow her on Twitter: @PetzGlenda

Follow her on Instagram: PahokeeAuthor729

Follow her on Facebook

Made in the USA
Coppell, TX
02 July 2022